FATED BONDS

ANGEL'S FATE: BOOK 1

TESSA COLE

Gryphon's Gate Publishing

Fated Bonds

Gryphon's Gate Publishing

550 King St. N.

PO Box 42088 Conestoga

Waterloo, ON

N2L 6K5

ebook ISBN: 978-1-988115-76-4

Print ISBN: 978-1-988115-75-7

AMIAH

I'D THOUGHT HE WAS *THE ONE*.

The moment I'd locked eyes with him, the ghostly swirling white lines of my not-yet-awakened angelic mating brand had started to ache, which meant he was my destiny.

Except the magic in the mark hadn't risen to the surface of my skin alight with the golden glow of our soul bond. It had remained buried, a constant throb, reminding me that he hadn't been ready. It hadn't been the right time. I'd needed to be patient.

And I had been. I'd been blessed with the sacred angelic mark and promised from the moment I was born that I'd have a love so rare and great and beautiful other angels would talk about it for centuries. The brand was eternal, destined, and could never be broken. I would wait centuries for him — if by a twist of magic his mortality let him live that long before our bond extended his life. I'd already waited one and a half centuries, keeping my secret because I didn't want all the curious looks and questions a formed but not awakened brand would get. What was a little more time?

I'd do whatever it took.

At least I thought I'd been willing to do whatever it took.

Until I met *her*.

Essie Shaw. His actual mate.

She'd shown me how horrifying the brand was, how it stole her independence and all her choices. She'd been crazy with fear and on-her-knees shattered when her mates had been injured and in trouble, and I had no reason to believe her situation was unusual. The angelic mating brand created a soul bond deeper than any other bond in all the realms. The death of one mate caused the death of the other — or drove her insane, which wasn't the better option.

I shuddered and wrapped my arms tighter around me even though the summer's night was still warm and muggy with almost no breeze sweeping across the Joined Parliament Operations Building's rooftop.

No, the cold was soul deep and had sunk into my core the moment I'd seen Essie on the floor, screaming in agony and fear.

I didn't want that. I couldn't live with that. I'd lost my freedom once before, and I swore I'd never lose it again. Just the thought of being trapped made my pulse race. And yet I was already branded, the ache growing stronger every day.

Another shudder slipped down my spine. My soul mate was drawing closer. It was the only explanation for the growing pain — although I had no idea why it had started four and a half years ago when I hadn't really met my true mate.

I swept my gaze over the skyline of Union City's Supernatural Quarter. This part of the city had been restored after Michael's war of extermination as a place to live for those supernatural beings who'd come out of hiding to defend humanity, and where I'd called home for the last twenty years.

Except I wasn't sure I could call it home anymore. I hadn't really lived since I'd met *him*.

I'd been waiting.

Like a good angel.

And I'd escaped that nightmare by the skin of my teeth... for now.

Before me, in an apartment building a few blocks away, a light turned off, while a streetlight on the next street over flickered off then back on. A car with blue neon glowing from underneath it sped by most likely headed to the vampire section of the Quarter, the heavy *thump thump* from its stereo so powerful I could feel it in my chest even five stories up.

If I looked to my right and slightly behind me, I'd be able to see the UV-blocking purple-glass canopy over the vampires' section catching hints of the light of the half moon along with the strobe lights from the half dozen nightclubs occupying the vampires' main strip.

There were some vampires and shifters who'd indulge in a flashy, obnoxious vehicle like that, but given that the car had come from the direction of the park separating the Quarter from the human part of the city, the occupants were more likely young human males out to party with the creatures of the night.

Which surprised me a little. But then the path to humans accepting supers hadn't been as rocky as I'd expected. The monsters who'd hidden in the dark had become saviors and for the most part, humanity was welcoming, or at least tolerant, of supernatural beings. Yes, there were a handful of humans who still feared supers, and many who still didn't want to live next door to them, but the terror of extinction from a common monstrous enemy had certainly eased a lot of fear between species.

It also didn't hurt that supers had representation in government in the Joined Parliament — and therefore weren't fighting to be recognized as citizens — as well, they had laws to abide by and an enforcement agency — the Joined Parliament Bureau of Supernatural Law Enforcement — with JP teams to uphold those laws.

And for the last three years, I'd been the chief physician for Union City's JP Operations' Building because *he* had joined Union City's JP team.

I'd thought if I was near him, my mating brand would be awakened and our bond would fully form and we become more than just friends. I yearned for our bond, for him. He was passionate and strong and fiercely protective. His shifter nature gave him a wild edge that I knew I'd never find in another angel, and I'd thought our bonding meant I needed a counterbalance to my reserved angelic nature and my need to always be in control.

I just hadn't realized how much our bond— *any* bond would rip away all control. I liked my life, liked who I was, liked how I had freedom and a job that released the constantly building pressure of my healing magic. A bond would take all that away.

And yet my heart ached for the loss of something I no longer wanted.

Which didn't make any sense.

How could I mourn something that terrified me?

Except it wasn't the angelic mating brand and everything it entailed that I was mourning. It was the loss of what could have been, the promise of joy, passion, unconditional love and acceptance, and the dream of a soul-deep connection with someone.

Well, no more! So the brand wasn't what I thought it was and its terrible fate was headed my way. I wasn't going to just accept its inevitability. Yes, a soul bond, once formed, was impossible to break, but my brand hadn't awakened yet. Maybe there was a way to remove it, or block it, or something before my soul bonded with a complete stranger's and made me fall in love with him.

And maybe I only *believed* a soul bond was impossible to break.

I'd been wrong about how beautiful the mating brand was. I could be wrong about the finality of its soul bond. The only way to know for sure was to stop feeling sorry for myself and do something, gather information, find someone powerful enough who might be able to break or suppress my mating brand—

I bit back a groan. There was only one person who could possibly be strong enough, and I really didn't want to see the arrogant, lascivious faekin again.

Except Sebastian Bane wasn't a faekin — half human

half fae — glyph witch. He was a full fae sorcerer in hiding... probably because he'd slept with someone's mate or sold stolen magical artifacts to the wrong super, or done something stupid and had a hit out on him.

He'd proposition every woman I'd seen him come in contact with, and while that hadn't been many, he was still at a hundred percent propositions to encountered women — myself included.

I'd promptly turned him down of course. There wasn't any way I'd have sexual intercourse with a man like him. I was saving myself for my soul mate—

Except I didn't want a soul mate any more.

And if I wasn't going to have a soul mate, why wouldn't I take a lover?

Because that lover could end up being my soul mate... although Sebastian and I were such opposites, there was no way he could be my mate.

Another shudder swept through me. I couldn't believe I was actually thinking of saying yes if he propositioned me again... which he wouldn't because I'd already clearly and firmly turned him down.

The door to the stairwell opened, and my heart skipped a beat. Essie liked to come up to the patio, her angelic nature drawing her to rooftops and open sky as much as it did me. And while I knew I needed to work on creating a truce between us — since I'd been less than kind to her when I thought she was going to emotionally shatter my mate — I wasn't ready. Every time I saw her, I saw my wasted years — thank goodness only four! — and my lifetime of naiveté.

Thankfully, Cassius stood in the doorway and not

Essie, although he appeared harder and more imposing than I'd ever seen him before, even in those darkest days during Michael's war. He looked like a statue who'd been sculpted by a master with his broad muscular shoulders straining his simple black T-shirt, strong chiseled jaw, and piercing blue eyes. He wore his blond hair buzzed short — something he'd started doing during the war — and it made him look like the dangerous warrior I knew he'd made himself into. Gone was the thoughtful warm angel I'd become friends with almost a hundred years ago, replaced with a solemn soldier.

And now that soldier was even more solemn, acting cold and angry toward everyone, including me. But then Essie Shaw's life hadn't been the only one to be turned upside down in the last couple of months, and while things had turned out all right in the end, it wasn't just Essie who'd gotten scars.

Except Cassius's scars weren't anything I could heal. My magic only worked on physical injuries, and the one person who could help him emotionally — Essie Shaw with her empathic healing magic — was the one person he was angry at.

"They're about to leave," he said. "Did you want to say goodbye?"

"They're only going to be in Rome for a few weeks. Why would I?" I asked, my anger at Cassius's anger making my tone sharper than I intended.

I wanted to heal him, heal all of them, everyone. It was a compulsion deep within my soul, one that had pulled me into the mortal realm when Michael had started his war, one stronger than my need for order, control, or open sky. I'd felt all those wounded souls crying, their physical agony making my magic burn through my whole body even while I was in the Realm of Celestial Light, and even if Cassius hadn't asked me to join the Angelic Defense with him, I would have joined.

"Right." The muscles in Cassius's jaw flexed and he turned his gaze to the Quarter's skyline.

The weight of his judgment sat heavy between us. I wasn't being a team player. I'd been purposefully mean to Essie to get her to leave in order to protect Marcus and the rest of the team... and, if I was being honest, to protect myself. I knew I should have chosen a different way to protect everyone, but I'd been shocked seeing her there in my office. Four and a half years ago, she'd been the cause of enormous physical and emotional pain to Marcus, pain my magic hadn't been able to ease, and I didn't want that for him again or anyone else.

Except I'd been fighting destiny, and it didn't care who it hurt to reach its outcome.

At least everyone had survived the terrible battles that had happened about a month ago — although I had no idea how — and life had returned to a new normal with Essie as part of the team.

But that meant I needed to admit I was wrong and make nice with the new girl. And I would. I wanted to. Just as soon as looking at her didn't remind me of the nightmare coming my way, and the heartache of an illogical loss.

And really, Cassius should talk. Really. He should. As far as I could tell, he'd barely said more than a dozen words to Essie or anyone of her guys with the exception of his brother. He needed to make nice as much as I did.

"The sooner you work it out with Marcus—"

"There's nothing to work out." Jeez. Did everyone know that I'd been an idiot over him? Cassius had been on assignment out of town for the last two and a half years and had only returned for a visit once. Someone must have told him about Marcus... probably Cassius's brother, Gideon. Gideon had seen and heard enough to have known how I'd felt about Marcus.

And while yes, I'd admit, I'd had an emotional attachment to Marcus, everything I'd done had also been practical. Essie hadn't branded him at the time, and her bonds with her other men would have made her love them more. Marcus hadn't deserved to be slowly abandoned, his love unrequited. No one did.

And no one deserved the nightmare of the angelic mating brand. Not even Essie Shaw.

Another shudder swept over me and I pushed my fear of my fate as deep down inside me as possible. "I was looking out for the health of Union City's JP team. That's my job. She didn't understand the nature of the mating brand." And neither had I. "If they hadn't had a soul bond, it would have eventually shattered him no matter how strong his will."

"But they do have a bond." Cassius kept his gaze locked on the skyline, his posture rigid, and for a second it felt like he was talking about his brother, one of Essie's other mates, and not Marcus.

"And now we have the strongest JP team in the mortal realm," I said. This wasn't the conversation I wanted to have. As much as Cassius and I had been good friends, we'd never really talked about our romantic relationships — or rather, he never talked about his, since I'd spent my life secretly and stupidly waiting for my soul mate and hadn't had any. "Have you talked with Nathaniel and Chris?"

They worked as operational support but the head office had decided that with Cassius as team leader, the three of them could handle the day-to-day activities of the JP in Union City, first for the two and a half weeks while the primary team was out of commission recovering from their terrible ordeal, and now when they went to Rome for advanced training.

"They've been briefed. They—" He cocked his head to the side and squinted as my magic swelled under my skin. It rushed into my palms not yet manifested and visible, but ready to burst free at my command.

Someone was in desperate need of immediate medical attention, and my magic had latched onto them. I gritted my teeth. I hated when my power did this, hated the lack of control and choice. But there wasn't anything I could do once my healing magic had connected with a soul in need, so I yanked my gaze to follow Cassius's and caught a hint of shadow rushing past a pale gray cloud. The shape hurtled across the front of the Quarter's tallest building and a bank of windows with the lights still on.

My pulse stalled. "Is that a person?"

The big, bulky shape took out the top of the spire of the next building, careened off the wall of the six-story high rise beside it, and crashed into the park ring forest with a resounding *boom*.

My thoughts lurched as my power surged, burning up my forearms to my elbows. That *was* a person. A man. A big one by his size and build. Even if I hadn't clearly seen him, my magic knew it.

I reached for my phone but realized I'd left it in my office and there wasn't time to go and get it. There also wasn't time to change out of my pastel blue silk camisole and tan linen pantsuit. But this wasn't the first time I'd ruined my clothes to save a life, and I doubted it would be the last.

"Tell Cassey to prep triage." I pushed a trickle of power into my back and, with a white flash of angelic light, released my wings, the magic allowing them to manifest through my clothing without damaging what I was wearing — something I highly appreciated. I didn't release my wings often, but when I did, it was usually an emergency and while my clothes might end up bloody, they could sometimes be saved. Very little would save them if my wings had ripped massive holes in the back.

"Amiah, wait." Cassius grabbed for me, but I leaped off the roof before he could stop me. Light flashed at the corner of my eye as he released his wings and flew after me. "Just wait."

"Some supers can survive a fall like that, and my magic says he's still alive." But he wouldn't be if I didn't get to him right away.

I pushed myself to fly faster headlong into the breeze that hadn't been there moments ago. It whipped my long blond hair out of its tight chignon and away from my face and cut through my thin clothes, chilling my skin everywhere except for my hands and forearms where my magic pulsed.

Everything within me narrowed to a pinpoint focus on the man. I could get to him in time. I could save him. I had to save him—

My thoughts lurched at that. I'd never *had* to save anyone before. The possibility of death had always been an option. My magic knew that. As long as I did everything in my power to save someone, I didn't experience any backlash. If I didn't do everything possible, my magic turned inward, sweeping through me and painfully incapacitating me.

"Stop. I'm the agent in charge. We know nothing about this situation." Cassius flew close and tried to grab me again.

I jerked away and held up my now-glowing palms. "We know someone down there needs medical attention." I dove into the alley between two four-story buildings. There was no way I could shake him or even out fly him. He was the stronger flyer, the stronger angel in every way, but maybe I could dodge him long enough to get to whoever had fallen out of the sky.

I took a quick turn out of the alley onto the next major street. Cassius drew close and reached for my ankle again, but I darted back into another alley and jerked to the side narrowly avoiding the metal fire escape clinging to the building's red-brick wall.

"I don't want to write you up," Cassius said. "Amiah, please. We have to follow protocol. We're already on probation with head office."

"You know I *have* to go to him." He knew how my

magic worked, knew that if I fought it when it locked on to someone like this, I'd be useless for hours, sometimes even days.

"I promise. You'll go to him. But we have to follow protocol."

"I can't wait for protocol. If I don't want to be useless tomorrow, I can't." No matter how much it made my heart race to disobey the rules, the call of my magic was the stronger compulsion. It always was.

I shot out of the alley, across the empty two-lane street at the edge of the Quarter, flying so low I skimmed the roof of a small silver sports car parked at the curb, and barreled into the dark shadows between the thick tree trunks into the park ring.

My magic urged me on. *Fly faster. Save him. Go go go.*

I twisted avoiding branches and kept low to the ground, half trusting my night vision that allowed me to see reasonably well in low light and half trusting my instincts as I followed a dirt path heading deeper into the forest.

Cassius was right on my heels. If he put in a push, he'd be able to grab me. I didn't know why he didn't, but I was grateful he let me keep going. Probably the practicality of not wanting Operations' chief physician incapacitated by something that could be avoided. And with the amount of magic building in my hands, if I didn't try to save whoever had fallen out of the sky, I'd be out of commission for days.

My magic jerked me to the left toward thick underbrush and dense evergreens. With a pulse of power to my back, I yanked my wings into my body, hit the ground running, and shoved through the foliage.

I broke through into a clearing illuminated by the pale light of the half moon. A wide deep groove had been cut into the forest floor, the dirt pushed to the sides and heaped at the back, and broken branches littered the area.

At the far end, Sebastian Bane, his skin so pale it seemed translucent and radiating a pale icy blue light, knelt beside the broken, bleeding body of a massive, completely naked man.

AMIAH

"Amiah?" Sebastian's eyes widened at our arrival. "Cassius?"

My thoughts stuttered over his presence... and, if I was being honest with myself, his breathtaking appearance. If the man had been a demon, he'd have been an incubus. And a part of me wondered — since no one knew much about fae or their realm — if he wasn't the fae equivalent of one given his lascivious nature.

His stunning good looks, unusual pale eyes, and spiky white and silver hair gave him an exotic appearance, and with a body that I knew from treating him was all sculpted lean muscles covered in mesmerizing black tattoos, he probably had just as much success satisfying his needs as an incubus. He'd certainly know what he was doing—

"What the hell—?" Sebastian said, leaning forward, pressing his hands harder against a laceration in the naked man's abdomen and doing little to slow the blood oozing between his pale fingers. "What are you doing here?"

I ignored him and heaved my thoughts back to the immediate problem. Assess the situation and save the man. From his essence and his lack of clothing, I guessed he was some kind of shifter — since a shifter's magic destroyed his clothing when he shifted — but I wasn't sure what type. His essence seemed wilder, more primal than Marcus's, so I didn't think the man was a werewolf, but he also didn't have the sleek predatory feel of a feline.

Whatever he was, he was something that could survive that terrible fall, although just from looking at him, I was certain he'd broken every bone in his body, and his left fibula and ulna protruded through his skin. He probably had ruptured organs as well. This was going to take everything I had and then some. If we could get him to Operations, I'd be able to supplement my magic with human surgery, but first I'd need to stabilize him so we could move him.

"Why aren't you calling triage?" I snapped at Cassius. I didn't wait to see if he pulled out his phone or not, and dropped to my knees in the dry crunchy summer weeds on the other side of the man from Sebastian.

Even broken and bloody, the naked man was a stunning specimen, his massive body a study in powerful musculature. He wasn't as gorgeous as Sebastian or handsome as Cassius, but with his mussed dark red hair — longer than that of both Cassius and Sebastian — and a few days' worth of scruff along his jaw, he had a hard, rugged appearance that spoke tantalizingly of power and passion which was just as attractive.

The pressure of my magic grew stronger, the glow from my palms bright in the dark forest. If I didn't connect with him soon, I'd pay the price.

I placed my hands over his heart and let my senses slide into his body. It didn't matter if Sebastian still kept pressure on the man's wound. Until my magic released me, it would heal the most grievous injuries first, not letting me go until this man was stable or someone else was in greater need. Given the state of the naked man, I doubted any of my magic would go into Sebastian at all before I ran out.

My power connected and I instantly knew that yes, almost every bone in his body had been broken, some, like his right femur had been shattered. Both of his lungs had been pierced by broken ribs, his spleen had ruptured, and he was bleeding out from numerous deep lacerations.

It was a miracle he was still alive, and I could feel his life rushing out of him. There wasn't time to be gentle and slowly seep my power into him. But in his condition, I doubted he'd feel the painful burn of being healed too quickly, so I drew in a steadying breath and released my magic without restraint. It crashed into him, a massive, hot wave, that always felt like blood pouring down my arms and over my hands and into my patient even though it wasn't actually blood.

He screamed and jerked upright.

Oh, my goodness!

With his eyes still closed, he rammed his palm into my chest. The air burst from my lungs, and I flew back, slamming into a large rock at the edge of the clearing.

Hot agony blazed through my chest and the forest lurched around me as my power surged inward, threatening to drown me.

Sebastian grabbed the naked man's arm — too little too late — and the man collapsed back to the ground as if he hadn't just sat up and hit me with his broken arm.

Cassius scrambled to my side and cupped my cheeks between his palms, trying to lock gazes with me. But I couldn't get my vision to steady. It had been a long time since I'd been hit so hard that the world spun, my breath had been knocked out of me, and my ribs had been cracked — which I knew with certainty two of them were. And never before had I been hit by a patient like that. Yes, I'd been hit and clawed and bitten, but that—

"Amiah." The angelic light radiating from Cassius's eyes flared as his concern intensified.

"I'm okay," I gasped, trying to push his hands aside. The naked man was still dying and my pain was nothing compared to that. I could deal with it later, and even if I hadn't been okay, my magic still wouldn't have allowed me to leave him.

Cassius didn't let go and his eyes narrowed. "You're not okay."

"And he's dying." I matched his glare. "Call triage."

"No, don't," Sebastian said, his hands back on the gushing gut wound, seemingly unaware that his white button-down was getting bloody. "It's too dangerous. Just get him stable. I'll take it from there."

"Stable doesn't mean he's out of the woods." I shoved at Cassius, shooting agony through my chest. He glared at me but sat back, letting me pass, and I scrambled back to the naked man.

Sebastian's lips quirked and he rolled his pale eyes at me. "You did not just say that."

"Say what?" I placed my hands back over the naked man's heart but held my power back. I didn't want a repeat of the first time I'd flooded him. "Both of you hold him down. I don't want to get hit again."

The hint of Sebastian's smile turned wicked, heating my insides with a yearning I'd spent my entire adult life ignoring and one I was going to continue ignoring because I was certain Sebastian was about to make fun of me.

"If you stabilize him," he said, "I'm pretty sure he *will* get out of the woods."

...because Sebastian would drag whoever this man was out of the park ring... which was more of a woods than a park.

"That wasn't in the least bit amusing," I huffed.

"You just don't want to admit you like a little word play," he said, making *word play* sound like it was supposed to be something else, something hot and dirty, that increased the aching heat inside me.

Cassius grabbed the naked man's shoulders, and Sebastian pressed down hard on the man's gut wound.

I drew in another steadying breath and, even though I didn't really have the time for it, strained to release my magic slowly, praying I could increase the flow without making him lash out again. All the while my magic screamed to work faster. *Hurry up. Save him.*

My power flowed back into him, thick and viscous

and clinging to his damaged cells while the excess leaked down my forearms, making them burn. *Slow and steady. Build it up gently.* I'd resisted the compulsion before — not often, but I had — and I could do it again.

"Okay, Bane," Cassius said. "Start talking. Why is it dangerous to take this guy to Operations?"

"Titus is—" Light flashed from a small tattoo almost completely covered in blood on the inside of Sebastian's wrist. "Fuck."

He jerked around as a man materialized out of the shadows behind him. One moment there was nothing, the next, a man — or rather fae from his delicately pointed ears — had appeared, the shadows partially bleeding out of his face and hands, leaving a few billowing clouds of darkness undulating under his skin. He wore all black and had a scarf pulled up covering his mouth and nose like a bandit... or an assassin.

He stabbed at Sebastian's heart with a knife the length of my forearm, and only Sebastian's sudden turn to face the other fae saved him. The blade sliced into Sebastian's side, his white button-down soaking up his blood in a dark, growing stain. With a grunt of pain, Sebastian seized the man's wrist, but the man jerked back, breaking free of Sebastian's hold, and lunged in again.

My power flared, the sudden shock of being attacked breaking my control of my magic. The power leaking down my forearms slammed into the naked man— what had Sebastian called him? Titus? It burned through his body, making him scream and his muscles seize.

"Because of this," Sebastian gasped, as he twisted just

enough so the blade cut his shirt but not skin, allowing him to get close to his assailant. He seized the man's wrist again and punched him in the gut, drawing a surprised *oomph*.

Cassius leaped to his feet, his fire magic bursting around his right hand, and he snapped a fire whip around the assailant's neck, but another man— no— demon from the hellfire in his eyes— no— vampire from his still lifeless essence rushed out of the shadows, his long black hair tied back in a ponytail sweeping behind him with the movement.

He sliced Cassius's whip with a black katana, the blade only visible from the momentary glint of moonlight and firelight off the metal, and sparks showered the ground, catching in the dry weeds and turning into small fires that were sure to get out of hand quickly.

They did, however, offer better illumination, and it was clear I'd been right about Cassius's assailant on both accounts. The man had both the hellfire of a demon in his eyes and the fangs of a vampire, which meant he had to have been half demon half human in order to be turned by a master vampire since the ritual didn't work on pure demons.

He, too, wore all black: black leather pants and a black wrap tunic with an East Asian feel to the cut and fabric. It hung past his knees, was bound tight across his chest, and secured by a wide sash and a leather belt.

He barreled toward Cassius and slashed at him with his katana. Cassius drew the flames in the weeds back into his palms putting out the mini fires as he jerked out of the way of the blade, but the demon-vampire didn't press his attack, instead shifting to lunge at me.

My pulse froze. I had to move, get out of the way, but my magic held me captive, refusing to release me until Titus was healed enough to move or I was physically pulled away.

This was why I never did field work. It was too dangerous. No matter how hard I concentrated or mentally fought my power, if it had locked onto someone, it wouldn't let go, even if I was in danger.

"Amiah, move," Sebastian shouted, but the glow of my power burned brighter and the hot sticky flow seized my muscles, keeping me locked in place.

Cassius snapped his fire whip around the demon-vampire's neck as a force-wave rushed from Sebastian's palms and slammed into me, ripping my hands away from Titus and knocking me onto my back. Pain sliced through my chest from my cracked ribs, stealing my breath, and my magic surged inward with the promise of a crushing backlash.

The demon-vampire staggered but didn't go down, and Cassius yanked him a few steps away from me with his fire whip before the demon-vampire twisted and severed the whip with his katana.

I heaved myself back to Titus, my power reconnecting with his injuries and taking control of my body as the weeds beside me caught fire.

"Cassius." I gritted my teeth and forced my hands to slide down Titus's body to get away from the flames. But I only managed to get to his abs before my power jerked me to a stop, not allowing me to move farther from his heart, the place where my magic had the easiest access into his body since he didn't have just one grave injury to concentrate on.

My heart pounded with a mix of fear and frustration. If I hadn't been locked onto him, I'd have been able to move my hands anywhere. It had been years since I'd let myself end up in a situation like this. Working in a medical center, first for the war, then the emergency department at the supers' hospital in the Quarter, and then in Operations had been enough to keep this nasty part of my magic at bay.

"Cassius. Your fire," I said, determined to keep my voice stern but calm. No one liked it when their physician panicked.

Except everything within me screamed. *Fire!* But also *save him!*

The heat seared my skin, the flames singeing my pantleg. Even if Titus's condition wasn't dire, I didn't want to have to waste magic healing myself since it took a lot more magic to heal myself than someone else.

I scrambled over Titus to his other side to get away from the flames and, grabbing his shoulder while my other hand was still stuck on his heart, tried to roll him out of danger. But the man was heavy — he must have been solid muscle — and I couldn't get him to roll, at least not while my healing magic was still rushing out of me into him, taking my strength with it.

"Cassius!" I wrenched my attention from my patient and the flames in search of help.

Sebastian still fought hand-to-hand with the shadowy fae, with two more growing blood patches staining his sliced shirt and a black tattooed glyph near his neck glowing with icy-blue light.

Cassius was a few feet away, his flames dancing around him and the demon-vampire, who lunged in with a quick jab. Cassius started to sidestep, then froze, the angelic light glowing in his eyes flaring. The blade plunged toward his chest and my pulse tripped. If I was still locked on Titus, I might not be able to save Cassius if he took a serious injury. But at the last minute, with a burst of fire around his hands and a scream, he heaved to the side.

For a second it looked like he'd managed to avoid getting cut, then the firelight shimmered in the blood soaking into his black T-shirt and the fabric parted revealing a laceration slicing across his upper chest from shoulder to shoulder.

"Don't make eye contact with the nightmare," Cassius gasped. He shot a ball of fire into the trees directly across from him as he scrambled out of the way of another sweep of the demon-vampire's katana.

A demon with hellfire hair licking around tall thick horns that protruded from his forehead burst from the shadows. He was, without a doubt, a nightmare, a demon who, in both his human and horse form, could paralyze you with fear.

"Amiah, can you run?" Cassius asked.

"Not even to get away from your fire," I snapped back. The flames now burned my patient's shoulder and the pressure of my magic surged.

"How long until he's stable?" Sebastian asked, slapping his ribs and activating another tattoo, although it didn't seem as if anything magical had happened.

"I—" I scrambled to hold back my rushing power, but with a scream, Titus jerked awake again, and his eyes flew open revealing striking golden irises that stole whatever I was going to say. For a second there was just him, his predatory gaze boring into me, seeing straight into my soul.

Then pain twisted his expression. His breath turned into ragged gasps, and he grabbed the front of my suit jacket and shoved me to the ground, impossibly rolling on top of me and pinning me with his still mostly broken body, his weight crushing me. The movement, with the strength and power rushing out of me, made my head spin.

Blood from his wounds splattered on my face and clothes, and he snarled, revealing pointed elongated canines, suggesting that maybe he was a werewolf.

"You can't have it," he growled, his eyes wild as he clamped a huge hand around my neck and squeezed.

AMIAH

I GASPED, CLAWING AT TITUS'S HAND WITH MY WEAK STILL-glowing fingers, my other hand still pressed against his chest. I tried to tell him I didn't want whatever it was he was protecting, but couldn't draw enough breath to speak. Without a doubt, all he needed to do was tighten his grip and he'd crush my windpipe.

"I won't let you have it," he growled, but for some reason, his grip didn't tighten, and his body trembled, his strange golden eyes wide with fear and pain.

"Amiah, is he stable?" Sebastian asked, either not noticing I was in trouble or not caring.

Help me!

I whimpered, the most noise I could make, but knew the moment the pathetic sound came out it wasn't loud enough to draw anyone's attention.

Please, look at me.

The forest grew darker. I was going to pass out soon.

I heaved against Titus's massive weight but couldn't move him.

"Doesn't matter, we have to get out of here," Cassius said, also not looking my way or he definitely would have come to my rescue. "Teleport us."

I dug my short nails into Titus's wrist. His gaze never left mine, his expression more dangerous beast than logical man.

Help.

The trembling in his body increased. "You can't have it. I won't let you." Now it sounded like he was begging.

"A teleport is not happening," Sebastian said. "We have to run for it. I can put them down long enough to get to my car if you can carry Titus— Oh, fuck. Titus. Let her go." Out of the corner of my eye, I saw Sebastian leap toward me, and Titus's attention jerked to the fae.

"Seireadan?" Titus gasped, and his eyes rolled back. He collapsed on top of me, stealing what little breath I had left and sending agony screaming through my chest.

My magical compulsion to heal him until he was stable finally released me — thank goodness for that! — leaving me weak with miniature convulsions racing through my muscles. I struggled to push him off, even just enough to squirm free, but I'd used too much magic too quickly and barely had the strength to breathe against his weight.

Cassius shot another fireball at the demon-vampire, tossing him into the nightmare although not dropping either of them, and heaved Titus off me as Sebastian slapped two more tattoos and hissed a sibilant — probably fae — word.

Another force-wave shot from his hand, this one stronger than before, picking up rocks, fallen branches, and flaming weeds. It put out all the fire and slammed into the fae, the demon-vampire, and the nightmare, tossing them deeper into the forest.

Sebastian jerked to face us. "I wove a bit of sleep in with that blast but that won't keep them down for long." He held his hand out to me and I batted it away and scrambled to my feet.

The forest darkened and lurched, and my legs shook, but I gritted my teeth. There was no way I was going to let Sebastian see how dizzy I was. It would just give him more to make fun of and the dizziness would pass... eventually.

"I'm parked down the path," Sebastian said, and Cassius hefted Titus over his shoulders.

We crashed through the underbrush and back down the path. Sebastian ran straight to the small, sleek silver two-door sports car parked at the side of the road and opened the passenger side door.

"Are you kidding me?" Cassius asked. "You came here in that?"

"If I'd known you were coming, I would have driven a bigger vehicle," Sebastian said, his tone dripping with sarcasm. "You're welcome to run with him all the way back to my place."

Cassius's eyes narrowed and the muscles in his jaw flexed. "We're not going back to your place."

Oh, my goodness.

The street darkened and whirled and I fought to keep standing.

Were they really having this conversation right now? "You're all bleeding. Those men could catch up with us any minute. Get in the car!"

Cassius stiffened and Sebastian's eyes widened and I realized my tone had been a lot sharper than I intended. But I wasn't going to take it back. I didn't need them to like me. I just needed them to not get hurt any worse than they already were, because I was already running low.

"You heard the lady," Sebastian said, gesturing to the open passenger door.

Titus was too big to fit in the back with someone else even if Sebastian pulled the front seats all the way forward, so Cassius set the big man in the front passenger seat and squeezed his not-nearly-as-big but still pretty-big frame into the barely there back seat.

I squished in beside him onto the soft black leather, grateful that I was about average size and build, and grabbed Titus's shoulder, easing more healing magic into him, and assessing his condition. Yes, he'd been well enough to be moved, but that didn't really mean much. Most of his organs and some of his bones had barely been stitched back together while other bones were still broken, and he still bled profusely. At least most of the internal bleeding had stopped.

Sebastian hopped into the driver's seat, drew in a shuddering breath, and activated another glyph along his right ribs. Icy blue-white light flared from the tattoo, turning his white shirt see-through, revealing the dark swirling lines covering his torso but also accentuating the large patches of blood soaking the fabric. He was going to need medical attention, if not my healing magic — which I could give him now that I'd been released from the need to heal Titus even though I didn't have much left — then certainly stitches, and Cassius would as well.

With another shuddering breath and a grip on the steering wheel that made the tendons in his forearms flex, Sebastian sped away from the curb, the wheels squealing against the asphalt.

"Okay," Cassius said, his voice low. "What was that?"

Sebastian swerved around a corner, putting a three-story building between us and the entrance to the park then took a hard left and raced down the road.

Cassius bit back a strangled grunt. "And that was a red light."

Titus moaned, my healing magic starting to pull him out of unconsciousness even though it would be better if he didn't wake. The agony of his broken body would still be overwhelming, and given his strength and violent reactions, it would be best if he didn't lash out while we were all crammed into Sebastian's tiny car. Except there wasn't anything I could do. My magic knitted broken bodies back together. It didn't sedate or dull pain.

"He needs a sedative and more medical attention. All of you need medical attention," I said, forcing my words to be firm and professional, and not letting my increasing dizziness and weakness affect my tone. I didn't want an argument. And I didn't want either of them to see how surging that much magic into someone affected me. Knowing Cassius, he'd get all worried and treat me as if I was fragile. He hadn't looked at me as if I was fragile in a long time and I intended to keep it that way. Because no one took a fragile woman seriously and I wasn't going to let anyone take my control away like that. "You're taking us to Operations."

"No." Sebastian's gaze jumped to the rear-view mirror and caught mine, his expression deadly serious. "You saw what happened. I'm taking Titus to my apartment."

"You don't think we can protect him?" Cassius's eyes narrowed. "Or will I find out the truth and have to arrest him?"

"Neither," Sebastian said. "I can only keep the protection spell I cast on Titus going for so long, and Operations doesn't have the kind of protections my apartment has. Those men will still be coming after him."

"What kind of protection?" Cassius demanded.

Sebastian snorted. "A glyph witch never casts and tells."

"So an illegal spell," Cassius huffed.

"Go ahead and prove it." Sebastian sped around a corner, going through another red light and making the muscles in Cassius's jaw flex.

With a scream, Titus jerked in his seat and slammed his knee into the dashboard, cracking it.

I pushed more magic into him, repeating my mantra in my head over and over again.

Just keep looking strong and calm. Just a little longer. Strong and calm.

But the speeding car did little to ease the growing whirl in my head, and my hunched forward position to maintain contact with Titus made it painful to draw each breath. That and my neck where he'd grabbed me was starting to hurt, which meant he'd squeezed hard enough to bruise. "He needs to be properly sedated. He's dangerous in this condition."

"He's dangerous in any condition." Sebastian pulled into a short driveway leading into the underground parking for a four-story office building. The heavy metal door rolled open, and he drove down the steep ramp, past row upon row of mostly empty parking spots, to the back of the garage that I was pretty sure was now in the basement of the next building over.

"This is none of your business, angel." Sebastian parked between an expensive looking SUV and another sleek sports car, this one black. He shoved open his door and got out, revealing that the whole left side of his button-down was soaked with blood.

Cassius climbed out after him. "A fight between supers makes it my business. I could bring you in for running those red lights."

"No you can't. You can only write me a ticket. Call a cab and go home." Sebastian shoved past Cassius, limped around the front of the car, and opened the passenger door. His breath was too fast and his expression tight. Even without my magic telling me, I knew he was in pain.

Titus moaned again, and Sebastian turned his attention to me. "Can you revive him? It'll be easier if I don't have to carry him."

"His broken legs are barely knitted back together, and even if I could revive him, given his injuries and his violent outbursts, that's a bad idea."

"Right. Of course. Dangerous in any condition," Sebastian said, his tone clear he thought he was stupid for having forgotten what he'd just said. He pressed his forehead against the doorframe and squeezed his eyes shut. "You God damn fucking idiot."

"Bane—" Cassius growled, but I cut him off before he could utter whatever he was going to threaten Sebastian with.

"Pick him up, Cassius, and let's get him cleaned up and in a bed." I glared at Cassius. There was no point in Titus bleeding out in Sebastian's fancy sports car when it would be more comfortable for him and me to finish what I could in Sebastian's apartment. "You can arrest Sebastian, or both of them after *all* of you have stopped bleeding."

Cassius huffed but pulled Titus out of the car and hefted him over his shoulders again as Sebastian led the way to a plain, cinderblock wall. The fae pressed his palm to one of the bricks, and the illusion shimmered then vanished revealing an elevator door.

The door slid open and the guys marched in as I clenched my hands and squared my shoulders, struggling to not show how weak I was, then I joined them. Sebastian hit the top of two buttons and the door slid shut. Guess the elevator only went to two floors. The garage and up to wherever we were going now.

Tense silence broken by sharp breathing from all the men and punctuated by moaning gasps from Titus filled the elevator. Darkness danced at the edge of my vision, and I tightened my fists, determined not to grab the side of the wall to keep my balance.

I will not look weak. I will be strong and calm. I wouldn't ever be weak again.

A moment later, the door opened to a long opulent

hall. I'd only been to Sebastian's apartment once before, but I didn't think I'd ever forget the white marble floor or the complicated gilded frescoes on the walls and ceiling of the hall outside his door. All that money wasted on decorations when it could have been spent on medical attention for those less fortunate.

The elevator had opened at the end of the hall. A quarter of the way down stood a heavy door with a large frosted blue and white stained-glass window, and at the far end were the stairs leading up to the roof and directly down to the ground level without any doors to the three other floors in the building. The soft *thump thump* of music from the nightclub below filled the silence but wasn't nearly as loud as I'd have expected this close to midnight, which suggested Sebastian had enspelled his floor to mute the sounds below.

Sebastian unlocked his front door, flicked a switch turning on a shimmering crystal chandelier hanging from the vaulted ceiling, and limped across his stunning white-on-white with hints of blue and silver living room toward his kitchen, leaving a trail of blood droplets on the white marble floor.

"Put him in a bed," Sebastian said, "then go. I can take it from there. He's a pretty fast healer so he'll probably be fine soon."

I huffed. No one healed that fast.

"Are you going to tell us who he is?" Cassius asked, adjusting his grip on Titus, and I realized Cassius didn't know where the bedrooms were. "And who were those men who tried to kill you?"

The last time we'd been here— or rather *the only*

time was when Cassius had been magically poisoned and we, along with the main JP team, had been running for our lives. He probably didn't even remember arriving, and he certainly hadn't been conscious when we'd left. At the time, I'd been terrified I was going to lose him. Without Marcus, all I had were Cassius and my fellow healer, Priam. I didn't make friends easily and I'd thought I'd found my soul mate and hadn't needed anyone else. Even if Cassius did always take assignments out of town, he'd been my one constant for almost a century.

The room started to tilt and I dug my nails into my palms. I'd been conscious the last time I'd left, I'd be conscious this time, too.

"I've already told you," Sebastian called from the kitchen. "His name is Titus and that's all you need to know."

"Not good enough, Bane. There are three dangerous men in my city."

"It's not *your* city," Sebastian said. "It's your brother's. And there are lots of dangerous men and women here. Three more you're never going to see again are not your concern."

"They didn't look like the kind of men to give up. If they know anything about angels, they'll know Am—" The light in Cassius's eyes blazed. "They'll know all angels live in the JP Operations building. We left with their target. You or Titus. They're going to show up at Operations looking for you whether we like it or not."

Sebastian limped out of the kitchen with a small red first aid kit that I doubted had much of anything helpful in it. "They know Operations doesn't have an area concealment spell. They'll know Titus isn't there."

"You don't know that," Cassius said.

Titus moaned and jerked, forcing Cassius to shift to keep hold of the big man, the movement sliding his foot into the growing blood pool at his feet.

"The protection of everyone in that building and in this city are my responsibility right now."

"Then put Titus in a bed and go fucking protect them." Sebastian limped around his conversation area of two couches and a coffee table, past his grand piano to the hall with the apartment's other rooms, and threw open the first door on the right.

Cassius glared after him.

"Just follow him." I wasn't going to be able to remain standing, not with the whirling lightheadedness threatening to steal my consciousness, and I certainly wasn't going to be able to hide my trembling for much longer. I didn't want either Cassius or Sebastian to see me give in and sit. Or worse, pass out. "You can argue while I heal you two then finish with Titus."

With a grunt, Cassius marched to the door and pushed past Sebastian. Inside was a clean, elegant bedroom done in the same white, blues, and silver as the rest of Sebastian's apartment. The room was lit by another, smaller, crystal chandelier, had a king-sized bed with a pristine white duvet, and an en suite bathroom with marble countertops and a standup shower.

I yanked the duvet off the bed, tossed it on the floor out of the way, pulled off the white sheet underneath, and laid it on the bathroom floor. It wasn't ideal and there wasn't a whole lot of room in the bathroom for all four of us, but it was the best solution to clean Titus up.

"Oh, for the love of— Just put him in the bed," Sebastian said.

"Once I've stopped the bleeding and he's cleaned up, then yes, we'll put him in a bed." I pointed to the big, heavy man on Cassius's shoulder. "I doubt you want to have to remake the bed around him."

Cassius set Titus on the sheet then perched on the closed toilet lid, his knee bouncing with what I knew was pent-up frustration, his expression hard. A wisp of smoke curled around his fingers, the precursor to his fire magic escaping his control and wrapping around his hands with dangerous flames.

The muscles in his jaw clenched and the smoke broke apart as he got his emotions back under control.

I'd seen his control slip more times in the last few weeks than I ever had during our friendship, but I had hoped that with things finally settling down, he'd no longer be struggling to keep his flames at bay.

Of course, it probably didn't help that we were just attacked and he was in pain. Something I could take care of. But first—

I sank to the floor beside Titus and pressed my hands over his heart to assess if moving him had damaged any of the work I'd already done. Somehow, he'd gotten through being hauled out of the park ring and up to Sebastian's apartment without redamaging any of his still-fragile organs, leaving me a few bones and most of the lacerations to heal, many of which could wait until tomorrow when I'd recovered some of my power. And, much to my surprise, he didn't have a single burn on his body from Cassius's accidental flames.

"I'm assuming you don't have a suture kit," I said to Sebastian, "and that first aid kit isn't big enough for all the gauze and bandages I'll need so—"

"So come up with something. Fine." Sebastian dropped the first aid kit on the counter and ran a hand over his spiky white hair, streaking blood over the tips. "You're not going until he's stopped bleeding, are you?"

I met his crystalline gaze. "Until *everyone* has stopped bleeding."

His lips quirked and desire heated his eyes. "Does that mean we all have to get naked?"

A foolish shiver of need swept through me, but I was pretty sure he was flirting to change the topic, not because he was actually interested in me, so I squashed the emotion and forced my focus to the job at hand: healing my patients.

"Get her bandages, Bane," Cassius growled.

Sebastian snapped his attention to Cassius. "Only if you promise to get the hell out of my apartment."

"Tell me who's after your friend and we'll go."

Jeez, neither man was going to budge figuratively on the topic and likely literally with their physical positions. Which wasn't going to help me hurry through healing everyone. I hadn't thought Sebastian was as stubborn as Cassius, but then I guess I didn't really know him.

Either way, I couldn't let this go on.

I jerked to my feet, slicing pain through my chest, and pointed to the door behind Sebastian. The room spun and darkened, and I grabbed the counter to steady myself. "Bandages. And you—" I tightened my grip on the counter to keep my balance and forced my expression into a hard, professional mask, praying neither man noticed how weak I really was. "Take off your shirt so I can assess your injuries without using my magic."

Sebastian snickered. "So we *do* get to get naked." He limped out of the bedroom, leaving me with Cassius and his hardened emotions.

"He's as bad as an incubus," Cassius growled. "Couldn't get Gideon's mate so he's going after you."

"Which implies I'm second best. Gee, thank you."

Cassius's eyes widened as he realized what he'd said. "That's not what I meant."

But it wasn't wrong. I'd made a point of making it clear to everyone that I wasn't interested in a romantic relationship... well, everyone except Marcus, because I'd been waiting for *the one*. I doubted anyone at Operations ever saw me in a romantic way — including Marcus — and I had no one to blame but myself. Except that hadn't bothered me until I'd realized what a fool I'd been and how even just waiting for my inevitable soul mate took away my choice for who and how I wanted to first be intimate with someone.

And I *had* to stop thinking about that. There was no point wallowing when I had a job to do. There wasn't even any point in planning. Once I'd healed Cassius, Sebastian, and Titus and had recovered, *then* I'd take action.

Hunh. I could use the excuse of checking up on Titus to come back to Sebastian's. If I was lucky, Cassius would be busy and I'd be able to discreetly hire Sebastian to remove my mating brand.

The man would make a big deal about it, me coming to him, but I could live with a little humiliation if it meant I'd be free.

"You know that's not what I meant," Cassius said, a whisper of smoke curling from his hands.

"I know." I heaved my attention back to business. Why was it so hard to focus these days? "How badly are you hurt?" I asked as I shrugged out of my ruined suit jacket, turned on the tap, and pumped soap from the dispenser into my palm.

"I'll be okay." He shrugged and winced.

I cocked an eyebrow at him, dried my hands, and checked the first aid kit for gloves more out of habit from using a combination of human and angelic healing than anything else because my healing magic wouldn't let me transmit diseases or infections. The kit didn't have any gloves, so I turned my attention back to Cassius.

"I can manage," he said, his tone returning to hard and commanding as if I were an agent under his command... which I wasn't. Trauma trumped agent-in-charge every time. Just silly agents liked to forget that.

"I'm not letting you go after those men while injured," I replied, matching his tone because I knew once he'd pulled enough information out of Sebastian he was going after them. "Take off your shirt and let's see."

I didn't really need for him to disrobe for my magic to work, but given I was low and still had Sebastian to heal and Titus to top up and the fact that I was in a bathroom with limited resources and not an OR, I needed to be smart about how I used what I had left.

"Amiah, I'm—"

"You already know it's useless to lie about your physical condition. Why do you insist on it every time?" He always did this, always pretended he wasn't hurt, or it wasn't as bad as it was, and always told me to take care of someone else first, as if I couldn't assess how best to use my magic. "Take your shirt off, agent. Don't make me work any harder than I have to."

I shuffled past Titus to stand in front of Cassius. His eyes narrowed. The icy hard edge that had been his almost constant expression since he'd returned to Union City just under a month ago grew into a silent challenge to my command.

Well, he could challenge it all he liked. I wasn't giving in. I could be just as hard and icy as he could. I'd spent a lifetime hiding my emotions for the sake of my patients, and right now I was exhausted and dizzy and trying not to tremble. I had every reason to be angry, more reasons than he did. I just wanted to go home, crawl into bed, and pretend I could stop thinking about Marcus and my brand, but I couldn't ignore the compulsion to heal Cassius, Sebastian, and Titus. Even if my magic hadn't locked onto them, I was still compelled to help. It would drive me crazy if I had an opportunity to help and I didn't take it. At least now I could choose how much I healed them.

"You're the agent on duty, you're going to put yourself in a dangerous situation. I *can't* let you walk out of here still bleeding. Please."

The look in Cassius's eyes softened, and his piercing blue gaze locked with mine.

My breath caught and my pulse stuttered at the intensity in his eyes. It sent a shiver racing down my spine, bringing back with a vengeance the yearning Sebastian had awoken in the park ring, defying my iron grip on my emotions, and making my body throb with need.

Cassius dragged his sliced and bloody shirt up over his head, revealing his gorgeous sculpted body and making my pulse stall completely.

AMIAH

I WAS CERTAIN CASSIUS DIDN'T MEAN FOR HIS GAZE capturing mine to be sexual. We didn't have that kind of a relationship and never would. But I couldn't stop my thoughts from jumping straight to desire... for him?

That wasn't possible. We were friends. Nothing more.

No, I just yearned for anyone at this point. How long could an angel go without intimacy before she lost her mind? Especially knowing that my not-soul-mate was being intimate with his actual mate, quite possibly at this very moment.

Which I didn't want!

Why was that so hard to remember?

Because it wasn't intimacy I didn't want. I didn't want the control-stealing soul bond. And now my reason for celibacy was gone.

That, and I missed physical contact. We might have just been friends, but Marcus had needed physical contact. I doubted he'd even been aware of his need since he wasn't a naturally born shifter and probably didn't know shifters had a much smaller personal space than most people, especially angels. I'd selfishly not told him and allowed him to stand too close and to embrace me when he'd thought I needed comfort... when I *did* need comfort, and now that I'd gotten used to that kind of closeness, that touch, it was gone.

Except Cassius was the last person I'd get physical comfort from, even platonic comfort. That need for closeness just wasn't in his nature. He'd fight all my battles if I let him, but he'd never sit just a little too close. And now I'd gone weeks without something I'd had for the last four years. I hadn't thought I'd need physical contact on the same level as a shifter, but maybe I'd been wrong.

And again! I wasn't supposed to be thinking about that right now.

I refocused my attention on Cassius, his gaze still boring into me, his chiseled muscular torso on display. Blood smeared his skin and the parts not bloody were red and swelling with the beginning of heavy contusions. The laceration across his chest still wept, along with another gash at his ribs.

I contemplated telling him to take his pants off since his left pantleg was pasted to his thigh with blood, but we weren't in triage, and I doubted he'd appreciate me asking him to strip to his underwear in Sebastian's apartment... especially since Sebastian had already teased us about getting naked.

"Just slow the bleeding," Cassius said, dropping his gaze from mine, his voice strangely gruff.

"I know how to do my job." I sagged to the floor, using the counter to help lower myself, mindful of my cracked ribs, and laid my trembling hands against the laceration across his chest. If I didn't think he'd go headlong after those men, I *would* just heal him enough to slow the bleeding. Angels didn't have the fastest innate healing among supernatural beings, but they did have some, and with a partial healing, the wounds would be fully shut within twenty-four hours. They'd scar unless I gave him another session, but he'd survive.

Except I knew Cassius. He wouldn't allow those men to endanger anyone else, and he'd been more dogged about protecting everyone since the mess a few weeks ago where he'd helped his brother take down Lilith, the Hellfire Queen.

My magic swelled into my palms, the oozing heat weak compared to the flood I'd poured into Titus. I closed my eyes to concentrate and gently pushed my power into the wound. He didn't need to be healed quickly so there was no point in hurting him while I healed him.

My power billowed but instead of staying in the chest wound, it slipped down to the laceration in his side, heading to the worst injury first. Except the added distance thinned my magic, stretching it taut, and that required more magical strength to heal him, so I moved my left hand to his side to ease the pressure growing inside me.

A shiver trembled through his body and his muscles tensed. "You can go faster."

"This won't take long. You can wait." Through my connection to his body, I felt the flesh in his side start to knit together. And now that the laceration in his side was no longer the worst injury, a stream of my magic split off and sank into his thigh, thinning my power even more.

Another split and my magic swelled back through the laceration across his chest. My muscles contracted, my body drawing into my deepest reserves to keep going, and even with my eyes closed, I could feel the bathroom spinning.

"Amiah."

The voice was far away and yet close at the same time. Tender yet stern.

Just a little more, just to ensure he was at full strength when he put his life on the line again.

"Amiah."

Fingers clasped around my wrists — Cassius's fingers — and he jerked my hands from his body.

The connection between us snapped, jolting through me with a ghost of a backlash and another sharp slice of pain from my ribs, and I wrenched my attention up to him. Or at least I tried to. The light in the bathroom had dimmed and he was slightly out of focus.

"That's enough," Cassius said, and for a moment he had the same look of pity and concern that he'd had when he'd found me chained in that tent all those years ago. A look I swore I'd never see again on his face or anyone's. A look I desperately wanted to forget, but couldn't.

I wasn't helpless. I wasn't. And I'd never be helpless again.

I tightened my mask of cool professionalism and dropped my gaze, unable to hold his. The lacerations on his chest and side were sealed shut, but because he'd pulled me away and my magic hadn't withdrawn from him, I knew they weren't completely healed. They, along with the laceration in his thigh, were probably still tender to the touch under all that blood.

His eyes narrowed. "You need to rest."

As much as I wanted to argue with him, I couldn't. I was exhausted, except I wasn't done. Sebastian and Titus were still bleeding, and my compulsion to heal them, the compulsion that had left me weak and helpless all those years ago, made my pulse pick up.

I loved and hated my magic. I saved lives, gave people second chances, but I often did it whether I wanted to or not. Sometimes I could ignore the compulsion, but right now I was too tired to fight it. It was easier to just give in, finish what I could, and be done with it.

Which made me want to scream in frustration. It didn't matter how hard I tried to be in control, I never truly was.

I searched inside my palms, the place where I always felt my magic, to see how much I had left. A spark still warmed my hands. If I was careful, I could partially close the worst of Sebastian's and Titus's wounds, but that was the best I was going to get.

"I've a little left for Sebastian and Titus," I said, standing. The bathroom lurched and darkened, and I clutched the counter. "Then I'm done."

"You might be able to convince everyone else you're still fine, but I know you're more tired than you look," Cassius said, his expression softening even more, worry dimming the angel glow in his eyes. "Bane is a big boy. He can take care of himself."

"He sure is and he sure can," Sebastian said as he limped into the doorway, holding a pair of scissors and a folded white sheet. He'd thought to wash the blood from his hands and forearms, but hadn't changed his clothes yet. "Especially if that means you get out of my apartment."

Except he looked pale— or rather paler, which I hadn't thought was possible with his complexion, and his skin had a grayish hue and wasn't as luminescent as usual.

"Just sit and take off your shirt." I pointed to the toilet where Cassius sat then turned on the tap again out of habit and scrubbed Cassius's blood from my hands.

"No, Amiah," Cassius insisted, "you're going home."

"Don't tell me what I can and cannot do." And really, if I didn't want a bigger fight about it, I shouldn't waste time arguing. I should just heal Sebastian and Titus and end the conversation.

I split the magic I had left in half, lurched to Sebastian, and grabbed his forearm with my clean but still wet hand. With a forceful burst, I shoved one half of my power into him and partially knitted the worst of his injuries together. He screamed at the sudden painful blast of magic into his body and dropped the sheet and scissors to clutch the doorframe, his breath ragged his eyes wide.

"Jesus," he gasped.

The muscles in my legs gave out and I dropped to the floor at Titus's feet, painfully jarring my ribs. Cassius leaped from the toilet seat to grab me, but I shoved the rest of my power into Titus before he could reach me.

Titus howled and his eyes flew open. His hand snapped up to hit me, and Cassius seized it and yanked it back, as Sebastian pressed one hand to his shoulder activating a glyph, dropped to Titus's side, and placed his other hand over Titus's heart. The big man's eyes rolled back with Sebastian's spell and he collapsed, unconscious again, onto the bloody sheet on the floor.

"Jeez, Amiah," Cassius groaned as he leaned against the side of the counter. "Of all the stupid—"

"You don't want to finish that sentence." We'd argued before about me overexerting myself — a lot, actually, during the war — but I'd thought he understood how I had to help. I'd had power left and both Sebastian and Titus had needed it and I just couldn't fight the compulsion. It was really that simple.

I jerked a trembling hand over Titus, falling back on my cool professional persona to stay in control. "Now he still has a few broken bones and his condition is fragile. Clean him up, pack and bind the wounds that are still bleeding and get him into bed."

"You know that in your condition, I now have to escort you back to Operations," Cassius said, standing and washing his hands. At least he was going to do as I'd asked and finish with Titus first.

"You weren't going to before?" Sebastian rolled his eyes. "She just used who-knows-how-much magic. Chivalry really is dead."

"I was going to call her a cab and then ensure her safety by going after those men."

Which was such a Cassius thing to do. He didn't do

friendly, warm gestures. He abandoned you to go out and bring you justice.

"And I've already told you she's not in danger." Sebastian grabbed the scissors and cut into the sheet.

"Someone threw your friend out of a plane or helicopter and sent men after him to make sure he was dead," Cassius said, soaking a hand towel and ringing out the water. "They tried to kill him. Don't you want justice?"

"Capture him." Sebastian ripped a strip from the sheet.

"What?" The light in Cassius's eyes flared.

"They tried to kill *us* so they could *capture* him. I'm not bringing anyone else into this. Believe me when I say, if you're not near Titus, you're not in danger."

"You'll pardon me if I just don't take your word for it," Cassius said, kneeling beside Titus and getting to work on cleaning him up.

Oh, for goodness sake. Again? They were going to be stuck in a standoff all night and there wasn't any way now that Cassius would agree to let me leave by myself, no matter how much I argued with him. If I had more energy, I'd smack both of them. "Stop talking in circles. Sebastian, what's your evidence? How do you know for certain the Quarter and Operations are safe? Cassius isn't going to leave without more information."

A hint of a victorious smile curled Cassius's lips.

Yeah, no. You're not going to think you've won this. "And Cassius, believe him. He's helped the JP enough to get the benefit of the doubt."

"Yeah, but not out of the goodness of his heart. He sent us a bill," Cassius said.

Sebastian shrugged, and a whisper of wicked sexual playfulness gleamed in his eyes. "I had to see if the JP would pay."

"Your evidence," I repeated before Cassius could argue about that as well.

"Fine." Sebastian sighed. "Titus is from the fae realm and those men were bounty hunters of the Shadow Court. He's their only target." A ghost of something passed across his expression but vanished before I could figure out what it meant. "They won't make trouble in the mortal realm unless they have to, such as finding us with Titus, and they won't do a full assault of any place. That would draw too much attention. The only people in Union City in danger will be me and Titus as soon as you two get the hell out of my apartment." Sebastian tore another strip from the sheet with a sharp *riiiiip*. "Oh, and no, I don't want the JP's help."

"I'm going to hold you responsible if you're wrong." Which was as much of an acknowledgment as Sebastian was going to get from Cassius that he was backing down.

"You go right on ahead and do that," Sebastian shot back.

I was sure Cassius was going to go home, sleep on it, and return at the crack of dawn demanding answers, but that was a problem for tomorrow.

Cassius harrumphed, but he and Sebastian did get to work cleaning and dressing Titus's wounds. In strained silence, but they did it. At least they were no longer arguing.

By the time they were finished and had hauled Titus into the bed, I'd regained enough strength to stand and walk without assistance. I could almost pretend I hadn't been weak and had just been sitting and supervising the guys' work. Except if I'd said that out loud, I was sure neither man would have believed me. And if I thought too long about it, my cheeks would flush with embarrassment. I was supposed to be a professional. Calm, in control, a rock in the painful chaos of a patient's injuries. I wasn't the one who was supposed to need help, not ever again.

"I'll come back in the morning and check on you and Titus." I grabbed my bloody suit jacket from the bathroom floor, mindful of hiding my sore ribs from Cassius because he'd make a fuss over that if he knew about them.

"It's better if you don't," Sebastian said, escorting us to his front door. "Unless you want to stay the night?" His tone turned sultry, and that damned desire heated low within me again.

Except I was pretty sure his offer was to tease me and Cassius. It wasn't real. Not even in the sense of a one-night stand... which I wasn't interested in. Really. That, and I needed to get back home and have my friend Priam discreetly heal my cracked ribs and what I was sure was going to be a spectacular bruise around my throat.

Not to mention, I had no clothes here and mine were covered in blood. Oh, and I really wanted a shower. If I stayed, that meant getting naked... in Sebastian's apartment... with him close by.

A shudder swept through me, but with excitement at the prospect, not the nerves or fear I'd have expected.

I tightened my expression to hide my surprise. There was something very wrong with me.

What I needed Sebastian for was to see if he could remove my mating brand before it fully formed. Nothing more. *Then* I could find someone to ease my need for physical contact. Someone who wasn't flirting just to get a rise out of me. Someone more appropriate.

"I'll be by midmorning," I said, heading out the door before Sebastian could argue and making my head spin with the sudden movement.

Cassius fell into step beside me and Sebastian's door closed, the deadbolt sliding shut with a heavy *click*.

"I might not be able to escort you back here in the morning," Cassius said, his voice low. "And yes, I know you don't need someone to walk you around, but those guys are still out there."

The spinning didn't ease up as I reached the stairs, so I slowed my pace — hopefully not enough for Cassius to notice — and grabbed the railing to steady myself. As much as I wanted to remind him that I wasn't helpless, I couldn't argue with his assessment of the situation.

"There's no way I'm going to be able to convince Sebastian to bring Titus to Operations." I reached the landing of the third floor, my slower pace doing nothing to ease the spinning and my breath painful and shallow. "I don't believe for a minute his friend heals so fast that he'll be fine in the morning. He's going to need another session or a lot of bedrest."

"And given the situation, I doubt Sebastian will think bedrest is a good idea," Cassius said.

"Would you?" Even I knew enough that the longer they stayed in one place, the greater the chance of being caught. Just because Sebastian said those men weren't going to cause trouble, didn't mean they wouldn't start asking around about a faekin. There were so few of them in the world and only one in Union City. Sooner or later someone would point them to Sebastian.

"I'm just afraid of what he's going to do." Cassius blew out a heavy breath. "I shouldn't have let it go."

"You should have figured out how to get him onto your side." I let go of the railing to go around the corner on the second-floor landing, and stumbled, just a little bit, but managed to catch my balance by leaning against the wall as I walked. "You've worked with him before."

"Not sure the fight against Lilith counts. He was working with Gideon's team. I was setting my career on fire."

"You did what you thought was right." I struggled to draw in a deeper breath. The shallow pants weren't enough and my dizziness was growing, and now it felt as if Titus was lying on top of me again, crushing my chest.

Cassius glanced at me and frowned. "You don't look good."

"Just tired." He was one of a very few who knew first-hand what overtaxing myself did to me. Although it was starting to worry me that maybe I wasn't recovering as quickly as usual because I'd completely drained myself too soon after the last time I'd drained myself — that being the fight against Lilith a few weeks ago.

"You know finishing Titus's healing isn't your responsibility," he said. "Bane has more than enough money to afford medical attention."

"But it wouldn't be magical," I gasped, struggling to breathe. Only angels had the ability to magically heal, and the three other angels in Union with healing worked at Mercy Memorial. They didn't keep private practices.

"Still not your problem."

It wasn't, but I had every intention of returning to Sebastian's, might as well heal Titus when I did.

We reached the bottom of the stairs and stepped out onto a small patio lit by a single light hanging above the door. The *thump thump thump* of the music from the dance club throbbed in my chest the moment we'd passed through the doorway, adding more evidence to the theory that Sebastian had a sound-muting spell on his residence.

The patio was just big enough to comfortably hold a wrought-iron bistro table with two chairs, its boundaries marked by four planter boxes with evergreen shrubs. Beyond, cloaked in darkness, lay a narrow alley and our way out to the street to catch a cab.

I took three steps away from the door and the air around me vanished. One minute I could breathe, sort of, the next, nothing. The weight crushing my chest swelled, making the pressure from before seem like nothing, with a pain that went beyond just my cracked ribs, and my lungs burned, desperate for oxygen.

I staggered and grabbed the edge of the bistro table, but didn't have the strength to hold myself up. My knees smacked against the concrete ground and I crumpled onto my side. The patio spun around me, getting darker and darker, the light above the door growing smaller and smaller.

My pulse stuttered, fighting to keep going, and I desperately dug inside myself for magic, even just a spark, to save myself. But I was empty. I'd given everything to save Titus and heal Cassius and Sebastian.

And on top of that, I had no idea what was wrong with me! How could I not know? I could connect with the life force inside someone and know what was wrong with them in an instant, and that included me.

But I couldn't get my thoughts to focus past the encroaching darkness and the burning in my lungs. All I knew was that I was suffocating, but I had no idea why.

Cassius's face leaped into my line of vision. His expression was filled with fear and he cupped my cheeks between his strong hands, his skin hot against mine, his fire magic on the verge of releasing. His mouth moved, but I couldn't hear him past the rushing in my ears. The darkness swelled, blotting out everything except a weak glimmer from the angel glow in his eyes, and my fingers and toes went numb as a chill settled inside me.

AMIAH

TIME LURCHED, AND I GASPED IN A RAGGED BREATH THAT sent screaming agony through my chest. One minute I was on the ground dying, the next I was in Cassius's arms, my ear pressed against his chest hearing the rapid thud of his heart. It was like that day all over again when he'd found me. I'd been weak, barely alive not just because I'd been physically abused but because my own magic had compelled me to heal so many people without rest.

The worst part was that I'd had no one to blame but myself for my condition. If I'd resisted the urge, held my power back, I might have been strong enough to escape. But there'd been so many suffering people, many of them children. How could I have refused them? How could I have not helped them just to free myself?

Except by the time I'd realized saving my strength was my only way to escape, that the human who'd enslaved me was going to profit off my healing magic until I'd withered and died, I was too weak to resist my healing compulsion.

"Put her on the couch," Sebastian said from somewhere ahead of me.

"How did you not know this would happen?" Cassius demanded as he set me down on something soft. "You should have warned us there was a spell on her."

"Right, because I always know when there's a spell around."

I pried my eyes open and struggled to focus on my surroundings. We were back in Sebastian's apartment, and my gaze caught and stalled on a rainbow of refracted light from the crystal chandelier shining on the marble floor near my foot. My thoughts spun around and around, crushing pain still seized my chest, and I couldn't catch my breath.

"Don't you?" Cassius demanded. "Those men were dangerous. You should have checked or something. That should be standard practice."

"Not an agent," Sebastian shot back. "There is no standard practice."

"Not good enough." Cassius cupped my cheeks again with his too-warm hands, smoke curling from his skin. He was starting to lose control of his fire. He raised my head, pulling my attention away from the rainbow to meet his gaze, his eyes filled with worry.

I still couldn't figure out what was wrong with me, why I'd suffocated. It was like my mind had completely turned off and I couldn't get it started again. Draining myself might have made me blackout, but it shouldn't have suffocated me, and even if I had blacked out, it should have happened right after healing Titus.

"What happened?" I asked, my lips numb, my words

embarrassingly slurred. I needed to pull myself together so he'd stop looking at me like that.

"Just a minor complication," Sebastian said, drawing close and pressing a hand over my heart.

Cassius stiffened, his gaze dipping to Sebastian's hand just above my breast before leaping back to mine. "He says you're linked with Titus. That's why you passed out."

Everything within me froze. "I'm what?"

No.

No no no. This wasn't happening, it couldn't be happening, please don't let it be happening.

"No. I can't be. I won't be. I—" I lurched forward, but Sebastian pressed me back onto the couch, my body so weak I doubted he had to use much force.

"Just take it easy," he said.

Take it easy! As if this wasn't my worst fear come to life?

My pulse leaped into a rapid tattoo and panic stole what little breath I'd managed to recover. I couldn't be bonded. Not so soon. Not when there was a hope, albeit a slim hope, but a hope nonetheless, that I could escape that fate. I hadn't even had a moment to talk with Sebastian. But without a doubt, now that the brand had formed, it'd be impossible to break. The one shot I had at freedom was gone, all because my stupid magic had locked onto a stranger and compelled me to save him.

"It'll be okay," Sebastian said, and an icy tingle of his magic seeped into my skin, doing little to ease my panic. It tugged at something inside me then melted into nothing. "Damn. I was right. Well, no matter. I'll break it and then you can be on your merry way."

"You're just going to break it? Just like that?" A harsh laugh escaped my lips. If it was that easy to break a mating brand, surely angels would have known about it.

My thoughts stuttered over that. Unless maybe no one knew because no one wanted to know? Maybe he was right and I could be free before the brand compelled me to fall in love with Titus. I didn't even know Titus. How was that fair? I didn't want to lose my life to a stranger. I didn't—

Sebastian frowned. "Okay, maybe not *just* like that."

"Of course not." My heart sank and my eyes burned with tears that I was *not* going to cry. I needed to keep it together and regain control. If I looked strong and acted strong, eventually I'd be strong. I wouldn't let this define me. Not like it had for my whole life. I'd find a way out. I would. Please.

"Hey," Cassius said, shifting to sit beside me on the couch — with an appropriately modest amount of space between us — and drawing my attention back to him. "You're not trapped."

"Don't," I said, my throat tight. If he tried to convince me this was a good thing, I'd start crying. And I was *not* going to cry! "Don't tell me it's magical and beautiful and sacred."

Sebastian huffed. "A leash spell? Yeah. It's anything but. It's not even close to a soul bond and certainly not that kind of permanent. I can break it. I just need a resonance charm."

His words tripped in my mind. "So you're saying...?"

I pressed my hand against my hip where my aching mating brand was. It didn't hurt more than before and it wasn't warm like the stories said a newly formed brand felt like. The need to pull up my camisole and shove down the waistband of my pants to check made my pulse race even faster. But I couldn't do it in front of Sebastian or Cassius. Cassius would probably be awed and amazed that I was destined to have a soul mate, and Sebastian would make some remark about taking my clothes off.

Sebastian chuckled. "You thought you were branded?"

"What other option was there?" I glared at him, fighting tears that were a mix of panic and relief. I still had time. I could still be free.

"I suppose leash spells are rare here." He sat on the edge of his coffee table. He still wore his bloody clothes and blood still streaked the tips of his white and silver hair, and while I was sure he wasn't bleeding as badly as before I'd healed him, his complexion was still a little gray. "The good news is it won't fuck with your emotions like a soul bond and it's not permanent."

"And the bad news?" Cassius asked, his voice dark and dangerous.

"You can't go far. A leash spell links a prisoner to their master, so if the prisoner goes beyond the designated distance, they'll suffocate. Well, technically it removes the air around the prisoner and that suffocates them. And by the looks of it, you can't go more than a hundred feet from Titus."

My breath hitched, and the panic that had eased when I'd learned I wasn't mated to Titus surged, squeezing my chest and turning my breath into shallow quick gasps again. "So I'm Titus's prisoner?"

"No. Titus started suffocating as well. That's why I ran down to get you," Sebastian said. "I thought he was the prisoner half of the spell. But I think what happened is that he somehow managed to break a leash spell originally on him, but didn't completely dispel it. When you healed him, the spell must have reignited. But it's as if you're both the prisoner."

I couldn't be anyone's prisoner. Not again. Even if it hadn't been intended, I couldn't be trapped like this.

The urge to go, get as far away from Titus as possible, made my stomach roil because that was the very thing I couldn't do.

"And those men were the ones holding him captive?" Cassius asked.

"No." Sebastian rolled his eyes at Cassius. "Those were the men hired by the man holding him captive. Someone who casts a leash spell doesn't do his own dirty work."

Please. I can't be trapped.

And I couldn't let this fear control me. *You're stronger than this, remember?* There was a way out. Sebastian said he could break the spell.

I clung to that thought and sucked in a steadying breath that shot agony through my cracked ribs and drew a whimper that I couldn't keep back.

More smoke curled from Cassius's hands, and Sebastian sat forward, pressing his palms against my knees, the gesture honest and pure without any hint of sexual intent.

"Just take it slow," the fae said. "Depending on the spell, it could take a while for the effects to wear off."

Except everything within me screamed at the idea of being trapped a second longer.

"You said you need a resonance charm to break the spell," I forced out, fighting to keep my tone even and calm.

"Yeah, I need it to find your magical resonance, Titus's, and the spell's so I can get in and pull it apart." Sebastian squeezed my knees in reassurance, then stiffened as if he'd just realized what he was doing, and leaned back, drawing his hands away. "It's not simple, but I'm more than capable of handling it," he added, his tone deepening, turning his words into a sexual innuendo.

Cassius's eyes narrowed. "Then get the charm and break this spell."

"Would love to, because that would get you the hell out of my house, but I need sleep." He shoved up to his feet and stared down at me. "And since you can't get more than a hundred feet from Titus, it looks like you're staying the night."

"You're not going to do it now?" I squeaked. Now. I had to be free now. I couldn't be trapped. *Let-me-go-let-me-go-let-me-go.*

"You don't want me fucking this up," Sebastian said. "The spell won't do anything to you if you don't get too far from Titus. You'll be fine until the morning."

But I was trapped!

"All right then," Cassius said as he pulled out his phone. "I'll call Chris and get him to bring over a change of clothes for us."

"Of course, you're staying, too." Bane threw his hands

up. "Well, I hope you like sleeping together because I only have one other guestroom."

Cassius's eyes widened. "We're not— I mean—" He cleared his throat. "That wouldn't be appropriate."

"I'll take the couch in the study." I stood, the movement making the room tilt. My body trembled with the effort to hold my panic at bay and not let them see it. I wasn't going to last much longer. I needed to get alone before either of them realized the truth: that I couldn't handle what they thought was so simple, that I was weak.

Cassius jerked up and grabbed my elbow, helping me steady myself. "I'll take the couch. You should have the bed."

"Great. Now that you've got that all sorted, I'm going to bed." Sebastian shook his head and headed down the hall, not bothering to turn the light on.

"Do you know if the other guestroom has an en suite?" Cassius asked as Sebastian went into the room at the very end of the hall.

"It does." I dragged my attention back to Cassius. Surely he could feel my pulse racing, but he didn't react as if he knew I was falling apart. He wasn't even giving me *the look* any more. I just needed to hold out a little longer.

"Then have a shower. I'll leave your clothes outside the door," he said.

My gaze dipped over his still bare and bloody torso. "You should probably have a shower, too."

Which meant I'd have to hold out even longer while I waited for him to use my bathroom. My trembling increased, my mind screaming, *trapped, trapped, trapped*. I couldn't do it. I—

No. I wouldn't let him see me weak again. Ever. I squared my shoulders. "We're already unwanted house-guests. We shouldn't get blood on his furniture." I glanced at the blue-gray couch we'd been sitting on and the blood smeared on its cushions. "On any *more* furniture than we've already ruined."

"Yes," he said, his voice gruff. "Right. I'll wait out here until you're decent." The muscles in his jaw clenched, but I didn't know if it was because of his frustration at the situation or something else. "Unless... ah... you think you're too dizzy to shower by yourself."

My pulse leaped and my body heated with embarrassment and desire, which I quickly squashed, desperate to keep my expression from revealing my surprise and my unreasonable yearning.

This was all Sebastian's fault. Flirting with me and making me think of having sex — with apparently anyone if I was considering Cassius. Cassius's offer had been purely practical. I'd been perfectly fine all these years without sexual intercourse, educating and exploring myself so I wouldn't be a complete disappointment for my soul mate, and waiting. I would be perfectly fine now.

Except I wasn't fine. I was trapped and tired and heartbroken.

"I'll manage."

Cassius frowned.

"I'm already breathing better," I said, which was true. The massive weight of the leash spell had finally eased and now all I needed were shallow breaths to avoid aggravating my ribs. "And the dizziness has subsided."

Subsided but wasn't completely gone. But I was *not* going to get naked with Cassius. I needed a friend now more than ever, and, given my desires, showering together would ruin that.

I squared my shoulders and took a few steps past the coffee table, determined to look like the living room wasn't slowly spinning. "See. I'll be okay. Now call Chris and get us some clean clothes."

His frown deepened.

"The guestroom is the second door on the left." I turned and made it into the hall without staggering.

Behind me, I heard the front door open and close as Cassius went to get our clothes.

"Didn't take Cassius up on his offer to share a shower I see," Sebastian said from the far end of the hall, still wearing his bloody and ruined clothes while holding a pile of folded clean ones.

A shiver of anticipation trembled down my spine. I didn't understand how I kept responding to him like that. I *knew* he wasn't interested in me, that his flirting was just a game he played with every woman, and yet no one had ever really flirted with me before, and it made me feel... desired.

"It wasn't necessary," I forced out.

"It usually isn't." His clear gaze captured mine, and another shiver swept over me.

I clamped down on my yearning. "He only made that offer because he thinks I'm still dizzy." *And weak. So pathetically weak.*

"Sure he did," Sebastian said, crossing the distance between us.

"You know he did. Don't make it into something it isn't."

"You mean you and he haven't...?"

"Of course not!" How was I even having this conversation? Because I was trapped, bound to Sebastian's friend unable to leave his apartment. My pounding heart sped up and my trembling grew stronger. I gritted my teeth, forcing my expression icy. "Do you need something, Sebastian?"

His lips quirked.

Crap. That just opened me up for more teasing. *Please don't. Please just end this conversation.*

The sensual gleam in his eyes softened. "I thought you might want something to sleep in." He held out the clothes, a T-shirt and a pair of cotton knit shorts.

I didn't know what was more surprising. That the man who always wore a dress shirt and slacks had clothes like that or that he was thoughtful enough to offer them to me. Especially since I was sure he'd love to tease me in the morning about having no choice but to sleep in my underwear or worse, naked.

"Thank you," I said, taking the clothes, trying and failing to hide my shaking hands.

"Yeah, well, leash spells are nasty."

The look in his eyes softened even more, making my gut churn. He could see right through me. He knew I was weak and couldn't handle being trapped even for just a night, and yet I still squared my shoulders and hardened my expression to hide my emotions, the habit so ingrained that I couldn't stop myself even when I knew it was pointless.

"But *you* don't need anyone or anything, do you?" He rolled his eyes at me. "Accepting a little help won't kill you, you know."

"You should talk. Cassius has all but formally offered the JP's help for you and your friend."

"Not the same thing."

"Of course it is," I said. "He has the skills and assets you need to deal with those men, and you have the skills and assets I need to break this leash spell."

Sebastian's wicked smile tugged at his lips again and more need heated low within me. "So you admit it. I have something you need."

I opened my mouth to say I could easily call in another witch to break the spell. There were some powerful ones in the JP — although none of them as powerful as Sebastian — and I was sure they could handle this leash spell just as easily as Sebastian could — it would just be a matter of keeping it together long enough for them to get into town. But Sebastian *did* have something I needed... or at least I hoped he did: the power and knowledge to remove my not-yet-formed mating brand. And if I wanted his help, I was going to have to swallow my pride.

"You do," I said quietly.

His eyes widened. "You must really be exhausted. I expected more of a fight."

"I want—" I glanced behind me, checking for Cassius. He'd be furious to learn I was trying to remove the most sacred mark an angel could have.

He still hadn't returned with our clothes but that could change at any time, and if I was going to broach the subject with Sebastian tonight, I had to do it now.

"What do you want, Amiah?" Sebastian asked, his voice sliding into a low sensual drawl.

"I want to hire you to break a mating brand." The words came out in a rush and my pulse pounded with the fear that he'd laugh at me.

But his eyes narrowed instead. "I'm not breaking any of Esther's bonds," he said, jumping to the most natural conclusion. Angelic mating brands were rare and Essie's bonds were the only ones anyone in the realms knew about. But that he'd think I was so jealous of Essie that I'd want to break her soul bonds—?

Was that what everyone thought of me? I knew I wouldn't win any popularity contests, but I didn't think they thought I was heartless. I'd dedicated my life to saving people. People who, if they just thought things through and weren't so reckless, wouldn't need me.

Well, fine then. If that's what they thought, that's what they thought. I didn't need to be liked. Things were just fine the way they were.

Except they weren't. A part of my soul was missing. The aching brand was proof of that. It was also proof that I'd be trapped again.

"I have a partially formed mating brand that hasn't awakened," I said, fighting to keep my fear from my voice. "I want it gone before it turns into a soul bond."

"Holy fuck," Sebastian gasped. "An angel wants her brand gone."

"I won't be trapped like Essie. I won't lose my independence to a stranger." My breath picked up. I was going to lose control and have a panic attack in front of Sebastian. I clamped down hard on my fear. "I want it gone. Are you powerful enough to do that or do I need to look for someone else?"

"Oh sweetheart, there isn't anyone else." His wicked smile grew but didn't reach his eyes as if this was more of an act than anything else. "If I can't do it, no one can."

"But you'll try?" *Please say yes. Please.* He was my only hope.

"It'll cost you."

"I wouldn't have expected anything else." *Whatever the cost.* My fear melted into relief. I was going to be free. I'd be able to keep my life. "But I expect you to start as soon as possible."

"I have a leash spell and a group of kidnappers to deal with first," he said. "That could take some time."

"Not if you accept the JP's help." It was a win-win for everyone. Sebastian would be able to protect Titus, Cassius would know those men were in custody, and I'd deal with my brand before it was too late.

"Not happening," Sebastian said with a shudder. "Not until Esther gets better control of her magic."

"You don't have to worry about that. The primary team is in Rome. You'd be working with Cassius."

Sebastian's eyes narrowed. "That doesn't make it better."

"Sebastian, please." I couldn't risk the brand fully forming while I waited for him to deal with whatever was going on with Titus. "I know it'll be impossible to break if it forms and then..."

"Then you'll be stuck with someone forever."

I didn't want to beg, but I would if I had to. The mating brand could awaken at any time. "I know whatever is going on with Titus is complicated, but I'll pay—" God, I was going to regret this. "I'll pay whatever the price."

"Whatever?" This time his wicked smile did reach his eyes, filling them with heated sexual desire and making my body ache again with that frustrating need I desperately wanted to ignore.

I opened my mouth to tell him I wouldn't pay with sex, but the moment I thought that, I realized I would. Many supers used sex as a currency, and given Sebastian's constant flirtations, I should have expected it.

"Whatever the price." I held his gaze to show I was serious.

He stared back as if he was searching my soul for the truth in my words, and my skin heated with a mix of desire and embarrassment.

"Well, then," he purred. "Let's have a look at this unformed brand."

"You'll need more light," I said, my voice breathy.

"I meant look with my magical senses. I don't have to see it, just touch it to figure out what it is."

"Right." I knew that. His magic probably worked in similar ways to mine, sensing spells like I could sense injuries.

I set his clothes on the floor, not wanting to get them dirty before I'd even worn them, and tugged up the hem of my camisole and pushed down the waistband of my pants.

His gaze locked on my bared skin and my pulse pounded faster.

"The brand runs from just above my waist, over my hip, and down my thigh." The ghostly white lines curling under my skin were hard to see in good light unless you knew what you were looking for, but in the dim light in the hall, they were invisible.

Sebastian stepped close and brushed his fingers along the top of my hipbone with a whisper of a touch that made my not-yet-formed brand throb and my breath hitch.

"Ah, I see." His eyes fluttered shut and he traced the line that trailed up to my waist and curved around to my back with his index finger, the movement slow, sensual. My trembling increased, no longer with fear, but with that pesky yearning I'd been trying to ignore.

I fought to stay where I was and not lean into his touch. Maybe my willingness to pay with sex wasn't just because I'd do anything to not be trapped by a soul bond, but because I wanted it, wanted to be caressed and kissed and filled. There'd be no strings attached with Sebastian. I wouldn't have to continue aching like this while I waited for the right man to come along. I could satisfy a need and move on.

His icy magic prickled under my skin and raced along the brand's lines swirling over my abdomen. The sensation made my inner muscles clench and drew a surprised gasp of pleasure.

"I can't make any guarantees," he said as his magic slid down my thigh, drawing another breathy gasp. "And I still expect payment if I can't break it."

"I understand."

"But I'm sure we can work out a payment that'll suit both of us." He opened his eyes and raised a gaze without a hint of sexual invitation to mine. His expression was serious, all business, and it was clear, he'd just been toying with me, like all the other times before.

The heat of my desire swelled into embarrassment, burning my cheeks and twisting in my chest. He didn't want me. Of course, he didn't want me. How could I have been so foolish to think he'd actually be interested in me when he could have any number of strong, confident, easy-going, experienced women?

"I'll start tomorrow after I break the leash spell and —" He shuddered. "—after Cassius and I come up with a plan to help Titus. There should be some downtime while things are getting sorted for me to check my library."

"Thank you," I said, trying to keep my disappointment from my tone. I didn't know why his rejection stung so much. It was supposed to have been a transaction, nothing more.

CASSIUS

I CALLED AGENT KARSTEN FOR A CHANGE OF CLOTHES FOR Amiah and me, and, after checking to make sure I wouldn't be locked out, waited at the edge of Bane's patio. Fire dripped from my hands, sizzling on the concrete at my feet, small sharp flashes against the night as my emotions roiled in a furious, fearful sea. Amiah was enspelled and exhausted and there wasn't a damned thing I could do about it.

God, she was so willful. If she'd just listened to me, followed protocol, we wouldn't have been in this mess.

Except I knew that wasn't fair. Amiah had no control over who her magic locked onto. The best she could do was avoid situations where she was likely to come across someone gravely injured. If she hadn't been standing on Operations' roof or if I hadn't seen Titus and said something, she might have been fine.

But draining herself to exhaustion... that was her fault. She knew better. And yet she kept doing it over and over again.

I bit back a growl of frustration. Neither I nor Bane would have died from our injuries. She hadn't needed to heal either of us, and she certainly hadn't needed to completely seal shut all my wounds. It had been like she was in a trance, lost in her magic, and unaware of how much power she was pushing into me.

And I'd been an idiot, distracted by her kneeling close, her warm hands pressed against me, and her breath feathering over my aching flesh. I hadn't realized until it was too late that she was going to heal everything completely and drain herself dry.

My power flared and curled up my forearms, and molten fire poured onto the ground.

Shit.

I clenched my jaw and heaved my fire back under my skin. It writhed and snapped against my will, searing my insides as I fought to get my emotions back under control.

I needed to take another assignment out of town. It was the only way to regain what little hold I had on my emotions.

My brother was safe. He didn't need my protection — not that I'd been able to protect him or anyone in the last few weeks. Hell, he was mated to a powerful super who I had no doubt would destroy the world if something happened to him, and he was happy.

Amiah wasn't.

But I couldn't give her what she desired. Not without risking burning everything around me.

My emotions churned stronger, my fire threatening to break free. I hadn't realized I'd fallen in love with my best friend until the war had pulled us apart. When it was done, things between us were different. Because I was different.

She hadn't gotten through the war without psychological scars, I don't think anyone had, but my psychological scars were bigger and deeper. My magic was best suited for the front lines and special ops, and I'd turned myself into a force of destruction, my rage at the injustice of a senseless war turning my magic into a firestorm that burned everything to ash.

And a part of me had enjoyed it. I'd embraced the monster inside me, finally released my hold on my emotions, and wreaked vengeance on Michael's army for the murder of millions... for the murder of my youngest brother. I hadn't cared about rules or order, only justice.

I couldn't lose control like that again.

Except my fire magic had gained strength during the war and had become harder to control. Moderate levels of emotions that hadn't affected it before affected it now, and it wasn't just rage that made it burn hotter. It was every emotion.

And at the moment, I was barely holding on with the memory of that demon-vampire hybrid stabbing at Amiah playing over and over again in my mind. I'd almost failed her, just like I'd failed to protect my brother, Dominic, against Michael, and Gideon in the fight against Lilith.

I'd thought once I'd figured out how to control my fire, I could tell Amiah the truth, tell her that I'd really fallen in love with her the moment I found her chained in that faith healer's tent, drained, and clinging to life. But then she joined the JP to follow Marcus, and I realized I'd never be able to be the man she wanted.

Marcus was fierce, his emotions powerful and untamed like many shifters, and he was free to show them. Most shifters loved hard whether they were mated or not, and with Amiah setting her sights on Marcus, it was clear. She'd finally figured out what she wanted. Passion.

Which I had. But like all my emotions, rage, fear, joy, it too was connected to my fire, and I could never let go enough to fully show it.

A hot spark snapped against the concrete, the sound sharp and loud even against the noise from the nightclub under Bane's apartment.

I was barely holding it together as it was. Letting go to embrace and show my desires was too dangerous. People would get hurt. Amiah would get hurt.

She'd always been careful with her heart. I wasn't even sure I'd ever seen her show interest in anyone until Marcus, and even then, unless you knew her well, you probably wouldn't have noticed... not until Essie Shaw had shown up.

I didn't know what Amiah had been waiting for with him, but I was glad she'd never made a move on her feelings. It made me ache and my fire burn hotter knowing how hurt she must have been — must still be — when he formed a soul bond with Essie. I couldn't imagine how much more she'd be hurting if she'd actively pursued him or if they'd had an intimate relationship before everyone realized he was fated to love someone else.

But just because Marcus wasn't the one for her, didn't

mean she didn't still deserve the intense passion of a shifter. She deserved everything she wanted. And I was God damned going to protect her to make sure she got it.

An average-height, muscular figure dressed in typical black JP fatigues strode into sight from down the alley. He had a backpack slung over one shoulder and his gait was sure, strong, radiating the power of a werewolf. Chris Karsten. He and Nathaniel usually secured crime scenes after the main team had dealt with the dangerous situations, and from what I could tell from his JP files, he was easy-going, orderly, and highly competent. Competent enough that he could probably put in a transfer and request to join a primary team. Except his family and his pack were in Union and, in the time we'd spent working together over the last couple of weeks, I'd learned he was happy being a secondary agent in order to stay where he was.

I clamped down even harder on my emotions, turning my fire into curling smoke, before Chris realized how close I was to losing it. It wasn't good that I couldn't get my flames fully under control, but it was the best I was going to get, what with Amiah's condition and whatever this mess was with Bane and Titus.

"Jesus," Chris said, as he approached, his gaze sliding over my bruised, bloody, and shirtless body, his expression tight with concern. "What the hell happened? Is Amiah okay?"

"She is." No thanks to me. "She's fine." But that was all I was going to say. She wouldn't appreciate me saying she'd foolishly drained herself to exhaustion, and she certainly wouldn't want me mentioning the leash spell. Especially since she'd be free in the morning.

"Good. I figured something had happened if you both needed a change of clothes, but I didn't expect—" He blew out a heavy breath, and handed over the backpack.

"Thank you for this. Get Nathaniel, Jasmine, and Summer and go to the park ring. We were attacked by a male nightmare, a male demon-vampire hybrid, and a male shadow fae."

Chris's eyebrows shot up. "A shadow fae?"

"Yeah. He can blend into the shadows like a wraith." I pulled out my phone to send him the location of our fight. "I want everything you can find, forensics, tracks, if you pick up scents that don't match me, Amiah, or Bane. See if you can figure out where they came from or where they went. But," I said as I leveled a hard glare at him to ensure he understood I was serious, "if you see them, don't approach, not until we have a better idea who they are. These guys are dangerous."

"Copy that." Chris's attention shifted to the door behind me and I could see the question in his eyes. Why weren't we back at Operations? There was no reason for Amiah to treat someone outside of her medical facility. "Anything else I need to know?" he asked.

"I'm sure lots, but I don't know it either." The smoke curling from my hands thickened and I sucked it back before it turned into flames. "I hope I'll have more in the morning."

"Yes, sir," Chris said with a tight nod. "I'll text you if I find anything that can't wait."

"Thanks." I watched him stride back down the alley

as I took deep breaths that twinged the still tender cuts across my chest and side in an attempt to lock down my emotions before I went back inside. I still had to talk to Amiah again before this night was done, and I needed to lock everything down to do it. The moment Bane had told her she was magically linked to Titus that same look in her eyes that she'd had when I'd found her all those years ago had flashed across her expression. Desperate, terrified, hopeless.

A spark snapped from my hands.

She'd recovered her composure quickly, but it was all an act and I had no idea how to help her and that was making it nearly impossible to keep my emotions in check.

AMIAH

I slept fitfully, the agony in my chest and the ache around my throat, making it impossible to get comfortable. That, and my mind kept whirling, spinning between being trapped by the leash spell and having told Sebastian about my brand, something I'd never told anyone else about... not to mention how I'd actually considered paying Sebastian with sex or how much it had stung when he'd offered different payment terms.

I couldn't believe I'd done or thought that, and I prayed he wouldn't say anything about it in front of Cassius. I wouldn't be able to keep a strong appearance if Cassius's concern grew — I was barely holding it together as it was — and without a doubt, he'd be concerned that I'd want to get rid of my brand.

It also hadn't helped that I'd slept in Sebastian's borrowed clothes, too tired to change into the scrubs Chris had brought over after I'd dragged my exhausted, aching body out of the shower and let Cassius have his turn. I'd thought I'd be fine sleeping in Sebastian's T-shirt and shorts, but all night long, all I could smell was a fresh evergreen scent that without a doubt was Sebastian's. I hadn't been able to stop thinking about him, about the heated look in his eyes and that whisper of a touch that made my body throb and how he'd just turned it all off, clearly not interested.

I gave up on sleep just before dawn and went into the bathroom to splash water on my face in the hope that I wouldn't look as run down as I felt and Cassius wouldn't be as worried as he'd been last night.

Except a quick glance in the mirror revealed that splashing a little water wasn't going to do much to mitigate any of Cassius's concerns. Sure, he wasn't going to notice my dimmer than usual angel glow, or my tired expression, because he was going to be staring at the massive dark red bruise around my neck in the shape of Titus's large hand.

Just wonderful. If I didn't want him fussing, I was going to have to heal myself. Except my magic wasn't even halfway back to full and I'd need at least a full night's sleep more to recover all of it. Which meant I needed to see how much more healing Titus needed before turning my magic on myself. Because without a doubt, Sebastian would want to go on the run with Titus or start a fight or something dangerous to deal with those men, and I couldn't risk Titus still being injured when they did that.

My injuries could wait. It took a lot more magic to heal myself than everyone else and just like when I healed everyone else, I couldn't pick and choose what to heal. My magic always mended the worst injury first.

Which meant it would heal my cracked ribs before my bruise, and that meant healing to the point of getting rid of the bruise would drain what little power I'd managed to recover. I wasn't so vain as to let Titus continue suffering especially when his life was in danger just to avoid an argument with Cassius.

With a sigh, I ran my fingers through my long blond locks, combing out the tangles and braiding it back so it was out of my way — which was only a temporary solution because I didn't have anything to tie off the braid. I considered changing into the scrubs, but some of Titus's deepest lacerations could still be bleeding, and it was better to get Sebastian's clothes bloody than the only change of clothes I could reasonably wear to walk out of Sebastian's apartment. No way was I showing up at Operations wearing his clothes and giving everyone something to gossip about.

Besides, after this morning everything would be fine—

Well, maybe not *fine*, but at least on track. I'd no longer be trapped by the leash spell, I could get away from Sebastian and his flirtation and regain my composure, and I wouldn't have to worry about Cassius seeing me as that weak, pathetic angel he'd rescued all those years ago. I'd be back in control and soon free of my mating brand.

So long as I didn't think about the fear currently squeezing my heart — and the cause was going to be gone before the morning was out — I was okay. There was hope and I could hold out a few hours longer.

As quietly as possible, I tiptoed across the hall to

Sebastian's other guestroom and eased open the door, hoping Titus was still sleeping and I wouldn't wake him. Given his violent reaction last night, it was foolish of me to check on him without Sebastian or Cassius, but I'd snuck in and checked on hundreds of patients before, many with highly acute senses, without waking them. I could check on Titus, top him up, and be gone before he stirred without needing to bother anyone, and more importantly without Cassius realizing I'd slept in Sebastian's clothes.

And yes, that was an irrational thought. What did I care if Cassius saw me wearing Sebastian's clothes? What did I care if Sebastian saw me? But I did care. It would open me up to questions from Cassius and teasing from Sebastian, and after last night's concern and rejection, I didn't want to deal with either.

Inside the bedroom, Titus lay on his side facing me, his shaggy dark red hair veiling one eye, the other eye closed and his chest rising and falling with the steady breath of sleep. The comforter had slipped down to his waist, and in daylight, without the chaos of the fight, he looked even bigger and bulkier — and more intimidating — than he had last night.

A thick ragged scar encircled his one visible wrist, and I could see a hint of another scar on his neck, injuries I knew too well from healing Michael's captives.

The sight sent a shudder racing through me. My captivity at the hands of that human almost a hundred years before Michael's war hadn't resulted in physical scars, but I knew many held in captivity weren't so lucky.

Titus's skin, what I could see around the many

bandages, was mottled with dark purple bruises, some with hints of green as if they were almost a week old, not less than twelve hours old, and the lacerations that had been too small to worry about bandaging had sealed shut and were faint pink lines.

All of which spoke to an exceptional level of healing, and a deplorable degree of imprisonment.

If his healing was that good, it would have taken a lot for a long time to make scars like the ones he had on his wrist and neck.

At least his exceptional healing meant I wouldn't need to give him much more to finish knitting his broken bones back together and strengthen his newly healed organs. Then a quick shift into his beast would finish the job. That might even leave me enough magic to heal my ribs and my neck and avoid comments from Cassius.

I crept to Titus's bedside, placed a gentle hand on his massive biceps, and let my magic connect with his body.

All of his bones, even the ones I hadn't had enough power to heal, were healed, his organs were strong as if they hadn't been damaged at all, and every laceration had sealed shut, although the deepest ones looked like they were still tender.

Sebastian hadn't lied. Titus was a fast healer. I didn't think I'd ever come across someone — incubi and succubi excepted — who healed so quickly, not even a greater demon.

For a second, I contemplated leaving him as he was and letting his natural healing finish the job. If he shifted in and out of his beast form then stayed out of trouble, he'd be fine by the evening, even his bruises would be gone.

But those were the key words: if he stayed out of trouble.

I had no idea what Sebastian was planning, and while Titus was big and Sebastian magically powerful, that didn't mean they'd be able to get through the next fight without serious injury.

The thought of Sebastian gravely injured made my stomach churn. I might not like the way he did things or how he teased me, but he'd come through for the JP recently when we were desperate. That, and I'd already saved his life once before. I didn't want all that hard work to go to waste. I wouldn't be able to live with myself if I didn't finish healing Titus and something happened to Sebastian. And unlike Sebastian and Titus, I wasn't about to jump headlong into trouble.

I drew in a steadying breath, sliced agony through my chest, and pushed past the pain to reach the still-weak spark of magic in my palms. It flared at my mental touch, pushing against my mental grip, but I easily kept it contained. There was no need for this healing to be painful, and besides, painful would wake him up, defeating the purpose of healing him without him noticing.

I focused my magic into the hand I had pressed against his arm and released a small stream, but before the stream could flow into him, he seized my wrist and wrenched me forward.

With a yelp, I tumbled on top of him, and in one swift

movement, he rolled, pinning me under his massive body, shooting agony through my chest.

His hand clamped around my throat again and our gazes locked, his expression stunned.

For a second there was only him. No fear, no pain, nothing, as if my mind and soul had stalled unable to register on anything else but him, not even the danger he presented.

He radiated a wild, unbridled intensity that stole all breath and thought. My body heated at his quick exhales washing over my cheeks, the press of his thighs on either side of mine boxing me in, and his pelvis pinning me to the mattress.

The vein in his neck pulsed under the ragged scar, the beats growing faster, and with a blink, the shock vanished from his golden eyes. He jerked closer, lurching my thoughts back into action, and snarled, revealing sharp extended canines.

"Don't scream and answer my questions and I won't snap your neck." His grip around my throat tightened.

The fear I should have had the moment he'd grabbed me slammed into me and my lungs screamed for air. I clawed at his hands and jerked against his weight, but that only sliced more pain through me, stealing what little breath I had left and sending flecks of darkness across my vision.

"Nod if you understand," he said, his expression hard, his intention clear: if I even squeaked too loudly, he'd kill me. Rage and fear and determination now filled his eyes, I wasn't even sure if I'd seen his wide-eyed stunned look or just imagined it. What I did know was that someone had cast that horrible leash spell on him and imprisoned him. He'd do anything, kill anyone, to be free, and I was about to become a casualty.

I gasped against his grip, instinct making me continue to heave against him, desperate to be free. Pain burned my chest and the darkness in my vision swelled.

"Fucking hell," Sebastian said, his voice cutting through the darkness. "Don't kill her."

Titus stiffened, and his attention jerked to Sebastian standing in the doorway. He wore a pair of dark blue pajama pants that hung low on his hips and nothing else, giving me a spectacular view of his sculpted arms and torso and the swirl of black glyphs tattooed on his pale skin. Behind him stood Cassius with his angel glow blazing, his smoke curling around him, and fully dressed in a black T-shirt and fatigues as if he'd slept in his clean clothes.

"Get off her," Cassius commanded.

"Seireadan?" Titus's grip relaxed a bit, but he didn't let go or get off me. "Is she yours?"

"No," Sebastian said.

"But she smells like you."

"Because she borrowed my clothes." Sebastian took a slow step closer to the bed. "You bled all over hers."

"I said, get off." Cassius's smoke thickened.

Titus bared his canines and growled low in his throat. "No, not until I know I'm free."

"You honestly think I'd enslave you?" Sebastian asked, taking another step closer.

"Deaglan did," Titus growled.

"I said. Off." Cassius shoved Sebastian out of the way,

snapped a fire whip around Titus's throat, and yanked him off the bed with a vicious jerk.

Titus hit the floor with a heavy thump, the comforter tangling around his legs and tugging me half off the bed toward him. He grabbed the whip with his hands as if it wasn't made of flames, tore it apart, and lunged at Cassius, who snapped up another whip. But Titus tackled him, using his massive body to slam Cassius against the marble floor, throwing off Cassius's strike.

"Jeez, stop," Sebastian said, jerking out of the way of the two men and activating a glyph on his left forearm that curled from his wrist past his elbow, snaking in between other glyphs. "Deaglan betrayed me too."

Cassius shot a blinding spark into Titus's face. The big man flinched and Cassius managed to shove him off him with the help of a fire blast into Titus's chest. The bandage-made-of-sheet around his gut burst into flames and turned to ash, and my pulse stuttered. Cassius was going to ruin all the hard work I'd done last night, and there was no need for them to be fighting. Titus just needed to know he was safe.

More flames roared around Cassius's hand and I scrambled from the bed, agony blazing through my chest.

Titus's fingertips extended into thick claws with razor-sharp tips unlike any claws I'd ever seen on a shifter. He jerked his hand back to slash at Cassius, and I grabbed Titus's wrist.

"You're free," I said, praying my words would be enough to stop him since there was no way I was strong enough to hold him back.

He jerked to me, snarling, and I pressed my palms

around the ragged scar on his wrist. "I promise. No one here will hurt you."

My throat tightened. Those were the words Cassius had said to me when he'd rescued me. *He won't hurt you ever again. You're free.* Behind him, the burning tent and cart had lit up the twilight sky, brighter than the blazing sunset, a fiery announcement that Cassius's justice had been served.

And now I was trapped again.

Titus's eyes narrowed and he growled low in his throat, making Cassius tense and flick his wrist, reforming his whip.

"No," I said to Cassius then locked gazes with Titus. "You're free. I swear." *And I know how afraid you are to hope, and of the thousands of times you've dreamt of this moment. You'll be completely free just as soon as Sebastian breaks the leash spell.* But I couldn't mention that, not until he'd calmed down, because with his current fury, I doubted he realized being bound to me had been an accident.

"You are, Titus," Sebastian said, also not mentioning the still-active leash spell, his hand still on his glowing glyph. "Deaglan betrayed me too."

"Try to take me back and I'll kill you," Titus snarled, his voice low and dangerous, his gaze locked with mine.

"That would mean I'd have to go back." Out of the corner of my eye, I saw Sebastian drop his hand from his arm and release the power in the glyph, its light going out. "Not happening."

With a growl, Titus jerked his wrist out of my grasp and sat back, conceding the fight, but the tension didn't leave his body. He remained a predator, ready to pounce the moment he sensed danger... or weakness.

"If I'd known Deaglan had you, I would have come for you." Sebastian crouched beside me, his bare shoulder brushing mine, sending an inappropriate shiver of attraction through me. "If I'd known you'd ended your hibernation..."

"I'm not sure I would have trusted you," Titus said, his body language saying he still didn't trust him.

I inched away from Sebastian, but Cassius sat up on my other side and I couldn't put as much distance between me and Sebastian as I wanted. Cassius's gaze jumped to my neck and the muscles in his jaw flexed at what he saw.

Thankfully he didn't say anything — although it was clear he wanted to — and I fought to keep my shallow breaths even for fear Cassius would notice that I was in pain, too. That would only make it harder for me to look in control... which I wasn't. I was trapped—

Focus on Titus. Not the spell.

"You were seriously injured. Do you remember what happened?" I asked. Maybe a change of topic would help him relax. Especially since it was clear that right now there was no way he was going to let me put my hands on him to finish healing him.

I swept my gaze over him. Thankfully he didn't have a single burn from Cassius's fire, not even on his hands, which meant the plan for a little healing top up and a quick shift was still possible... if I could convince him it was safe.

"No." Titus snagged the comforter beside Sebastian

and covered himself with a surprising amount of modesty for a shifter. "Deaglan's leash spell weakened and I broke it. Then I ran. I thought I'd found a portal out of Faerie, but if you found me..." He glanced at Sebastian.

"No, you're out," Sebastian reassured him, his voice quiet and calm as if he, too, saw that Titus could snap again at any second. "We're in the mortal realm."

"You left Faerie?" Titus asked, surprised. "With Enowen?"

"No." Sebastian's expression grew grim. "And it's a long story, which—"

"Which you can talk about later. We need to deal with what's going on right now," Cassius said, smoke curling from his hands. "You said Deaglan is the leash spell guy and he's the one in charge of the men who attacked us? What do we know about them?"

Sebastian opened his mouth to say something, but Cassius cut him off.

"And I don't want an argument." The light in Cassius's eyes flared. "The JP *is* helping you deal with them. The sooner those guys are off the streets, the sooner your friend is safe."

I glanced at Sebastian, afraid of his response. Last night he'd said he'd work with Cassius, and now Cassius had actually offered assistance instead of taking over — which was a huge concession for Cassius — but there was still a chance Sebastian would go back on his word... or mention our deal.

"I was going to say before we *all* deal with Deaglan, we need to address the most immediate problems.

Breaking the leash spell between Titus and Amiah and getting proper protection spells on Titus."

"What?" Every muscle in Titus's big body tensed and the pulse in his neck picked up again. "You said I was free. I broke that spell."

"Technically you only disconnected it and when Amiah here—" Sebastian jerked his chin at me and Titus's gaze returned to mine, making my heart stutter at the intensity in his eyes along with the fear that I was magically bound to him. "When Amiah saved your ass with her healing magic, it latched onto her."

"So you lied," Titus said, his voice low. "I'm not free."

The panic I really needed to ignore surged, making my breath pick up. "Neither am I."

And I needed to be free. I had to be free. *Now. Please now. Never again.*

Something dark and sad flashed across his expression as if he could see the fear threatening to overwhelm me.

"You've both got the prisoner end of the spell, so it's sucky for both of you." Sebastian stood and headed to his office across the hall. "Let me get my resonance charm and fix that."

Titus's glare softened a bit, but he didn't look away and I couldn't tell if it was because he thought I was a fellow predator or prey... probably prey.

That, at least, was Cassius's assumption since he tugged on my elbow, urging me to put some distance between me and Titus. "Why don't you get off the floor?"

"How about I finish healing you first?" I said to Titus. "Why don't you shift then shift back and we'll see what's left."

"No."

I waited for him to say more, but he didn't.

"I'm not comfortable with you dealing with those men while you're injured."

"I don't care what makes you comfortable," Titus said, which made Cassius tense and more smoke curl from his hands.

"Titus, please. It'll only take a few minutes." *And it'll distract me from our situation.*

"What will?" Sebastian asked as he strode back into the bedroom carrying a small wooden box.

"Titus's healing. If he just shifts and shifts back, I'm sure there won't be much left." Why were people, particularly the men around me, so difficult? It wasn't as if I didn't know what I was doing.

"Yeah, no." Sebastian nudged Cassius with his foot. "You should move."

Cassius glared at him. "I'm not moving."

"You don't want to be too close to this and I really don't want to argue with Amiah about you being hurt. Especially when it'll be your own damned fault," Sebastian said as he cocked an eyebrow. "Do you?"

Cassius's fire flared, dancing over his forearms before sinking back under his skin, but he moved a few feet back.

"Don't change the topic," I said as Sebastian took Cassius's spot, sitting cross-legged on the floor beside me. "What do you mean, no? It's Titus's decision."

"And Titus is just as capable of doing the math as I am. He shifts into a thirty-foot dragon. He'd barely fit in this room and he'd break all the furniture." Sebastian

opened the box and pulled out a thin coin with a complicated glyph etched on its surface. "I like my furniture."

He said it so nonchalantly that his words almost
didn't register in my brain.

"You're a dragon?" I asked.

Titus couldn't possibly be a dragon. Dragons were
one of a few types of shifters natural only to the fae realm
and they'd been rare to begin with. And while I hadn't
spent any time researching dragons, all reports I'd heard
said they were extinct.

"I didn't think there were any dragons left," I said.
Which was the stupidest, most insensitive thing I could
say if he really was a dragon.

Titus harrumphed, but I couldn't tell if it was in
agreement or not. I supposed I could see it, his unusual
gold eyes unlike any shifter I'd ever seen, his wild
intense energy similar to a wolf's or a wild cat's and yet
more ferocious. If I really looked at him, there was a
sense of barely contained power radiating around him,
as if his human form was too small to hold in all his
energy.

"The last dragon died half a millennium ago," Cassius
said.

"No, the last dragon went into hibernation half a
millennium ago," Sebastian corrected.

"The last dragon was *leashed* half a millennium ago."
The rage and darkness I'd seen in Titus's eyes when he
thought he needed to take a hostage returned.

Sebastian's expression turned somber. "Never again. I
promise."

"Don't make promises you can't keep," Titus said.

"The Heart has awakened and the other courts will eventually learn I'm still alive. They're going to come for me."

"Which is why I need to separate you and Amiah." Sebastian held out his hand with the coin resting in his palm. "Both of you take my hand, palm over mine."

I set my hand on Sebastian's, our fingers brushing as my palm settled over his, sending another unwanted shiver of attraction sliding through me. I wished he'd never teased me by asking for his payment with sex. Or that he'd put a shirt on before running into the room. Now I couldn't keep my eyes off the mesmerizing swirls on his body, or the lines that disappeared past the waistband of his pants. All I could think about, when I managed to not think about being trapped, was having sex, as if that one teasing suggestion had shattered over a hundred years of restraint.

But it hadn't just been the suggestion that he wanted sex, it was the other times he'd propositioned me on top of learning that my hopes and dreams and the whole reason I'd been waiting had been a lie.

Titus laid his massive hand on top of mine, fully encompassing it and making my wrist look small and fragile in comparison to his. I was captured between his warm rough hand, and Sebastian's cool smooth one, a strange mix of hot and cold. Another shiver taunted me at the thought of being embraced between them. Essie had more than one mate. Why couldn't I have more than one lover?

Which — oh my goodness! — wasn't something I should be thinking about. Especially about Sebastian, who didn't really want me, and Titus, who was a complete stranger.

Sebastian's eyes narrowed. "It's just a little magic," he said, thankfully thinking my shiver was because I was afraid. "It'll be over before you know it."

"It didn't sound like just a little magic last night or just now when you told me to move," Cassius said. "Which is it?"

"Maybe I just wanted Amiah to stay the night." Sebastian flashed me a wicked grin, and I bit down on the desire swelling inside me. "Maybe I just wanted to get close to her."

All a game. Just a game. He isn't interested.

"So she *is* yours?" Titus growled.

"I'm not anyone's," I said before Sebastian could continue teasing me or reject me again — and I wasn't sure which response would upset me more. "Can we get on with this? I have things to attend to at Operations."

"Please," Cassius added. "The sooner Amiah is safe, the sooner we can go after those men."

Sebastian rolled his eyes. "One of these days I'm going to find an angel with a sense of humor."

"We have a sense of humor," Cassius said. "You're just not funny."

Sebastian snorted. "You keep thinking that."

Before Cassius could respond, Sebastian closed his eyes and set his other hand on top of Titus's.

Icy blue-white light rippled over the back of his hand and cold nipped just under my skin. He didn't activate any of the magical glyphs tattooed on his body which meant what he was doing was pure, fae sorcery, channeling raw magic from his core realm, Faerie, and weaving it into his spell by only the force of his willpower. Which was a lot more dangerous than using his essence to power the spell — in glyph form — already on his body. Too much magic too quickly and he could burn up. And given that Titus and I were connected to the spell, he could burn us up as well. I suspected the charm helped mitigate some of the dangers by focusing his power, but I had no idea by how much.

Cassius shifted and sparks danced over his forearms. He'd noticed that Sebastian wasn't using a glyph either, but he sucked in a quick breath and managed to quench his flames before something in the bedroom caught on fire. His angel glow, however, continued to blaze bright, revealing his worry.

The cold nipping under my skin turned to sharp, painful bites and crawled up my forearm to my elbow.

Across from me, Titus tensed, his hand on top of mine trembling and his gaze focused solely on me. The rage and fear had returned to his eyes, and for a second, a blink of an eye, it felt as if I was his lifeline, the only thing holding him in place. As much as he was participating in Sebastian's attempt to break the leash spell, he still didn't trust the fae. I didn't know if he trusted anyone.

I tried to reassure him with my eyes that it was going to be okay — afraid that if I said anything I'd break Sebastian's concentration. Sebastian was many things, but I'd yet to see him be malicious. Of course, I had very little experience with him. We'd only really met a few weeks ago, and before then, I'd only heard comments from the main team about buying hard-to-find magical items from him and his questionable morals.

The tendons in Sebastian's neck flexed and he rolled his shoulders, the soft glow emanating from his skin rolling down his body in a gentle wave. But instead of looking more relaxed, he looked worse, the light dimming, giving his complexion a grayish hue before flaring back to life.

"There you are," Sebastian whispered, and his cold magic swept into my chest and contracted around my heart.

I gasped, the sudden breath slicing pain through me, and fought the following whimper, afraid that if it looked like Sebastian was hurting me, Cassius would interfere. And I couldn't let Cassius interfere. I had to be free.

The cold burned, no longer just stinging bites, but a full-body burning, bringing with it a pressure that made every breath with my cracked ribs agonizing. The darkness of unconsciousness swelled at the edge of my vision, and I fought to hold on until Sebastian was done. Surely it wouldn't be much more. Surely I was strong enough to hold out—

No. I *was* strong enough. I wasn't weak. I'd never be weak again.

I ground my teeth. Across from me, Titus's whole body was also tense, his breath quick gasps. He growled low in his throat, and his pupils slitted as his dragon strained to rise to the surface.

"Seireadan," he hissed, his voice thick with warning.

"Just... a little... more," Sebastian gasped. "There."

The pressure snapped into a pull, ripping at my

insides with a pain unlike anything I'd ever experienced before, tearing a scream from my clenched jaw. The darkness in my vision swelled and tears streamed down my cheeks. Far off in the distance, Titus roared, the sound filled with agony, and someone else cried out.

Then the ripping pressure and cold vanished, leaving only pain and darkness, and I sagged forward, unable to stop my sobbing no matter how hard I tried to hold it back. God, I was so pathetic.

Strong hands drew me into a warm embrace, pulling me tight to a chest shuddering with ragged breaths, and I didn't bother fighting it. It was clear I was weak. I couldn't hide it if I wanted to.

"Is it done?" Cassius demanded... his voice across from me?

I dragged my eyes open, my throat tight as I fought to stop my tears. Cassius knelt in front of me, his hands on fire, glaring at Sebastian who sat with his forehead pressed against the floor, his back heaving with desperate breaths, while I lay in Titus's arms.

A spark caught in the comforter, igniting it, and Cassius's eyes flashed wide with fear. With a growl, he wrenched it and the rest of his flames back under his skin.

"Bane." He jerked to his feet and stormed into the en suite bathroom where there wasn't as much that could catch on fire, his body shaking with his bottled-up emotions. "Is she free?"

"No." Sebastian shuddered and his glow dimmed again, revealing that worrying ashen complexion.

No?

My pulse froze.

I wasn't free?

No, please. I can't stay like this. I can't. And I didn't want to go through that kind of agony again.

A tear trailed down my cheek and I leaned into Titus's embrace, not caring that he was a stranger, just needing the comfort of being held, something I hadn't had in over a month and desperately missed. I was still trapped and my heart ached. I was sure he would be back to keeping everyone at arm's length, including me, when this moment was done. It was just his shifter need for physical contact during stressful situations that made him hold me.

I could handle that. In fact, it was better than Cassius or Sebastian comforting me. I had no connection to Titus and he'd be gone once the leash spell was broken. It didn't matter if he judged me for leaning on him, and I could just tell Cassius that I didn't want to fight his shifter nature because he was so much stronger than me.

"I thought the charm was supposed to free her," Cassius said, as a spark snapped from his hand and hissed as it hit the marble floor.

"It was." Sebastian shuddered.

"You should have been able to break it," Titus said. "You're just as powerful as Deaglan."

"No shit." Sebastian turned his head just enough to glare at Titus with one eye, but surprise flashed across his expression when he saw me in Titus's arms.

Embarrassment heated my cheeks, but I was still sore and shaking too much to focus on rebuilding my in-control demeanor. And I missed this. Missed the heat and security and reassuring pulse of life from another being.

"So now what?" I asked, hoping to cut off any teasing before it started. "There has to be something else you can do." As soon as I voiced that out loud, my pulse beat faster with the fear that there wasn't anything else to do and I was stuck never able to leave Titus's side.

Titus's grip tightened, putting pressure on my cracked ribs and making me gasp. His eyes widened and his arms relaxed a bit, but he didn't let me go, as if he, too, still needed physical contact with someone, anyone.

"There is." Sebastian grabbed Titus's shoulder and sat up, using the big man to steady himself. "But it involves going to Left of Lincoln."

"Left of Lincoln?" That was the underground market that originally had been set up in an abandoned store-front just off the last left on Lincoln Street. Hence the name.

It wasn't there anymore and supposedly had grown from just a few illegal vendors to hundreds, but the name had stuck. After Michael's war, many people had decided to live off the grid, unwilling or unable to return to normal life, creating a whole underground society, and Left of Lincoln was the main place in Union City for those people to buy the supplies they needed or desired — be they legal or illegal — using a variety of currencies, including standard cash, magical essence, magical abili-ties, blood, and services that were more often than not sexual in nature... or at least so I'd heard. I'd never been to the market.

I hadn't needed to learn much about the off-grid

world, since all I did was heal people regardless of how they chose to live their lives. I only knew what Left of Lincoln was, and that the JP, for the most part, turned a blind eye to it in favor of going after more dangerous criminals.

"If the charm is specifically attuned to our resonance, it'll be easier to unravel the spell from your essences. But I don't want to risk waiting around on a specialist to come to us. It's better if we go to him. Which means all three of us have to go to Lincoln."

"You mean all four of us," Cassius said, stepping to the edge of the bathroom door, his fire gone but heavy smoke still curling from his hands and forearms. I was kind of surprised he hadn't set off the smoke detector yet.

"Of course you're coming," Sebastian groaned. "Fine. All four of us. I need a shower and Amiah and Titus need clothes."

"Amiah has clothes," Cassius said.

"I saw, but she can't go to Lincoln in scrubs. It's bad enough both of you are angels. You, in your military chic, I can pass off as hired muscle, there are a few angels that do that sort of thing, but Amiah can't go looking like a physician. Everyone will know she's with the JP and no one will do business with me."

"I'm not leaving to go to Operations to get a different change of clothes for Amiah," Cassius said.

"It's okay. I'll be fine," I assured him.

"Don't worry about it." Sebastian climbed to his feet. "My assistant has to bring clothes for Titus since nothing I own will fit him. I'll just get her to bring something for Amiah too." He staggered out of the bedroom, the soft glow emanating from his skin dimming and flaring back to life. "And Amiah, I suggest you do something about your neck. That bruise will attract all the wrong kind of attention."

Titus's golden gaze dipped to mine filled with a heart-stopping intensity. It made me ache, the look reminding me so much of Marcus and all his ferocious emotions. I hadn't experienced his all-in love, not the love he gave to his mate, but I'd desired it, thought if I was patient it would be mine.

I pushed out of Titus's arms and stood on shaky legs. It was a mistake to have let him hold me, to give in to my desire for physical contact. Now his embrace just reminded me of what I'd never have—

No, of what I didn't want. Really.

SEBASTIAN

I MADE IT INTO MY BEDROOM AND CLOSED THE DOOR before my knees gave out, dropping me to the hard marble floor, pain wracking my body.

Fuuuuck.

Fuck fuck fuck.

The resonance charm was supposed to have made it easier to break the leash spell. My old self would have been able to do it without the charm. A hard pull on my connection to the primal magic of Faerie combined with the charm should have been enough to do the trick.

But I wasn't my old self. I was the new fucked up version thanks to my inability to mind my own fucking business.

God. I shouldn't have agreed to help stop Lilith. What would it have mattered if she'd taken over this realm? There were other realms I could go to. I didn't have to go back to Faerie. But damned if I didn't like the mortal realm. No one gave a shit who I was, no one played sick games with me or anyone I cared about, and I'd been doing just fine until I'd stuck my nose where it didn't belong.

I pressed my forehead to the cool marble floor and dragged in a ragged breath, trying to ease the pain. It burned through my magical channels in my head, heart, and hell, to the tip of every nerve ending with the caustic poison of demonic magic, something that wasn't supposed to be in my body. Ever.

I couldn't connect with the Realm of Celestial Darkness to use its magic. I couldn't even make a connection to that realm. Which was why I couldn't get the damned magic out of my system and push out the poison.

Now, because the demonic magic kept getting in the way, I could barely reach the magic in Faerie, able to only channel a trickle of power when it used to be a flood. And yet I still risked all the side effects of channeling too much magic, because every time I tried to weave a spell, with or without a glyph to focus my power, the demonic magic exploded into an inferno, like a spark suddenly given oxygen.

As if just thinking about it gave it power, the demonic magic flared again, setting my skin on fire, forcing me to bite back a groan.

I doubted anyone was standing outside my door, but I didn't want to risk them hearing me, just in case. They needed to think I was powerful enough to break the leash spell. Hell, I *needed* to be powerful enough to break the leash spell, because Titus and Amiah needed to be free of each other. Not to mention if I couldn't break the leash spell, there was no way I'd be able to remove Amiah's not-yet-awakened mating brand... if there was even a way—

No. There had to be a way. There was always a way. A soul bond was similar to any bonding spell, just on a more powerful level. If I figured out how to break or block her soul's potential to make a bond, she should be able to live her life bond free.

And — I was a damned idiot — I really wanted her to have that. The idea of being permanently bound to someone for life was terrifying. I didn't care how happy Esther Shaw was with her mates, the idea scared the shit out of me, and I knew Amiah had the same fear.

I'd seen a hint of that fear in her eyes when she'd swallowed her pride to ask for my help, and I'd seen all of that fear, clear and raw, when she thought the leash spell had been her soul bond. It had been a look of absolute panic, just for a second, before she'd regained her composure, but it had been clear as day.

Except if I couldn't break a simple leash spell, how the hell was I going to deal with her soul bond?

I drew in another breath and, gripping the doorknob for balance, stood. I was going to have to get power from an outside source even though that still risked burning me up, and that was going to cost a lot... if I could even figure out how to break or block the mating brand.

Which wasn't the thing I should be worrying about.

Why the hell did I keep thinking of Amiah? And why had it scared the shit out of me to see Titus's hand around her throat, or pissed me off to see him mauling her like she was his security blanket while she'd been fighting her tears?

She was a pain in my ass with her ice queen attitude, and her sharp tongue, and her God damned insistence on spending every ounce of her magic healing people when she should just leave well enough alone.

Except fuck if I didn't just love seeing that little flash of surprise every time I hit on her and then her following angry frustration as she tried to hide the fact that I'd caught her off guard.

Although her reaction last night had been different. Yes to the surprise, but consideration instead of anger.

Which shocked the hell out of me. I couldn't believe she'd seriously thought about sleeping with me as payment to get rid of her mating brand.

But that only told me how desperate she was to have it gone.

Except that also pissed me off.

She thought I'd have sex with someone to make them pay off a debt. Yeah, there were a lot of supers who worked that way, but that was disgusting. A little no strings attached fucking was great. It was the way I preferred it. But everyone involved had to agree.

I staggered to my bathroom and turned on the shower, hoping the warm water would help me relax — since being tense made the demonic magic blaze hotter inside me even when I wasn't trying to use my magic.

What Amiah thought of me didn't matter. So what if we shared the same fear of being permanently bound to someone for the rest of our lives? I shouldn't let that influence how I did business, and I needed to come to terms now with the fact that I wouldn't be able to do anything for her and move on.

Which, God damn it, I didn't want to accept.

Jeez.

What I really should be thinking about was helping Titus and the fact that he hadn't been in hibernation all this time, but leashed like an animal in Deaglan's court.

After Deaglan's failed assassination attempt on me, I should have sent spies into his court. I shouldn't have said fuck it and abandoned everyone, and I sure as shit shouldn't have gone realm hopping without at least checking on Titus.

Except he hadn't told me where he'd been hibernating. No one was supposed to have known. He'd just said he'd wake and find me when Faerie's Heart started calling to him so I could remove or block that bond and he'd be free of his species' curse.

Which was yet another bond I was supposed to be able to break.

I pulled off my pajama pants, stepped into the shower, and pressed my palms against the cool tiles, trying to focus on the spray hitting me.

I couldn't believe the Heart had awakened already. Faerie was going to be a battleground with each court desperate to get their hands on it or stop someone else from getting it. That was how Titus ended up the last of his species. There hadn't been many dragons to begin with, but the last time the Heart had awakened, the Summer Court had decided no one should have it, and the only way to ensure that was to exterminate the only species with a direct connection to it: dragonkind.

I didn't know if the king of the Summer Court had changed his mind since then, but I had no doubt even if he had, some other monarch would decide Titus was too dangerous to live.

I couldn't allow Amiah to get caught up in this mess. She might be a pain in my ass, but she didn't deserve what was coming Titus's, and now my, way. I had to separate them as soon as possible, which meant I had to get my shit together.

And that started with telling Titus to stop calling me by my birth name. Seireadan had died the night Deaglan and Enowen, my betrothed, had tried to kill me, and I sure as shit didn't want to keep being reminded that I'd been a lovesick fool. I didn't need Titus bringing up details about a time I'd worked damned hard to forget, and I certainly didn't need Amiah asking questions about it.

TITUS

Seireadan — who didn't look or smell like Seireadan — left. The only reason I recognized him was because of the spell he'd wrapped in my soul so I could find him once I'd come out of hibernation and he could sever or block my connection to Faerie's Heart.

I didn't know why he had a glamour spell on him hiding his identity, and I had a terrible feeling a lot had happened in the five hundred years I'd been Deaglan's prisoner.

Amiah and the other angel left as well, closing the door behind them, and I headed into what had to be the bathing room to clean off the blood crusted to my now mostly healed body. My reflection in the large mirror over the white marble sink would have been laughable with all the bandages wrapped around me if it hadn't been proof of how injured I'd been — since Seireadan, who knew how fast I healed, had still let Amiah bind my wounds.

My pulse raced at the thought of her and I rubbed my

face as if that would help me think straight... which it didn't.

I sliced off the bandages with a claw then turned my attention to what I hoped was a waterfall or rain-shower stall. Even taking the time to figure out that the silver handle with the dial made water spray from a disk near the ceiling and that turning the handle adjusted the temperature — not like Faerie where magic adjusted the temperature with a thought — couldn't get her off my mind.

I had no idea why I'd grabbed her and held her close.

She'd been crying from what I knew was agonizing pain — a pain that had seized me as well — and my instincts had kicked in and all I'd wanted was to hold and reassure her.

Which was crazy. I didn't know her, and I sure as hell didn't know if anything was going to be okay.

But we were in the same boat, and I'd seen the fear and hurt in her eyes when she'd tried to tell me I was safe. She knew what it was like to be imprisoned. I didn't know how or why an angel like her would end up in such a terrible situation, but without a doubt, she'd felt that fear before.

With that look and her crying, I'd been unable to resist my nature, the nature that made dragons entwine their bodies with their mates. I had to touch her, steady her soul against mine, show her she wasn't alone — as well as use her to steady my own shaking soul.

I stepped into the washing stall that was barely wide enough for me and let the warm water rush over my skin.

It would have been even better if she'd been naked.

Full flesh to flesh contact to properly ground us... or rather me since she wasn't a dragon and didn't have the same need. Except that would have created a whole new problem.

My beast wanted her, and her being naked would have made it close to impossible to rein in that even more powerful primal emotion. An emotion that had roared to life the moment I'd pinned her to the bed and met her gaze — probably because I'd been without sex or even a compassionate touch for half a millennium and was starved for contact.

Yeah. That was it. My beast had latched onto the first female I'd encountered since escaping.

Except, as much as I wanted to deny it, there was more to my desire for Amiah than her just being female. While there'd been surprise and fear in her eyes when I'd grabbed her, there'd also been a fierce determination that had excited my beast.

That excitement had only grown when she'd risked her life to stop me from ripping out the other angel's throat even though she knew it'd take nothing for me to hurt her. And it had grown again with the look she'd given me when Seireadan had been trying to break the leash spell, as if she, by herself, would keep me safe from whatever was coming.

Which was the stupidest thing ever. She was small and fragile, and given that she had healing magic, I doubted she had another power that could hurt me or anyone else if she was threatened. She couldn't protect herself let alone me.

But that only made my beast more excited, and I was

glad I'd covered up before Seireadan had noticed my raging hard on. Because if she wasn't Seireadan's female like her scent implied — along with the fact that I couldn't smell the woman he'd been betrothed to on him or anywhere in the room — Amiah was surely the other angel's given how enraged he'd been to see me on top of her.

And my beast didn't give a fuck about that. Its desire for Amiah— No *any* female, Amiah was just an easy target, made my cock so hard it hurt.

This was going to be a problem. The best I could hope for was that getting myself off along with the promise of finding an appropriate female soon, would satisfy my beast.

I gripped my cock, and brought to mind the last female I'd had sex with. My female. She hadn't been my true mate, but not every dragon found their soul's mate. I'd won her affection and she would have been mine to the end of our days or until either of us found our soul's mate or another dragon challenged me for her and I lost the fight. She'd been a fire dragon like me, with red hair slightly paler than mine, gold-green eyes, and a powerful body — both in human and dragon form.

I pumped my hand up and down my length, remembering the intimate times we'd spent together, her hot flesh against mine, her lips teasing my body, and my cock sheathed in her tight heat. Except the moment I thought about driving into her, the image in my mind's eye shifted. The woman wrapped around my cock turned into delicate Amiah, with her blue glowing eyes partially hidden by lids lowered with pleasure, her long blond locks splayed on the pillow behind her giving her a shimmering halo, and her lips parted on a sensual moan.

My balls tightened and I tried to turn her back to my long-dead mate, hell, to anyone else, but couldn't. My beast wanted to be wrapped in *her* tight sheath, wanted to feel *her* come around my cock. Wanted to hear *her* moans and screams of pleasure.

My fantasy Amiah locked gazes with me as I drove into her, the look in her eyes said she understood me, understood the fear and hurt of being enslaved, and still wanted me, craved me as much as I craved her. Then her body tensed, her head tipped back exposing her delicate neck to my canines in invitation to mark her as mine, and she screamed her release which set off mine.

I came hard, biting back a roar, and digging my claws into the shower tiles to keep steady... and not to go storming out of the bathroom to find Amiah and make the fantasy real.

Fuck. This was really going to be a problem.

AMIAH

I LAY ON THE BED IN SEBASTIAN'S GUESTROOM, STARING AT the ceiling, exhausted and dizzy. Healing my cracked ribs and the bruise around my neck had taken everything I'd managed to regain with last night's meager sleep. All I wanted was to crawl into bed and sleep, but that would put off breaking the leash spell, and the panic of being trapped that had eased when I'd thought I'd be free in a few hours had returned with a vengeance.

I had to be free. *Now.*

Now now now.

Cassius was already back to looking at me like I was fragile, and I didn't know if I'd ever be able to get him to see me as an equal again, able to stand on my own just as much as he could. I shouldn't have let Titus hold me. But I was weak.

And now they all knew it.

The sooner Titus and I were separated the better. Cassius's honor wouldn't let him leave my side until he knew I was safe, which meant he wouldn't go after the men, and that would delay Sebastian in finding a solution to my problem.

A problem which I was now acutely aware of. With the pain from my ribs and throat gone, there was nothing distracting me from the warm ache running from the bottom of my ribcage, over my hip, and down my thigh. The pain in my not-yet-awakened mating brand felt stronger than before, but I had to be imagining that. It hadn't gotten worse. I was just more aware of it because I was trapped — *trapped trapped trapped!* — by the leash spell.

I drew in a slow pain-free breath, fighting to steady my nerves and to get the room to stop spinning.

I could handle this. Just a few more hours and I'd no longer have to act like I was strong and calm. I would be.

With another deep breath, I turned my attention to the scrubs sitting at the foot of the bed. I'd feel more like myself if I was dressed like myself, but that just seemed like too much work, especially since I was going to have to change again to go to Left of Lincoln. Better to have breakfast, regain some strength, and then change into whatever Sebastian's assistant was bringing over. Cassius had already seen me in Sebastian's clothes and hadn't said anything, so my irrational worry that he'd be upset had been unfounded and our friendship, the friendship I desperately needed right now, wasn't on rocky ground because of that.

No. It was because I'd never experienced such pain before and had given in to my weak, base need for physical comfort.

I pushed that thought aside. Regardless if Cassius

thought I was weak or not, he'd be there for me. Just like he always was.

I drew in another breath. *All right, Amiah. Time to get up and be a professional. Just a few more hours and you'll get your life back*

At least until my mating brand awakened.

My panic surged and I pushed that thought back.

Strong and calm. No one is supposed to worry about their physician. You can do this.

Another breath and I slowly sat up.

The room stayed at its ever-so-slight spinning but didn't get worse. That was the best I was going to get, so I squared my shoulders and made sure my mask of cool professionalism was in place and didn't reveal how exhausted I really was.

With my guard fully up, I carefully stepped into the hall and was met with the rich aromas of freshly brewed coffee and frying eggs.

Oh, thank goodness. Someone was making breakfast. I could only hope I could convince them to share since I wasn't sure I'd be able to stand at a stove long enough to make something at the moment.

I followed the smell to Sebastian's sleek high-end white and stainless-steel kitchen, where I found all of the guys.

Titus, sitting at the small kitchen table tucked into a corner by a tall window with the purplish hue of UV-blocking glass, was the first to notice me. He sat with his back to the wall with a towel, barely big enough to cover all of him, wrapped around his hips. His attention jumped to me the moment I stepped through the wide opening, his gaze filled with a confusing mix of emotions.

At first glance, he looked... hungry and not in the way a beast looked at dinner but in the way a man looked at a woman he desired. But that quickly shifted to a banked anger, which I couldn't blame him for. I'd been angry at everyone for a long time after my rescue even though I knew I had no reason to be angry with them.

Sebastian sat beside him, dressed in beige summer slacks and a light-blue button-down. His lips were quirked in their perpetual mischievous smile as if he knew a dirty joke, most likely about me, and was dying to share it in front of everyone to embarrass me. The grayish hue to his complexion was gone, and he looked like he always did, with a blue-white glow emanating from his skin at the soft, almost imperceptible levels of a faekin, not the more powerful glow of the full fae that he really was.

Cassius, much to my surprise, stood at the stove frying up a big pan of scrambled eggs. He had his back to me and didn't notice my arrival, and I took the moment to appreciate his broad shoulders, narrow waist, and firm glutes. A part of me was surprised he hadn't settled down in a serious relationship by now. He was a good, handsome man who cared deeply, or at least he'd cared before the war. Now I was sure he still cared, but the signs were harder to notice and he hid it behind an overbearing protectiveness.

"How can I help?" I asked, the idea of Cassius making me breakfast without me at least helping suddenly making me uncomfortable despite my exhaustion. I could probably lean on the counter and make toast or something. Really.

Cassius glanced at me and his eyes narrowed. "I'd rather you sit and eat before you pass out."

"I'm not going to pass out," I said, old habits making me square my shoulders as I headed to the sleek, single-serve coffee machine. But Sebastian stood, blocking my way, and held out his chair for me.

"I need a refill," he said, his cup still half full. "I'll make yours while I'm up."

"I—" I bit back my sharp response. I couldn't afford to alienate him and risk him refusing to remove my brand, but I also didn't like him doing something for me that I could just as easily do myself, especially when it was clear he was just getting up for me.

He cocked an eyebrow as if daring me to finish what I was going to say.

This wasn't the conversation I wanted to have so I pressed my lips together and sagged into the offered chair.

"Atta girl," he chuckled as if he'd just scored a point, making me bristle because he had. I'd just given in and sat like he'd asked.

"She takes a little sugar and a lot of cream," Cassius said, dividing the finished eggs onto four plates. "What's the ETA on the clothes?"

"Anytime now." Sebastian grabbed a mug from the cupboard above the coffee maker and set it in the machine. "I'd like to get to Lincoln as soon as possible. Titus is going to stick out like a sore thumb so the fewer people who see him, the better."

My stomach tightened. That meant I'd be free soon. Likely within an hour or two.

"You honestly think less of a crowd will be better?" Cassius asked going to the fridge and pouring a glass of orange juice. "There'll be fewer people to blend in with."

He set the juice, a plate of eggs, and a fork in front of me as the tightness in my stomach turned into a cold stone. Waiting until there were more people in Lincoln was the better plan no matter how much I wanted to be free. *Right now.*

Sebastian rolled his eyes and jerked his thumb at Titus. "Don't tell me you think he's going to blend in with anyone. He's as big as a greater demon or an ogre but with the wrong essence and the wrong coloring. It doesn't matter how big the crowd is, everyone is going to notice him."

I took a bite of the eggs not really tasting them. "We should get a glamour and a concealment spell on him first." If Titus was going to draw attention, magically changing his appearance was the most logical first step. It was illegal for anyone except the military or the JP to cast those spells but we were trying to hide from dangerous men. We were going to have to break the rules.

That thought made my stomach churn, adding to the worry that getting concealment and glamour spells on Titus meant putting off breaking the leash spell for even longer.

I glanced at Titus, fighting to keep my expression calm. "Can you handle being leashed a little longer to get a proper glamour put in place?"

Could I?

My heart raced at the thought. But disguising Titus first was the safest plan.

"Sure," he said, his voice gruff, his gaze dropping to his breakfast.

"A glamour first would be logical if you two weren't bound with a leash spell." Sebastian set my coffee on the table and slid into the chair beside me. "The glamour, along with a concealment spell, needs to be strong and long lasting. The leash spell will suck power during the casting, making it harder to cast and set the spells. I'm not sure whoever we get to set the spells will be able to do it while you two are connected. At least not someone I completely trust."

"You can't set them?" Cassius took the last chair between Sebastian and Titus and shot me a worried glance. He was still looking at me like I was fragile and a part of me feared he'd never stop. At least he wasn't freaking out over the conversation about casting illegal spells... which only spoke to how serious the situation was.

"I can do a lot of things," Sebastian said, "but I can't set a spell in someone."

Cassius sighed. "And there isn't anyone at Operations right now who's strong enough to set one."

Which left us with the risk of Titus being seen or waiting until a strong enough witch flew in to Union City to meet us.

Cassius pinched the bridge of his nose and a wisp of smoke curled from his hand. "This is a terrible idea. We're just going to walk around Left of Lincoln without a glamour or a concealment spell. That's almost as bad as putting up a billboard saying where we are."

"Jeez, I'm not that stupid." Sebastian took a sip of his coffee. "Yes, we're going to be walking around Lincoln without a glamour, but I have a group concealment glyph. I can keep it active long enough to get the charm attuned to our resonance and get back here, so they at least won't be able to track us with magic."

The muscles in Cassius's jaw twitched, likely at Sebastian's confession that he had an illegal spell tattooed on his body. "That's another issue. Those men saw you. They're going to start asking about you and someone is going to point them here." He frowned and shoved his fork into his eggs with an angry thrust. "I'm surprised they haven't shown up by now."

"They haven't because I have a look-away spell on the apartment. Yeah, people know I do business in the office I keep downstairs, but only a select few know I actually live here." Sebastian drained his coffee mug. "Anyone who shows up looking for me will find my office closed and leave."

"What about your landlord?" Cassius asked. The master vampire who owned the building wasn't the most trustworthy and wasn't on the best of terms with the JP.

Sebastian's expression hardened. "She won't be a problem," he said, and I didn't want to ask what that meant. It was probably something illegal, and while I might be able to look the other way, Cassius would have a harder time doing so.

More smoke curled around Cassius and he shifted, clearly coming to the same conclusion, but his phone chirped, saving him from having to decide if he should push for more details or not.

He answered and had a quick conversation, most likely with Chris, then hung up. "Chris lost the trail of those men in the middle of the Quarter near Winfield, and Summer is still working on the forensics they found in the park ring—"

"Tell her not to bother. She won't find anything useful," Sebastian said. "Those were professionals. They probably cast a spell to remove all trace of themselves and Titus. The only DNA she's going to find is yours, mine, and Amiah's, which means the JP won't be able to cast a tracking spell. This can't be handled in your traditional ways. The only way to get these men are for them to come to us."

"Which we're not going to let happen until Amiah is free of this situation," Cassius said.

Yes, free. Now. I had to be free. I took a large sip of my orange juice, grasping the glass in both hands to hide the fact that I was shaking.

Come on. It's just a few more hours.

And while I logically knew that, I couldn't convince the rest of me of it.

"You say that as if we have a choice in when they find us." Sebastian met Cassius's glare, all mirth gone from his expression. "Like I've been saying from the beginning of this clusterfuck, the first priority is separating Amiah and Titus."

"So long as we understand each other—" Cassius stiffened and held up his hand for silence. "Someone's here."

"Sebastian," a sultry alto called, the word punctuated with the sharp click of heels on the marble floor.

"It's my assistant." Sebastian stood, and took his empty plate and mug to the dishwasher. "In the kitchen, Nova," he called as a stunningly beautiful demon with the onyx skin of a babaus stepped into the archway between the living room and the kitchen.

She wore a vibrant green pantsuit, but only in the pretext of appearing professional since the skirt was obscenely short, showing off her long, shapely legs, and the form-fitting top under her jacket showed an equally obscene amount of cleavage.

But despite that, she didn't come across as cheap. It was more like she oozed sex as if she was a succubus, even though babaus didn't possess sexual magic. And with her lingering gaze on Cassius and Titus, she knew how alluring she was.

Cassius drew in a sharp breath and gave her a tight nod, before turning his back on me to go to the sink, so I had no idea what he thought of Nova. She wasn't like any of the women he'd dated in the past, but then as far as I knew he'd only ever dated angels, and angels, no matter how beautiful, just didn't have that kind of sexual magnetism. And really, Cassius could be attracted to her. He had needs, just like everyone else.

Which made me think of Titus and the hungry look he'd given me when I'd first entered the kitchen.

My gaze jumped to him of its own volition. As irrational and ridiculous as it was, I didn't want to see his desire for this woman, and yet I couldn't help looking. The man had spent a long time in captivity where I doubted his needs had been met. He was going to look at every woman that way. Except instead of the hunger I'd seen when I'd first entered the kitchen, his expression was pained. Then he shifted and grunted and his banked anger returned.

"You've *come* right on time," Sebastian said with a hint of his wicked smile, his inflection turning his words dirty.

"Don't I always," she purred, and his smile deepened, making embarrassment heat my cheeks.

To think I'd actually considered accepting his proposition for sex... if he ever propositioned me again. But of course he wouldn't. He wasn't interested in me. Why would he? Not when he had someone like Nova in his life. He probably had dozens of Novas at his beck and call, and I was a naive, inexperienced angel. All I had was research and self-exploration. No firsthand experience and that was probably clear as day to someone like Sebastian, which was why he teased me in the first place.

And jeez, why did that even bother me?

Because I'd been a fool to even entertain the possibility of releasing my own pent-up needs with him.

Nothing more.

Nova prowled to the table and set a full cloth bag in front of Titus. "I take it you're the big and tall—" Her gaze dipped to the towel around his hips. "—and extra large."

Titus sat forward, a strange desperate hope flashing across his expression for a second before returning to anger. With a huff, he grabbed the bag — and the ends of his towel to keep it secure — and marched out of the kitchen

"And you're the sundress." Nova set a second bag in

front of me and sank into the chair across from me, but her attention was back on Sebastian and Cassius, barely giving me a cursory glance. "I changed today's meeting to tomorrow like you asked."

"You really think this will be solved by tomorrow?" Cassius handed Sebastian his dirty plate to put into the dishwasher.

I prayed it would be. Then he could get to work removing my brand.

"Maybe we'll get lucky." Except Sebastian didn't sound as if he believed that, making my hope wither. "But I'm meeting someone I don't want to piss off."

"That would be a first," Cassius said.

"There are lots of people I don't want to piss off." Sebastian's smile turned wicked. "But you're just too much fun."

"Oh? You think it's fun to piss me off?" Cassius demanded.

"Guys—" I bit the inside of my cheek. What was the point? At least they weren't arguing about anything serious.

Sebastian chuckled and glanced at me, but I grabbed the bag with the sundress and left the kitchen. The sooner I changed, the sooner we could get to Left of Lincoln and separate me and Titus.

I reached the bedroom and for a second I wasn't sure I wanted to look inside the bag. Whatever the dress was, it wasn't going to be appropriate for the chief physician of Operations.

But then not looking like myself was the whole point, and I wouldn't have to wear it for long.

Much to my surprise, the dress was tasteful. It was white with large blue flowers the color of my eyes and skimmed my curves perfectly. The skirt flared a bit and hung a modest one inch above my knees, and the sexiest things about it were the sweetheart neckline revealing a little more cleavage than I usually liked and its behind-the-neck strap that exposed most of my back, forcing me to go without a bra. Thankfully, I wasn't as well-endowed as Nova and there was enough support in the dress for me to feel comfortable going without.

To top it off, a pair of white sandals in my size with a practical heel had been included.

I was dressed and about to put on the sandals when someone knocked on the door.

"Are you decent?" Cassius asked.

"Just putting on my sandals."

"Not what I asked," he said as he opened the door.

His gaze swept over me, his eyes wide with surprise, and a hot curl of desire unfurled low within me even though I was sure his surprise wasn't at my appearance. He'd seen me in a dress... although not recently. But still—

"It surprised me too." I gave a slow twirl — still mindful of how tired I was — making the skirt gently swish around my legs. "I can't believe Sebastian had his assistant pick up something reasonable."

"Ah... yeah," Cassius said, his voice gruff. "I expect Nova has a different taste in clothes than you."

"That much is obvious." I sat on the edge of the bed to put on the sandals. "Is everyone waiting on me?" I hadn't spent a lot of time changing, but I had moved slower than usual. Breakfast had helped a little and now the room wasn't spinning, but I was still exhausted and my magic was still low and I was struggling to keep my fear at bay.

"Yeah." He crossed his arms and his expression hardened. "I called Priam to cover your shift at Operations."

"Good." My fingers shook as I tried to secure the catch on the sandal, but the more I fought to still my hands and not let Cassius see me tremble, the stronger my shaking became. "Tell him I should be able to take the afternoon portion of the shift," I said with as even a tone as possible.

"No." He knelt and nudged my hands away to buckle my sandal. "You look almost as exhausted as you did last night. If the situation wasn't so urgent, I'd make Bane wait a day."

"And by urgent you mean those men coming after Titus." Not the fact that I was trapped. Again. Which, if the idea of being controlled by someone didn't terrify me so much it wouldn't have been the most urgent issue to me. Without the men coming after Titus, being leashed to him didn't endanger me.

"I mean this whole mess," he said as he buckled my other sandal. "You're magically bound to a man we know nothing about, who has dangerous men coming after him for reasons we also know nothing about. For all we know, Titus broke out of jail where he was sent for committing a crime."

"You don't really believe that?" I didn't. Although I didn't know why. Titus's hurt and anger didn't seem like it came from a criminal who'd been caught. Except I had no proof. All I had to go on was my instinct. Cassius, however, was right. We didn't know anything about Titus or Sebastian for that matter... and if I couldn't get rid of my mating brand, I could find myself trapped in the same situation, bound to a man who I knew nothing about. "If those men had been fae law enforcement officers they would have identified themselves, not tried to stab Sebastian in the back."

"I'm not willing to risk your life by letting you stay around Bane and his friend to find out." He finished with the buckle on my sandal and stood.

He did *not* just say that! "Not *letting*?"

"The situation is dangerous," he insisted, missing the point.

"And I don't need your permission." I pushed past him and strode out of the bedroom. "I'm as capable of assessing this situation as you."

"No. You're not," he said, falling into step beside me, smoke curling from his hands. "You don't have any tactical training."

"I don't need to have tactical training. I healed your injuries. I know how dangerous they are."

Cassius huffed. "You have no idea how dangerous these men are."

"I do know." I glared at him even though I knew I'd never win this fight.

The light in Cassius's eyes flared. "No, you don't."

"You know, you two should just fuck and get it over with," Sebastian said from his spot by the door.

Titus, standing beside him dressed in a black T-shirt, black fatigues, and combat boots like Cassius, stiffened.

"Don't be crude," Cassius snapped.

"Don't be a prude," Sebastian shot back. "Man with

all that *restrained decorum,* angel sex must be boring... or fucking wild as hell." His pale gaze met mine, making me instantly throb with need. "Which is it? Are you an animal in bed?"

I bit back my frustration. How was this the same man who'd offered me something to sleep in and bought me a tasteful dress? And why did I still react to him like this? It was just a game. *Just. A. Game*

"My sexual predilections are none of your business," I said, painfully aware that just saying *predilections* made me sound like a prude as well. "Are we getting this leash spell broken or not?"

Sebastian snorted and opened his front door, gesturing for all of us to leave. Titus marched out first and Cassius followed.

"Sweetheart, you need to work on your comebacks," Sebastian said as I passed.

"Well then," I replied, pitching my voice so only Sebastian could hear me, "given that we're going to work out a type of payment suitable for both of us, I guess you'll never know what I'm like in bed."

Heat flooded my face and I quickly turned away from him.

Why did I just say that? Words had just come out of my mouth and—

And now he was going to tease me more. There'd be no end to it, and with it just being a game to him, all it would do would rub in the fact that I irrationally ached for him and he didn't want me.

AMIAH

THE RIDE IN THE ELEVATOR DOWN TO THE PARKING GARAGE was tense. Cassius stood stiffly at the back with Titus, who didn't even look at me as I entered, while Sebastian stood beside me with that look in his eyes that said he knew a secret dirty joke about me. I prayed he wouldn't carry on our conversation where Cassius and Titus could hear—

Actually, I prayed he wouldn't continue our conversation at all.

Why had I said that! If anything proved that I was losing my self-control, that was it, and without a doubt, given the heat in my face, my cheeks were bright red, giving it all away.

The door slid open to the cool damp underground garage, and I hurried out needing space. I couldn't think with the guys standing so close and having just been reminded of what I'd been avoiding for years and painfully ached for.

Sebastian walked past the SUV and sports cars to an

old maroon sedan with a dented front fender, parked in a dark corner of the garage, and opened the driver's side door without unlocking it.

"I see we're traveling in style," Cassius said, his tone dry.

"You wanted bigger," Sebastian replied with a shrug. "Flashing too much money around Lincoln is dangerous. It's bad enough it looks like I have two bodyguards and angel arm candy."

Cassius got into the front passenger seat. "Amiah is *not* arm candy."

"She looks pretty hot to me." Sebastian flashed me his wicked smile, making my insides warm with desire and frustration, and slid into the driver's seat.

Titus grunted, but I didn't know if it was in agreement or not and, eyeing the car with suspicion, got in the seat behind him.

"Flattery wouldn't get you into my bed," I said, shoving my feelings down and getting in as well.

"Oh?" Sebastian asked as he started the engine, his gaze meeting mine through the rear-view mirror. "Does that mean something else will?"

No, because you don't really mean it.

A hint of smoke wrapped around Cassius and he rolled down his window. "Can we focus on the job at hand?"

"There isn't much more to it," Sebastian said, pressing a hand to his side and activating a glyph. Light flared from the glyph, bright in the garage's low illumination, before dimming to an almost imperceptible level against his natural glow. "We go to Lincoln and get the resonance charm attuned to our resonances. And you—"

He pulled out of the garage into early morning sunlight. The street was empty since we were in the vampire section of the Quarter and even with the UV-blocking canopy vampires were still mostly creatures of the night, but he still promptly stopped at a red light even though there wasn't a single car on the road. "You keep yourself under control and don't arrest anyone."

"I've already promised I wouldn't," Cassius said, surprising me. Upholding the law was one of the main things that drove him, and he clung to it as if it kept him steady in a world of chaos. He hadn't been so strict with rules and regulations before the war. He could let things slide if it meant justice prevailed. But after the war, it was as if the rules were the only thing holding him together, and while that had eased a bit in the last twenty years, it hadn't gone away... and had gotten worse again in the last month. "Breaking the leash spell is the priority. Anything else would jeopardize that."

Sebastian turned onto the main street leading out of the Quarter and headed to the park ring that separated the supers' part of town from the humans' part. "You just remember that once we get there."

Dappled early morning sunlight flickered through the thick branches overhead as we drove into the park then filled the car in full as we crossed its threshold into the human part of Union City.

I didn't often leave the Quarter, and I was always a little amazed at how different and modern the rest of Union felt compared to the Quarter.

The Quarter had originally been an older part of town, expropriated by the city to create an area for supers so they could live with humans but not necessarily right beside them. No one had known how the supernatural beings who'd come out of hiding to help save humanity from Michael would be received, but almost everyone had agreed they had as much right to live out in the open as humans. And while yes, there were modern buildings in the Quarter, most of the original structures had survived Michael's assaults giving the Quarter an older feel with its nineteenth century brick buildings.

The buildings directly on the other side of the ring, however, were towering residential high rises that had been built in the mid to late twentieth century. Most were plain utilitarian concrete without any charm, and I had no idea why anyone would want to live there, although I suspected people did because they couldn't afford some place better.

Which spoke volumes for those living there since a number of nice neighborhoods in Union had survived the assault while a significant number of the population hadn't, making good places to live cheap and plentiful in the beginning. But that left out those from the smaller towns in the area who'd been forced to abandon their communities and move to Union. Those who took too long to realize the Joined Parliament wasn't going to send revitalization money to their small town and instead focus on the larger cities lost out.

Sebastian headed south and I rolled down my window to alleviate the growing heat. Titus, after watching me, did the same. The day's humidity was already building and without a cloud in the sky, it was going to be another beautiful, hot summer's day. The breeze ruffled his shaggy red hair, and he leaned into it with his eyes closed and drew in a deep breath that expanded his massive chest.

"They didn't let you fly, did they?" I said, the sudden realization breaking my heart. Not letting a dragon fly had to be as horrible as not letting a wolf run.

"No."

"Did they even let you shift?" He'd been imprisoned for five hundred years. Not flying was terrible. Not shifting and releasing his beast would be soul crushing.

While shifters were still one being, they had two very distinct aspects to their soul that often made them feel like they were two separate entities in one body. And not being allowed to embrace both halves, be it beast or man, was psychologically and physically damaging. It was why shifters who weren't naturally born shifters, those rare few infected with lycanthropy, had difficult transitions. Not only did the lycanthropy painfully rewrite their DNA, but they often saw their beast as a separate being and fought it instead of accepted it.

"No," Titus said, his voice low, making my throat tighten.

"Have you shifted since you escaped?" I asked, trying to focus on his situation clinically and not emotionally. If he hadn't, he was going to need to do so soon and appease his primal nature.

"Yes."

Oh, thank goodness.

"You flew out of Faerie, didn't you?" Sebastian said,

driving into a deserted part of town, the buildings mostly rubble. "That's why you fell out of the sky. You found a sky portal but didn't account for the fact that if you have a shape more acceptable to the mortal realm a Faerie portal will shift you into that."

"And I was struck just before I went through and couldn't shift back in time," Titus said, his face still turned to the wind and sun.

Sebastian swerved around a pothole. "That must have been some blow. You used to be one of the fastest shifters I knew."

And it had been. My magic had locked onto Titus the moment he'd materialized in the mortal realm, which meant he'd already been seriously injured before he'd even hit the ground.

Titus grunted.

I reached out and firmly pressed my palm against his biceps, hoping that my small skin to skin touch would help calm his shifter's soul. There wasn't much I could do for the psychological trauma, but I could at least help steady him.

He stiffened, and for a moment I feared I'd gone too far by invading his personal space. Then, without turning away from the sun and wind, he rumbled low in his throat and captured my hand under his.

We stayed that way until Sebastian parked the sedan at the still-standing support for an overpass that ended fifty feet away in a nasty drop.

As if stopping was his cue, Titus climbed out of the car before Sebastian had even shut off the engine, and pulled on a black ball cap that shaded his eyes so I couldn't easily read his expression.

A mix of disappointment and sadness churned in my gut, fueled by my compulsion to heal. I understood, in part, the wounds in his soul, and I yearned, not for the first time, that my power was stronger and more complex. There was more to healing someone than just fixing his or her body and at times it felt like I was working with one hand tied behind my back.

Cassius pulled on a ball cap as well and added sunglasses that hid the glow from his eyes, although that wasn't a perfect disguise. Yes, no one would be able to see his eyes, but anyone with the ability to sense essences — which was most of the super population — would know he was an angel. It was, however, better than nothing. Especially if the whole point was to avoid as much attention as possible given our unusual party.

I got out as well, forcing my gaze over the area to distract myself from my need to help Titus and my inability to do so. The area looked like it had been a mix of residential and small commercial buildings. Those behind us in the direction we'd come from were mostly leveled with only a few concrete shells of three- and four-story apartment buildings standing ghostly sentinel.

The destruction lessened as I turned my attention to what lay in front of the car as if we were standing at the edge of the radius of a tremendous blast. And given the powerful magic Michael had commanded during the war, it could have been just one blast.

Ahead stood a modest, two-door mechanic's garage. The roof had been ripped off — probably from the blast

— and so had half of the sign, leaving only "& Son" creaking in the breeze. On its left sat another business, the sign gone so I had no idea what it had been. The big front window was broken, and the insides had been torn apart, likely from people scavenging everything that could be reused or recycled.

Sebastian led us down an alley between the two businesses that was so narrow Titus's shoulders brushed either side and along an uneven dirt path heading down into a wooded ravine.

"I would have thought Left of Lincoln would be easier to get to," Cassius said.

Sebastian skidded down a sharp incline in the path with the ease of someone who'd done that before. "We're coming in the back way. There's parking and easier access if you arrive by the main roads, but also a lot of people just hanging around. I'd rather avoid that kind of notice."

Cassius huffed. "So you actually can come up with a plan." He followed Sebastian down the slope then held out his hand to help me.

I contemplated not accepting his help. The way he looked at me was still verging on that same look of worry and pity he'd had all those years ago, and every part of me screamed that I needed to look stronger, *be* stronger.

But his look would only get worse if I slipped and landed on my rear end. And with my luck as of late, my skirt would fly up and I'd end up flashing all of them.

And then Sebastian would have something else to tease me about.

I took Cassius's hand and half skidded like Sebastian and Cassius. But the skid quickly turned into a slip, toppling me forward, and I crashed into Cassius's firm body.

His arm wrapped around me — it had to have been instinct, nothing else — and he held me close.

Unable to help myself, I melted into his embrace. I always felt safe in those rare instances when he held me, and I wanted to savor this moment, wanted it to last longer than I knew it would. It wouldn't come again anytime soon, even though I needed it.

"You okay?" he murmured, making my pulse pick up... because Sebastian had teased me and now I craved a connection with anyone, even Cassius. Except...

Was his faster too?

It couldn't be.

But before I could figure that out, he gripped my shoulders and took a step back, putting an appropriate amount of distance between us.

Sebastian rolled his eyes and for a second it looked like he was going to comment — probably say something snide — but he snapped his mouth shut and continued down the path. Maybe he, too, realized we all needed to play nice with each other to get through this.

I bit back a huff of frustration. It was more likely he was just waiting for a better opportunity to make a stinging remark.

A few minutes later, we stepped out of the woods into an alley of sorts running between the forest and behind a row of tents, trucks, and trailers.

Even at this early hour, standing in the shadow of a large red nylon tent, my senses were assaulted with the rumble of many voices and the smell of cooking food and pungent spices, reminding me of the Middle Eastern bazaar I'd visited — modern tents and vehicles aside — a few years before my abduction.

My impression didn't change when we made our way between the tent and a blue van and stepped onto a narrow street half full with people. It was almost hard to see that the area originally had been a small parking lot — most likely for access to the forested ravine — across the street from an unusual V-intersection where one street ran parallel to the ravine and two other streets met it in a V.

At the center of the market, standing in the point of the V, was an intact narrow three-story building with a sign advertising blood bunnies — for any vampire who'd managed to purchase a rare and expensive charm against the sun or were visiting after sunset — and prostitutes for everyone else. A few other buildings — a couple of small houses and three small storefronts — also remained standing, while the rest of Left of Lincoln were tents and vehicles crowded down the streets and around rubble creating a maze of passageways.

Sebastian held out his elbow and flashed me his wicked smile, making my pulse frustratingly stutter. "Remember who we're supposed to be, Angel Arm Candy."

I took his arm and he tugged me close, reigniting my desire, while Cassius glowered, and Titus focused on the area around us, his gaze darting over everything, his body tense.

"Hawk keeps a tent on the edge of the market. It's

usually this way," Sebastian said, heading toward the three-story building.

"Usually?" Cassius asked. "I don't particularly want to be wandering around. It's bad enough that we're already drawing attention."

And we were. People were looking at us with a mix of curiosity, suspicion, and jealousy. I felt like I was on display, and in a way I was. I didn't know how many people here knew or knew of Sebastian Bane, but he was still a rare faekin, and at the moment, he had two angels and a massive shifter with him. And while there were a few men with bodyguards and pretty young women hanging on their arms, there weren't a lot and none in as an unusual combination as us.

"Lincoln never stays the same," Sebastian said as if he didn't notice the stares. "Hell, two months ago it was on the other side of town near the old arena and last year it was about ten miles out of town."

Cassius harrumphed. "We should ask for directions."

"I agree," Titus rumbled.

"I'm not asking for directions." Sebastian tugged me even closer to avoid running into a monstrously large ogre with thick, grayish-green skin who was even bigger than Titus.

"The sooner we find Hawk, the sooner we get out of here," Cassius pressed.

"Asking for directions will just make us more memorable," Sebastian replied, leading us past a food truck with whole plucked chickens and skinned rabbits hanging from the metal awning. "Surely you're smart enough to know memorable is bad."

"So is spending more time than necessary," Cassius said.

For the love of—!

"This is Sebastian's turf. He knows the area and the people best."

Sebastian flashed me a satisfied smile, and Cassius's glower deepened.

Yeah, I don't think so.

"If you can't find this Hawk person in ten minutes," I added, "*I'm* going to ask for directions."

Sebastian rolled his eyes at me. "That's not—"

"Nine minutes and fifty seconds," I said. "Or do I start asking now?"

I started to step away from him to talk to a heavyset woman selling...? I had no idea.

But Sebastian tightened his grip on my arm and tugged me back to his side. "Fine. Ten minutes."

"Nine minutes and thirty seconds, now," Titus rumbled.

Sebastian glared at him. "You, too?"

We hurried past the unofficial blood house/brothel down the narrower of the two streets that made up the V-intersection and made our way past a pickup truck with — probably stolen — electronics, a tent with colorful lady's clothing, and a cube van with a complicated glyph painted on the side. The van's back door was open, revealing stacks of old-looking books, and wooden and metal boxes of various shapes and sizes.

If I was magically sensitive, I was sure that van would have been glowing like a sun or pulsing like a pressure wave with all the magic inside... *if* the woman standing at the open door selling the magical items wasn't trying to cheat her customers. But by the sudden tightness in Sebastian's body and the way he picked up his pace to move past the van, I was certain the woman was selling the real, magical deal.

We left the road two trucks and a small still-standing house later, moving into a tent city with even narrower passageways. Here the smells of cooked food, smoke, sweat, and urine clashed with each other in a strange mix of appealing and disgusting. People talked in hushed voices, stared at us as we passed, or hurried inside their tents.

The tension in Sebastian's body didn't ease and neither did his pace.

"You okay?" I asked softly, although I was pretty sure Cassius and Titus were still able to hear me.

"Yeah," he said, "just a lot of magic in this area. Not really a fan of letting it all hang out like this."

"You never were," an incubus said, stepping out of a large white canvas tent, far too similar to the tent I'd been kept in all those years ago.

I shuddered and the gorgeous demon slid his attention to me, hellfire simmering in shockingly gray-blue eyes — a rare color for a demon.

He radiated raw, unbridled sex that stole my breath, and he made no attempt to hide it like the other incubus I knew. It made me ache to run my hands through his jaw-length sandy blond hair, tease the base of his small horns fully knowing they were an erogenous zone, and let him do whatever he wanted to me. Like all incubi, he'd be perfection under his T-shirt and shorts, all sleek, sculpted muscle, and I instantly needed to see him naked, run my hands over him, have him pressed against me, inside me—

"Hawk," Sebastian said, making my pulse pick up.

This was who we were meeting? An incubus? I was already having trouble closing the floodgate on my desire. How was I going to hold myself together sitting near sex incarnate and not look like I was affected while Sebastian conducted his business?

AMIAH

Desire throbbed between my thighs as if proving the point that I no longer had any restraint, and the hellfire in the incubus's eyes swelled.

"You moved your tent," Sebastian said.

"I got pushed out by a blood witch." Hawk gave a sensual shrug, his gaze never leaving mine. "You here on business?"

"Yeah." Sebastian drew closer — and as a result, drew me closer.

My pulse beat even faster and I struggled to get myself back under control. I'd been around incubi before. This shouldn't be that difficult.

"Well, then." Hawk raised the flap on his tent and gestured for us to enter.

A whisper of fear fluttered through my chest, chilling my desire. I didn't want to go inside even though I *knew* it wasn't *that* tent. Cassius had burned it almost a hundred years ago, and if he hadn't killed the human who'd enslaved me, that human would still be long dead, not here in Left of Lincoln.

The thought made me furious.

All these years later and that human was still controlling me. How many times was I going to have to tell myself I was strong, I was in control, I was free before my soul believed it?

And maybe yesterday I would have believed it.

But today, I wasn't free.

I was magically bound to Titus and soon I'd be magically bound to someone else if Sebastian couldn't remove my mating brand.

Well, the first problem I could take care of. It was just a matter of going inside that tent. And the sooner I dealt with the leash spell, the sooner Sebastian could get to work on my brand.

Sebastian frowned and tugged gently on my arm, urging me forward and making embarrassment heat my cheeks. I'd hesitated for too long and now he knew something was wrong.

Fighting the urge to straighten my back — that would give me away even more — I made myself enter with him.

Inside was completely different to the traveling faith healer's tent from my past. That man had tried to portray a pious nature — even though he was nothing of the sort. He'd kept a clean tent with a simple cot for my patients during the day and him at night, a table with his bible, a wash basin, clean rags, and a locked chest filled with stones that was too heavy to move, which he chained my ankle to during the night.

Hawk's tent was stuffed with multi-colored pillows,

Persian rugs, and gauzy curtains. The morning sun shone fully on the tent top, providing more than enough light to see clearly, and yet the space still had a soft, intimate feel. The temperature was also comfortable — most likely cooled by magic. A large chest with an intricate design carved into its wooden surface sat at the back, and a low table sat in the center. At the edge of the table, on a metal tray, was a pitcher of pale yellow liquid with condensation beading on its glass surface along with two delicate wine glasses beside it.

Hawk gestured to the pillows in front of the table, but walked to the chest at the back and pulled out a third wine glass.

Sebastian sat on one of the cushions, drawing me down to sit beside him, and glanced at Cassius who gave a tight nod, his expression icy. He stayed at the entrance, just inside the flap, while Titus took up position kneeling at the side of the tent halfway between Cassius and the table — since he was too tall to fully stand.

"You don't usually come with muscle," Hawk said, oozing sexual grace as he eased into a cushion across from us and poured the yellow liquid into one of the wine glasses. "You also never come with a companion. Have you decided on an alternative payment this time?"

He flashed me a heart-stopping smile and Sebastian huffed.

"No," the fae said.

"Too bad." Hawk handed me the glass, brushing his index finger along my baby finger as I took it and sending his sensual magic rushing straight to my core. "I find angels intriguing."

I fought to keep my expression the same and not shift to ease the heat and pressure building low within me before remembering that it didn't matter what my outward appearance was, the incubus could sense my desire.

My cheeks heated and Hawk's smile deepened.

"Very intriguing," he purred, the hellfire in his eyes flaring.

"Are you planning on doing business today?" Sebastian demanded. "There are half a dozen Sensitives in Lincoln who can do what I need done."

"We both know you'd never go to those hacks." Hawk turned his attention to Sebastian, releasing me from his captivating gaze, and his smile shifted from sensual to friendly. "What do you need?"

Sebastian pulled the resonance charm from his pocket and set it on the table. "I need a three-way alignment."

Hawk cocked an eyebrow. "You can do a three-way alignment."

"I wouldn't be here if that had worked. The spell I'm breaking is warped and I need the charm aligned with more precision than I'm capable of."

"How much more?" Hawk asked, his expression becoming serious, all sense of sensuality or even warm friendship gone.

"As much as you can manage," Sebastian replied, just as seriously.

Hawk poured another glass of the pale yellow liquid and took a long sip. I watched the muscles in his neck flex as he swallowed, unable to help myself, fully knowing that was the effect of his magic.

"That'll cost you," Hawk said.

"I expected it would."

Hawk's eyes widened. "You're a better haggler than that."

Sebastian leaned forward, his expression hard. "Which should tell you how serious I am about you doing your best work."

"It tells me you're rattled." Hawk took another sip and closed his eyes. "Let's just see what you're up against—" He sucked in a sharp breath. "Shit. A leash spell?"

"You're familiar with it?" Sebastian asked, his voice grim.

"Yeah." Hawk opened his eyes now fully consumed by hellfire and turned his attention to me, his expression fierce. "Whoever cast that should be shot. Keep your money, Bane, and let's free the angel and the—" He glanced at Titus then turned back to Sebastian, his eyes wide. "Are you shitting me?"

"Nope," Sebastian said. "What's your usual order for the alignment?"

"You first. You're the one breaking the spell. Then the —" Hawk shook his head as if he still didn't believe what he was going to say. "Then the dragon, the origin of the spell, and finally Miss Angel here."

He finished his drink, picked up the charm, and stood.

Sebastian jerked his chin at the wine glass still in my hand as Hawk knelt behind him. "You're going to want to drink that."

I brought the glass to my lips and took a quick sniff

then a sip. It was wine. One with a nice light slightly sweet flavor, but wine nonetheless. "It's the middle of the morning."

"Trust me." Sebastian turned to face Hawk. "You're going to want it."

"If it's that bad, why aren't you or Titus drinking?"

Sebastian quirked an eyebrow at me as if I should have already figured out the answer. "This isn't going to affect me or Titus as much as it will you. Guys aren't our thing."

My thoughts tripped over that.

Right. Hawk was an incubus.

Heat seared my cheeks again and my pulse picked up. I was about to get firsthand experience with an incubus's sex magic, and Sebastian wanted me to drink first. Of course he wanted me intoxicated. That would offer the best opportunity for me to embarrass myself and give him more fodder to tease me with.

"One drink isn't going to release my inhibitions," I said, putting the glass on the table.

Sebastian drew in a deep breath and rolled his shoulders making his glow undulate down his body. "No, but it might relax you."

"And it's always better if you don't fight me," Hawk added, using his palm to press the charm against Sebastian's chest over his heart. "You ready?"

"To get blue balls? Oh, yeah," Sebastian said, his tone dripping with sarcasm. "Always."

Hawk chuckled and closed his eyes. "Pretty sure you'll be able to remedy that soon enough like you always do."

Sebastian shuddered and bit back a sensual groan that made my pulse pick up.

"Jeez, man," Hawk hissed. "You're spun so tight, it's painful. Take your own advice." He slid his free hand to the back of Sebastian's head and urged him forward to lean his forehead against his shoulder. "Just take a—"

Both of them stiffened and Sebastian's soft glow flickered, revealing that sickly gray pallor for a second. Then Sebastian groaned again, but this one sounded more like pain than pleasure.

"Shit, Bane." The muscles in Hawk's jaw flexed, and a surge of sensual desire brushed against my senses. "What the hell did you do?"

A husky moan escaped Sebastian's clenched jaw the sound back to pleasure and starting a slow throb between my thighs. "It'll be dealt with tomorrow," he said through gritted teeth.

"Then use the charm before then. That shit has messed with your resonance." Hawk drew in a deep, slow breath, and the heated desire that had been caressing my skin without me really knowing it, vanished, leaving me cold and aching. He must have released his power.

That thought made my pulse race even faster. If that was what his magic felt like without him touching me, what would it feel like to have his hands on me?

Hawk nudged Sebastian to sit back and withdrew his hand from Sebastian's heart, his expression tight with worry. He opened his mouth to say something but Sebastian's eyes darted to me and Hawk gave a tight nod.

Gasping, Sebastian leaned back against the table, his breath still too fast, and poured himself a glass of wine.

He emptied it in one gulp and turned his gaze, heavy with desire, toward me, making me think of how much I ached for him—

No. Anyone. I ached for *anyone*, not Sebastian specifically.

"You really should drink yours," he said, his voice husky, sending a thrill racing through me.

I yanked my attention away as Hawk turned to Titus, who watched the incubus with the eyes of a predator ready to attack.

"May I?" Hawk asked.

Titus grunted and nodded his assent, his body stiff and his expression hard.

"You might want to relax." Hawk pressed the charm over Titus's heart like he had with Sebastian, and closed his eyes.

Now that I was aware of it, I could feel Hawk's sensual magic whispering against my skin as he released his power. It made my insides heat but seemed to make every muscle in Titus's body tense.

"Take a breath," Hawk said. "Don't fight me."

Titus drew in a huge breath, expanding his massive chest, and released it on a shuddering growl.

Hawk's magic swelled and Titus's growl turned into a strangled groan. With another groan, he tipped forward, his breath suddenly fast, and Hawk caught Titus's forehead on his shoulder like he had with Sebastian, cupping the back of Titus's head. The tendon in Titus's neck flexed, and his face scrunched in pain as another groan, a strange mix of pain and pleasure, tore from his throat, sending more heated desire sweeping through me.

"How much longer?" Titus gasped, his back heaving with ragged breaths.

My breath picked up, matching his, and I fought to regain control over myself, but that only increased my fear. Hawk hadn't even touched me yet, and his power already made me ache for him.

"Just.... a little... more." Hawk's power swelled, stealing my breath, and Titus slammed his fist into the tent floor, his whole body shaking.

"And we're done." Hawk's power snapped off leaving me cold.

He withdrew his hand from Titus's heart and urged him to sit back like he had with Sebastian. With a snarl, Titus jerked away from Hawk, his eyes still closed, his body even more tense than before they'd started.

Then Hawk turned to me and my pulse stalled.

I didn't want his magic to affect me like Titus or even Sebastian... Except Sebastian had said Hawk's magic was going to affect me more.

Oh, God.

I downed the wine.

Hawk's lips quirked and he held up the charm. "May I?"

A part of me wanted to say no and run out of the tent. I didn't want to risk losing control, and without a doubt, Hawk's magic was going to make me want sex even more than I already did. But saying no wasn't an option. I had to be free. Now. I couldn't hold back my fear for much longer, which meant I had to suck it up and let Hawk touch me.

Please, touch me.

No! Don't.

I nodded, afraid I wouldn't be able to get any words out. Hawk lifted the charm to place it over my heart and I realized with horror that I didn't have the protection of clothing that Sebastian and Titus had. The neckline of my dress was too low. His flesh would be touching mine and that only enhanced an incubus's connection with his lover.

Hawk shifted closer. Heat from his demonic body temperature radiated from his hands as he raised them to set the charm over my heart and press his hot palm over top of that.

My mouth went dry and I wished I'd had another glass of wine. I wasn't relaxed enough for this. I didn't think I'd ever be.

"Just take a breath," Hawk murmured, his tone like silk against my senses.

I forced myself to inhale, and as I released it, he released his magic. It unfurled hot and slick and sensual, and I instantly ached for his touch. I needed to be caressed and kissed. I needed to know what it felt like for a man to move inside me and I was tired of waiting.

I can't be patient anymore. Please release this ache. Please, please touch me.

But that wasn't why I was in Hawk's tent. He was using his magic sensitivity to reach deep into my soul to attune the resonance charm to my resonance. That was it. Not to mention I would hate myself if I begged Hawk — like all but a small part of me wanted to do — to take me with Sebastian, Cassius, and Titus watching. Cassius would never look at me the same and it would just become more fodder for Sebastian's teasing.

My heart pounded faster and my body throbbed with need. I had to hold on until Hawk was done. My yearning would ease up once he withdrew his magic. Surely I could last for the few minutes it took for Hawk to get my resonance.

But his power swelled, and I released an embarrassingly sensual moan then another one as he slid his fingers into my hair and urged me to rest my forehead on his shoulder.

Except I didn't want to just lean on his shoulder, I wanted to rip off our clothes and take him deep inside me.

Now. God. Please now.

"So much desire," he whispered, his breath feathering across my neck and his magic swelling in my core. "Wound so tight. I can help you release it."

Yes. God, yes!

My breath grew ragged, each inhalation reminding me that Hawk's hand was on my breast and I desperately wanted it to move lower, to tease my nipple, taunt me in the best way before satisfying me.

I slipped my hands inside his shirt, trailing my fingers over his six-pack, making him hum with pleasure. The sound twisted my desire tighter, and I reached for the button on his fly when my brain finally caught up to my need.

Cassius, Sebastian, and Titus were in the tent! Watching. Had they noticed I was about to undress Hawk?

I glanced at Sebastian through a veil of lashes afraid

of seeing that wicked smile that said he was never going to let me live down that I wanted to have sex with an incubus I'd just met. Surely he saw where my hands were. He was the closest.

But instead of mischief, his gaze was heavy with raw desire, his pupils dilated. He was turned on and I got the sense he wanted to watch Hawk pleasure me.

And that idea excited me even more. My muscles clenched and my body trembled on the verge of an orgasm.

"Sweet Jesus," Hawk groaned, his voice so low I could barely hear him. "When you're free of the leash spell come find me."

He shot a hot spike of magic straight to my core and ignited my orgasm. My breath caught as the pleasure swept through me and I clutched the waistband of his shorts — only because that's where my hands had been when he made me come.

"That's just a taste," he murmured in my ear and his sensual magic melted away, leaving me panting and trembling and craving more.

I clung to him, fighting to catch my breath and regain my composure before I lifted my head and faced the guys. Embarrassment heated my cheeks that I'd orgasmed with everyone watching, but so, too, did excited desire for the same reason. And while it could have been Hawk's magic influencing me, I had a suspicion it wasn't.

"We need to go," Cassius said, his tone sharp, jerking my attention from my still trembling body. Something was wrong.

Hawk chuckled, the sound thick with male satisfaction. "Pretty sure Miss Angel can't walk yet."

"Then Bane, carry her," Cassius commanded. "It's gotten too quiet outside."

I drew in a ragged breath and forced myself to sit up.

"What do you mean too quiet?" Hawk asked.

"You might want to close up shop for a month or so," Sebastian said to Hawk as he stood and held out his hand to me.

"I can't afford to close up shop for a—"

A sharp *rip* came from the back of the tent, and with a yell, a wiry man with a knife leaped inside through the large slit he'd just made.

AMIAH

SEBASTIAN GRABBED HIS LEFT FOREARM AND HISSED A SOFT sibilant word as two more men leaped through the slit at the back of the tent. The glyph on his arm lit up and a moderately powerful force-wave shot from his left hand and knocked the men over, tumbling them into the tent's canvas back.

"Grab Amiah and let's go," he said to Hawk and staggered toward the flap at the front.

Hawk threw me over his shoulder before I could tell him I could manage.

The three assailants, all human males with similar builds to Sebastian and all with foot-long knives, scrambled to their feet and raced after us.

We ran out of the tent, and Hawk dropped me to my feet and shoved me into Sebastian's arms. "You should take her."

He then turned to face the men, and I pushed away from Sebastian before he could get a good grip on me.

"I can stand," I said, even if I was still a little unsteady.

Behind him Cassius and Titus fought with at least a dozen more assailants, a mix of men and women, humans and shifters, while people screamed and ran away, tripping over each other, tent lines, and knocked-over merchandise.

Cassius side-stepped a jab from one of the men, snapped a small fire whip around his neck — mindful of all the flammable tents and people around us — and wrenched him into a shifter behind him. Another shifter leaped at him, her claws aimed for his back, and he jerked around to face her, blocking her attack with his forearm and pushing her claws away from his body.

Titus snarled and slashed at a man with a sword, tossing him into a small red tent, as another man, a shifter, took the man's place. Inside the damaged tent, someone screamed and a woman scrambled out the front flap as the man Titus hit staggered to his feet then dropped to his hands and knees, gasping.

My magic surged to my palms and locked onto him, even though I'd only recovered a little magic from this morning.

Oh, no. My pulse stuttered. I didn't want to go running into a fight to heal someone let alone someone trying to hurt us. But my magic didn't care if that man was trying to hurt us or not. He was gravely injured and I *had* to try to save him.

I strained to stay where I was. I wasn't a reckless fool. The worse thing I could do was run into danger. That could distract Cassius and he could be killed. But the burning pressure to go to the injured assailant jerked me forward despite my desires.

Sebastian grabbed my arm. "What are you doing?"

"Keep me here," I gasped.

"Keep yourself here."

Behind me, someone yelled, and Sebastian yanked me out of the way to the other side of the narrow path by a pair of tall metal trailers. Hawk and the man who'd first entered the tent tumbled onto the ground where I'd just been standing, and Hawk rammed his elbow into the guy's face while Sebastian shot another small force-wave at a man about to stab Hawk in the back.

"What the hell have you gotten me into?" Hawk demanded, as more men hurried out of the tent.

"You really want an explanation right now?" Sebastian shot another force-wave, but my body jerked me away before I could see the results.

Weak light radiated from my palms, visible only to me, a testament to how little power I had, but the pressure to use it on the dying man was just as ferocious as if I was at full.

I stumbled, fighting the pull, but I had no idea if I'd be able to resist long enough for the fight to end and Cassius to drag me away.

Someone yelled and a woman tumbled to the ground beside me unconscious. Not dead. All around me, people yelled and screamed. Cassius had released more of his fire, his whip almost full size now, hissing and crackling as it struck flesh. Titus snarled and slashed someone else. Both Cassius and Titus were bleeding, their T-shirts cut, and blood splattered the hard-packed dirt at their feet.

Ahead, the injured man, still on his hands and knees, panted short shallow gasps, each breath coming farther and farther apart. Blood gushed from the wound Titus had inflicted with his claws, and from the amount on the ground, he was losing it quickly.

Pressure screamed through me with the promise of an excruciating backlash if I resisted much longer.

The man sagged to his side and I lurched forward another step. I was now at the edge of the chaos. There was no point in fighting the compulsion now. I was already in danger.

I scrambled to the fallen man's side just as the pressure inside me vanished, releasing me, replaced with anger and frustration. He was dead and I'd been forced to run into danger for no good reason.

A woman landed beside me with a *thud* and a heavy *oomph*. Her attention jerked to me and I froze. But a tall muscular man with a stern expression yelled at her and she scrambled back into the fight, only to be replaced by another man with a compound fracture, the bone protruding through the flesh of his right arm.

My magic flickered and I lunged for Titus. He was the closest, and if I wanted to get out of danger, I needed to use up my magic so it wouldn't lock onto someone else.

Titus jerked around to swipe at me but froze, and I slapped my palms against his side and released my magic. The sudden surge drew a wild howl filled with pain and Cassius wrenched around to face us.

"What are you doing?" He grabbed my arm and yanked me away before I'd given Titus all my power.

A slice of backlash cut through me, stealing my breath, and I grabbed Cassius's wrist and gave him the rest, all but the little bit that was always in the core of my being deep in my palms, a flame of magic that never went out.

He grunted against the pain of suddenly being healed and his gaze met mine, hard and icy with understanding.

Exhaustion flooded me and the world lurched and darkened, but at least I wasn't going to heal the enemy.

"Bane," Cassius yelled, seizing the assailant between him and Sebastian with his fire whip and slamming him into the side of a pickup truck. "Get her out of the way."

Bane's attention jerked toward us and Cassius shoved me toward him.

I staggered, fighting to stay upright and conscious. The weariness would pass. I just needed time to recover.

Sebastian yanked me to his side. "What the fuck is wrong with you?"

I opened my mouth to respond but he jerked his gaze away from me.

"Fucking crazy angels," he hissed and sent another force-wave into two shifters barreling down the path toward Hawk.

I swept my gaze around the chaos. There were dozens of assailants, and they were making no attempt to go unnoticed. The stern man yelled something else and two more men scrambled back into the fight. "I thought you said they wouldn't make a public attack."

"That was the Shadow Court. My glyph would light up if they were shadow fae." Sebastian pointed to a small glyph on the inside of his wrist, which flared to life with a brilliant white glow. "Oh, come on!"

With a curse, he shoved me back, hard. I lost my balance and fell onto my rear end, the impact jarring up my spine and sending darkness shuddering across my vision, but it saved my life as the fae with the shadows writhing under his skin darted out from between the two trailers his blade slicing the air where I'd just been.

He swiped his knife again, this time at Sebastian, who jerked out of the way. The blade cut through Sebastian's shirt, but thankfully didn't draw blood, and Sebastian grabbed the shadow fae's wrist and twisted it in an attempt to disarm him. But the shadow fae rammed his heel into Sebastian's knee, knocking him off balance, and wrenched his wrist free.

I staggered to my feet and scanned the area for somewhere to hide. The best place for me was out of the way. Even if I had combat skills, I was in no condition to fight, but a shifter, who'd been knocked to the ground by Hawk, noticed me and bolted toward me.

I glanced at Sebastian. He was busy with the shadow fae. And while Hawk had managed to get one of his assailants' knives, he was still fighting with four of them.

No one was going to help me, so I squeezed a trickle of magic out of the core of my being and released my wings. Up was the best place to go. Everyone would be able to see me — and up my skirt — but at least they wouldn't be able to get to me.

I leaped, caught the wind, reached the top of the trailers, and the nightmare from the park ring lunged out from behind one of the trailers and grabbed my ankle. He wrenched me down, slamming my back against the hardpacked dirt and knocking the wind from me.

For a second I was drifting in quiet darkness, then my

vision partially cleared and the sounds of the fight roared back to life around me.

"No flying away and going for help," the nightmare sneered, capturing me with his hellfire gaze.

Icy fear seized me. The faith healer's tent materialized around me and he smashed his Bible against the side of my head, making the world spin. I'd displeased him. I'd been unable to heal as many people as he'd wanted before I'd run out of magic, and he hadn't made the profits that he'd wanted.

With a snarl, he seized my throat and pushed me onto the table. Would this be the time he raped me? I'd told him I'd lose my magic if I wasn't pure, but I had no idea how long he'd believe that lie.

Tears streamed down my cheeks and his grip tightened, cutting off my air. *Please, don't. Please—*

Except the faith healer had never raped me and I wasn't in his tent. Cassius had freed me. This wasn't real. It was the nightmare's magic.

I gritted my teeth and felt for his magic in my mind. There. A sour, nauseating darkness.

The faith healer squeezed tighter and reached for his belt buckle.

No. Please no.

My thoughts stuttered, my fear swelling, and I heaved my focus back to the nightmare's magic. With a scream, I mentally shoved him out of my mind and the faith healer's tent vanished.

The nightmare snarled and lunged at me, but the demon-vampire, now beside him, grabbed his arm, stopping him.

"Not our target," he said to the nightmare, his voice so soft I could barely hear him above the roar of the fight.

The nightmare glared at him, the hellfire in his eyes blazing, then he jerked his arm free. He slammed his fist into the face of one of the other assailants, knocking him to the ground, and charged down the path toward Titus and Cassius.

"This doesn't involve you, angel," the demon-vampire said. "You should run."

In one swift motion, he drew his katana, turned, decapitated an assailant rushing up behind him, and strode after the nightmare.

I stared at the headless body, its blood rushing into a thick pool and soaking into the ground. It had happened so fast I almost couldn't make myself believe what I'd just seen. Sure, I'd just seen Titus kill someone, and I'd watched people kill and die during the war, but that man's death had been so quick and emotionless. As if the demon-vampire had felt nothing when he'd taken that life.

Sebastian dropped to the ground beside me as I sat up and pulled in my wings. Behind him, Hawk now fought with the shadow fae, his attacks with his knife not as sleek or efficient as the fae's but still confident as if he'd fought with a knife before.

"Are you hurt?" Sebastian asked.

"No. I'm—" I tried to catch my breath, still stunned from my fall and the horror of the nightmare's magic. The world was still spinning and I was so exhausted it was hard to keep my head up. "I'm—"

I dragged in another breath, this one harder than the last.

Hawk grunted and Sebastian's attention jumped back to him. The shadow fae yanked his dagger from Hawk's shoulder and rammed his fist into Hawk's gut.

"I'm—" I fought to draw my next breath against a rising pressure squeezing my insides. It was as if I'd cracked my ribs again. Each inhalation was agonizing, and darkness started to creep around the edges of my vision. "I'm—"

An invisible weight slammed into my chest, stealing what little air I had left and making my pulse race. I gasped, but there was no air to breathe in. Every muscle in my body tensed and I collapsed onto my side, my lungs burning.

"Amiah!" Sebastian's eyes flashed wide. His attention jerked up, and he yelled for Titus.

The world spun faster as the darkness in my vision swelled. I desperately reached for any glimmer of magic I had to save myself. But just like the last time, I had nothing left. And even if I did have magic, it wouldn't save me. There was no air to breathe. That wasn't something I could fix.

AMIAH

"Where the fuck is Titus?" Sebastian yelled and he rolled me to my back, captured my face with his cool palms, and pressed his lips against mine.

I froze. Shocked. Sebastian was kissing me. I was dying, and he was kissing me. I'd wondered what it would be like to kiss him, how it would make me feel. Would he surprise me and tease me with something gentle or be strong and brash like he always was? Except I couldn't tell if I felt anything. Everything within me was howling, desperate to breathe.

Then he released his breath into my mouth and I gasped it in against the pressure in my chest.

He turned his attention back to the fight around us. "Find Titus!"

"Little busy," Hawk said, his voice barely audible against the rushing in my ears.

Sebastian gave me another breath. "You're going to need to hold the next one." He pressed his lips against mine and gave me a bigger breath.

I tried to gasp in as much as I could, forcing my burning lungs to expand against the invisible weight crushing me.

"Find Titus. The big guy. Now." Sebastian pressed his hands to his chest, and both the sleep glyph on his shoulder and the force-wave glyph on his forearm burst to life, along with a third glyph that curled across his ribs.

With a scream, he released a massive blast of power that swept dust into my eyes and made the world darken and spin. Hawk staggered into the trailer, leaning against it to keep standing, while the shadow fae fell to his hands and knees. Beyond them, everyone along the path collapsed, some completely unconscious. All except the tall stern guy. He staggered, dropped to one knee, and his attention jerked to us.

"Fucking hell," Hawk hissed and he jabbed his blade toward the shadow fae's back, but the fae dropped and rolled under the trailer.

Gasping and trembling, Sebastian gave me another shallow breath, and Hawk dropped to his knees to chase after the shadow fae.

"No. Titus," Sebastian barked. "They're too far apart and everyone won't be down for long."

Hawk's attention jumped to me. "Shit." He bolted down the path.

Sebastian gave me another weak breath, his expression tight with pain and his eyes filled with fear. The glow in his skin was gone and his complexion was gray. Whatever he'd cast, it had taken a lot out of him.

The darkness in my vision swelled. His breaths weren't going to sustain me for much longer.

Another warm breath filled my mouth and, too late, I tried to breathe it in, but it vanished before I could inhale it. Sebastian's hands, back on my cheeks holding me steady, trembled and he gave me another shallow breath.

Someone yelled. Sebastian's cool presence disappeared and strong hands picked me up.

Whoever held me clutched me tight and started running, and I gasped in a painful breath, the crushing pressure still present, but at least the air was back.

Titus had to be near. I dragged my eyes open to find him and looked up into his ferocious golden gaze. He didn't look nearly as affected as I was, and I didn't know if I should be furious or grateful for that.

He barreled around the only remaining brick wall of what used to be a house into another tent alley. Ahead, Hawk and Sebastian — Hawk with his arm slung around Sebastian's waist helping him — slipped between a wooden stall with a red awning and a blue pickup truck, and Titus followed.

"We can't keep running," Cassius said from behind Titus.

"There's a storm drain overflow up ahead. Do you have enough juice to eliminate our trail?" Hawk asked Sebastian, who nodded.

We cut between two more tents, across ten feet of waist-high grass and weeds, and skidded down the concrete incline into the currently dry, man-made runoff creek. Ahead lay the dark mouth of the storm drain, its metal grate twisted back providing an opening big enough for us to enter.

The guys didn't slow once inside. They kept running

deeper into the cool, damp darkness, Hawk leading us down one pipe then another and another until we reached a hole where part of the wall had collapsed.

"We can catch our breath in here," Hawk said, helping Sebastian climb over the rubble and up a short, steep incline.

Titus set me on the ground at the top of the incline — which was actually a blue-tiled floor littered with debris, rubble, broken glass, and dirt. I lifted my gaze to a high, domed ceiling covered with a blue and white mosaic. The intricate design flowed around tall windows close to the ceiling, letting in just enough light to soften the darkness — the glass long broken — and ran down the walls and the half dozen pillars supporting the dome. A few feet away sat a curved bench, one of many ringing a large recessed area in the center. It looked like we'd entered what had once been a fancy European bathhouse.

With a grunt of pain, Titus climbed up beside me then moved past me so Cassius could climb in as well. He stopped beside me on his knees, his expression icy and his angel glow blazing.

"You okay?" A spark snapped from his hand and he shifted away from me.

"Are you?" I asked back.

Blood oozed down his cheek from a gash above his left eye and his T-shirt had been cut in numerous places.

"Nothing you can do about it," he said.

"I've more than just my magic." I could still treat them with non-magical methods. Even dizzy and exhausted, I was sure I could manage something. "We still need to take stock. What's everyone's condition?"

And I wasn't going to think about how I'd almost died because Titus had moved too far away from me.

I struggled to push away my fear and turned to face the rest of the guys to assess their conditions.

Except Hawk knelt in front of me, blocking my view. He ducked in close, grabbed the back of my head, and before I could say anything or pull away, captured my lips with his.

I gasped in surprise and he pushed his tongue into my mouth, raking it against mine.

Holy smokes. *This* was a real kiss.

Desire ignited within me. All the desperate need I'd been fighting for far too long, need that had been behind a wall of restraint that Sebastian and now Hawk had shattered, surged inside me.

I tangled my fingers in his hair, purposefully brushing the base of his horns, and kissed him back. He groaned, the sound low and dark, and his kiss turned ferocious. His grip in my hair tightened and he pulled my head back, arching my back and pushing my breasts forward. His other hand plunged down the front of my dress and he roughly palmed my breast, the sensation rushing through me, drawing a moan.

My core throbbed and I strained to move against his grip and straddle him, but he held me firm, fully controlling my body. Then a whisper of his sensual magic caressed inside of me and a soft climax rolled through me.

I shuddered with my release and whimpered into his mouth, satisfied and yet disappointed it had happened so fast and softly.

"Let her go." Cassius wrenched me out of Hawk's embrace and slammed his fist into the incubus's face with a resounding *crunch*.

"Fucking hell," Hawk gasped, blood running from his nose. "I just needed a top up."

And boy had I given him a top up. Succubi and Incubi survived on sexual energy. Anything that was lustful: thoughts, kissing, touching, and of course intercourse. And while they didn't need to participate in any of the activities, flesh-to-flesh contact provided more powerful energy than just standing nearby, and being the focus of the lust and participating was the most powerful of all.

He pushed his broken nose back into place, his enhanced healing stopping the bleeding and starting to set it already, proving just how much of a top up I'd given him.

"Pretty sure she didn't mind," he said, giving me a smug smile and making my cheeks heat with embarrassment. "And I didn't just take. I'm generous like that."

Oh, my God! If it hadn't been obvious to the others that I'd orgasmed — again — it was now.

"Just because you seduced her with magic doesn't mean she consented." Smoke billowed around me and Cassius's hands grew searing hot, stinging my skin.

"Cassius." His lack of control was really starting to concern me. I tried to push out of his embrace before his fire manifested and burned me. "Cassius, please."

His attention dropped to me and his smoke.

"Shit." With a growl, he set me on the floor and wrenched away. His smoke vanished but now he was so tense, trying to hold it back, he shook. "You don't get to use your magic on anyone you like."

"Oh, there was no magic involved." Hawk's smile turned wicked, renewing my aching desire. "Well, not until—"

"That's enough," I said before Hawk could go on. "I'm exhausted—" And embarrassed and frustrated on so many levels. "And my chest still hurts from the leash spell."

And I'm still trapped.

I fought to shove down everything I was feeling and focus on the situation. "Hawk is now healed. Who else is bleeding and how badly?"

"I'll manage," Cassius said, even though his clothes were ripped and bloody and the right side of his face was starting to swell, making it hard for him to fully open his eye. "If everyone else can manage as well, we should get back to Bane's and regroup."

"Not until we stop leaving a blood trail," Sebastian said, leaning back against the pillar beside us, his appearance the opposite of Cassius's. His shirt wasn't overly bloody, but he must have had a serious injury somewhere because his complexion was still gray and there was a small pool of blood beside him. "Both the Shadow and Spring Courts will be able to track us by our blood, and I don't have enough juice to hold up the group concealment spell *and* remove all traces of us as we make our way back home. The minute we move on and our blood is no longer within the concealment spell, they'll be able to hone in on it."

"Which means none of us can bleed until the samples

they've no doubt taken from our fight degrade." Cassius shifted, sucked in a sharp breath, and pressed his arm to his side. He probably had broken ribs as well. "In fifteen or sixteen hours?"

"I'd go with at least twenty-four to be safe," Sebastian said. "And I can't keep up the concealment that long without a break. Amiah, have you got enough magic to stop our bleeding?"

"No." I had nothing. "If I rest, I can recover some. How long can you hold the concealment?"

"If I'm just holding the concealment spell, I can keep it up for a while. How long do you need?" Sebastian asked.

"Honest inventory everyone," Cassius said, saving me from confessing I didn't even have enough magic to assess anyone's injuries. "I took some really nasty cuts from some of those shifters, but I've seared the worst of them shut so I'm not even close to bleeding out." Which had to have been excruciating.

Sure, his fire magic gave him the ability to cauterize wounds that regularly couldn't be cauterized and he now wasn't bleeding, but he'd replaced those lacerations with nasty burns. Burns he normally wouldn't have because unless he purposely set his mind to it, his fire didn't burn him. "I'm also pretty sure I have at least one broken rib."

I started to stand to move to him, but the room twisted and darkened before I'd even gotten off my knees, and I sagged back down to the floor. "Come here and take off your shirt so I can see just how many ribs you've broken."

The muscles in his jaw flexed and his expression grew

icier. But he got up, knelt before me, and pulled off his ruined T-shirt, revealing an angry patchwork of second degree burns and lacerations, many of which were oozing blood, along with bruises and swelling skin.

Hawk drew in a sharp breath. "Jeez. I'd hate to see how bad it gets that you can't manage."

"I fought on the front line in the war. I've been hurt worse," Cassius said, his voice gruff.

My throat tightened. He *had* been hurt worse. A number of times. And every time he'd come back to me a little harder and colder.

I ran my hands over his ribs trying not to think about his pain or how stunning he normally looked or how much I still ached with desire.

Because I had no magic, I had to put pressure on each rib and judge by feel and his reaction to determine how many were actually cracked or broken. "You've got three broken ribs on your left side, and I'm worried about two more on your right."

This was going to take a lot more magic than just healing lacerations. If Sebastian wanted me to stop all of the bleeding, I was going to have to heal Cassius's ribs first — and no way was I going to let him use his fire magic to burn the rest of his wounds shut.

"Titus?" I asked, turning to the dragon. He looked the best out of everyone, but then the people who'd attacked us weren't trying to kill him, just hurt him enough to abduct him. Yes, his shirt was also ripped and bloody, but I suspected the lacerations weren't serious, and even if they were, Titus was a fast healer.

"If we sit here for a few hours, I'll be fine," Titus said.

Hawk huffed. "The angel said honest inventory. I saw you get run through with a sword. A shifter can't heal that fast in a few hours."

"It wasn't that bad." Titus shrugged, and I didn't know if he was telling the truth or lying to hide how fast he healed. As it was, there was no blood gathering around him and his complexion was good, so he'd probably be in decent shape by the time I had enough magic to heal Cassius's ribs.

I shifted my attention back to Sebastian and fought to keep my expression even. It wasn't good if your physician looked worried, but he looked terrible. The blood pool by his leg had grown in the few minutes we'd been talking, his breath was shallow, and the light in his skin still hadn't recovered.

"I was cut a few times and I think the one on my thigh is pretty deep," he said.

"Let me see." I prayed it wouldn't need a tourniquet. I'd already need at least five hours of rest to recover enough magic to heal Cassius's ribs and cuts. That would leave the tourniquet on for too long, which could cause nerve damage and would require even more magic to fix.

He shifted so I could get a better look at the nasty laceration on the side of his upper right thigh without any comment about needing to take his pants off.

Jeez, he really was in bad shape.

I tore the hole in his pantleg wider and tried to get a good look without having anything to wipe the blood away.

The wound was deep and long, and blood flowed slowly and steadily. It cut through muscle, but, given the pace of his blood loss and the laceration's location, he'd gotten lucky and no major vessels had been severed. Yes, it would take at least a few more hours of rest for me to recover enough magic to heal it and any other injuries he had, but he wasn't in immediate danger.

"I'd like to just bind this and avoid a tourniquet. Take off your shirt."

"Pretty sure that's the wrong article of clothing. Or do you finally want to see me naked?" Sebastian's lips quirked and a glimmer of the annoying man I knew flickered in his pale eyes. Thank goodness.

"You have the cleanest shirt," I said, too exhausted and worried and relieved to give him the reaction he was probably looking for.

He unbuttoned his shirt and shrugged out of it as I fought to keep my expression even. He was even more breathtaking than Cassius, with his sculpted muscles and the dark tattoos swirling over him, and I'd clearly lost my mind because I couldn't stop thinking about sex.

I handed the dress shirt to Titus, who was the most capable of the group to make me a bandage with his strength and claws. "Please tear off the longest piece you can."

"Sure." Titus took the shirt and, with a sharp claw, cut a piece off the bottom, keeping the seams intact to make one long strip.

"So, given everyone's injuries and the fact that we can't lose a drop of blood, we're going to be here for a while." I took the rest of the shirt from Titus and folded it into a makeshift dressing and pressed it against Sebastian's wound. "Hold this here. I'll need at least eight hours of rest."

Which meant eight more hours magically bound to Titus.

No. I can handle this. I'm strong. Just a little longer.

Sebastian held the dressing in place and I secured it with the bandage Titus had cut.

"I'll need less if I can fall asleep, but given that we've just run for our lives and have people hunting us, I doubt I'd be able to relax enough to get a deep enough sleep. Unless..." Sebastian had a sleep glyph. But was I comfortable enough around these men to be magically put to sleep?

And did it really matter? We couldn't hide there forever. We needed to get back to Sebastian's apartment, and the sooner the better. Having to wait six hours was bad enough. What I was and wasn't comfortable with was nothing compared to the danger we were in.

"If you use your sleep glyph," I said to Sebastian, "we can take two hours off the time I need. Do you have enough power for that?" Technically, because he was a sorcerer he had all the power in Faerie, but the more exhausted he was, the harder it would be to control the flow into his body and avoid burning up.

"Six is better than eight," Sebastian said. "Get comfortable."

"Is it even safe to be here for that long?" Hawk asked.

Cassius wiped away the blood from the gash over his eye. "It'll have to be."

I settled against the pillar beside Sebastian so he wouldn't have to move to put me to sleep. It wasn't the most comfortable way to sleep, and I didn't know how I felt about passing out beside him, but I didn't really have much of an option since I didn't want to make him move and make the laceration in his thigh worse.

With a soft word, Sebastian activated his sleep glyph, pressed his hand over my heart, and a cool thread of his magic slipped into me, bringing with it a frustrating shiver of desire.

I bit back a groan. I shouldn't be thinking about sex. Even if I was pretty sure Sebastian wasn't my soul mate, we were running for our lives. That, and he'd already made it clear he wasn't interested.

Why did my desire keep going back to him? If I really wanted my first time to be with someone experienced, Hawk was the one to go to. He at least was interested. Of course, he was an incubus, he was always interested. But that also meant he wouldn't fall in love — well, it was rare if an incubus did — which meant the odds of Hawk being my soul mate were even less than Sebastian's.

Hmm. Maybe when all of this was done I *would* seek out Hawk.

SEBASTIAN

A‌MIAH'S EYES CLOSED AS MY SLEEP SPELL TOOK HER, AND she sagged against me, her head on my shoulder. Just that little touch made my already hard cock harder.

I was going to fucking kill Hawk. It was bad enough his magic made me hard as hell, but then to make Amiah come twice right in front of me—

I bit back a groan. She'd come in front of *all* of us. The show hadn't just been for me... which wasn't really a problem for me, either.

And man, when her guard was down and that bitchy ice queen act was gone, she was so fucking sexy. The sounds she'd made and the look on her face when she came... and that had just been a taste. It was obvious she'd tried to hide her reaction to Hawk's magic, and that he'd only given her a small amount of it — full power, and she would have come screaming then passed out. What would she be like if she truly let go?

And why the fuck did I want to make that happen? I wasn't interested in her. I didn't even like her.

Except the image of her lying on the ground suffocating flashed through my mind's eye and a whisper of the panic I'd felt trembled through me... because she was a valuable healer and leashed to Titus. That was all.

She sighed, turned into me, and wrapped her arm across my waist. Her warm breath feathered across my bare chest which brought back the memory of Hawk kissing her, his hand shoved down the front of her dress, and the mewling gasp she'd made.

Fuck. I couldn't do this.

I raised my gaze to Cassius sitting across from me. Wisps of smoke curled from his hands, a precursor to his fire reigniting, which would be bad for Amiah. Titus, to my left, was tense. Holding Amiah would be good for him, but he, too, probably had a raging hard on from Hawk's magic and the man had been imprisoned for half a millennium. Letting him be her pillow right now would be cruel.

Which left Hawk, who I wasn't handing her to, and me.

Swell.

"So," Hawk said with a smirk that said he knew exactly what his magic and Amiah had done to me. Asshole. "I'm not going to be able to return to my business even after our blood samples degrade, am I?"

"Not until things with Titus are cleared up," I replied, struggling to keep my tone even and not show how much I needed my own release not to mention the agony of the demonic magic screaming through my body from the fight. He already knew I was infected with power from the Realm of Celestial Darkness. I couldn't let him see how badly it affected me.

Except every inch of me burned like I'd been dipped in acid, and the pain wasn't letting up because I had to keep pushing power into my group concealment glyph. I couldn't even feel my injuries. The only reason I'd known the cut in my leg had been bad was because of the growing pool of blood on the floor beside me.

I shouldn't have cast that last force-wave. I shouldn't have woven in sleep, which meant I'd needed to weave in an exclusion for Titus, Cassius, and Hawk. I'd needed to channel too much raw magic to do all that and I was paying for it now.

But Amiah had been dying, and as much as I hated to admit it, I'd panicked.

Cassius sat forward. "What exactly are *things*?" He frowned. "And why did Amiah nearly die but Titus could keep fighting?"

"His leash has to be longer. I must have stretched it when I first tried to break the spell." And I really didn't want to think about that because that meant the spell was completely warped and was going to be challenging to rip apart even with a perfectly attuned resonance charm.

"I don't think my end is as strong, either," Titus said. "I felt a pressure and there were moments when it was hard to breathe, but it didn't come close to suffocating me. I thought she was okay." He clenched his hands and stared at Amiah, his gaze so intense it hurt to watch. "Things are only going to get worse. You have to separate us."

"One problem at a time." The demonic magic swelled.

I bit back a groan and Hawk's eyes narrowed. "We can't risk another mess like that. We need to get a proper concealment spell and glamour on you first."

If I could get a concealment spell on Titus along with a glamour that changed his appearance as well as his essence, we could run and hide until this mess blew over.

But the Spring Court was now involved and unlike the Shadow Court, they'd go after everyone who'd had contact with Titus. Amiah, Cassius, and Hawk were now in the middle of it, and it was going to be hard to convince the angels to abandon their lives until Faerie's Heart went back to sleep.

Except they were going to have to if they wanted to live... or until one of us could come up with a better plan to defend ourselves against all of the courts in Faerie.

"I thought you said breaking the leash spell was our first priority." Fire sparked from Cassius's hands even though his expression remained hard. "Amiah almost died. We've set the resonance charm, what more do you need?"

"To recover all the magic I spent saving her ass. Just like she needs sleep, so do I." The demonic magic swelled again, stealing my breath. Fuck. "Breaking the leash spell will use a lot of magic which will leave me vulnerable."

"And you think the original caster will be able to sense the spell when you pull it apart and use that to track you?" Hawk asked.

"Isn't that what you wanted?" Cassius asked. "To lure those men to us so I can arrest them."

"That was before the Spring Court showed up a hell of a lot sooner than I anticipated." Plus, despite my confidence earlier, a part of me feared that shadow fae had somehow seen through my glamour and recognized me, which was why he'd come after me again and let his friends go after Titus.

I'd hoped after all these years Deaglan had given up on trying to kill me. And maybe he had. No one had come looking for me for over a century. Running into me was probably just a bonus to his hunt for Titus.

"So that's why those men from the park ring were killing the other guys coming after us," Cassius said.

"Is that also why half of those guys who looked like humans were glamoured?" Hawk asked. "They weren't really human, were they?"

"No. They were spring fae. Their seneschal, Balwyrdan, is a sorcerer with a particular talent for glamour." Only those with a high magic sensitivity were able to sense his glamour, and even then, you had to be on guard to catch it. Just one of the many reasons I'd gotten out of Faerie.

Balwyrdan also had a vicious streak. I'd been surprised to see him commanding the spring fae assault team, and even more surprised he hadn't joined the fight.

"The fae might not be members of the Joined Parliament, but they do recognize the mortal realm as a sovereign realm," Cassius said. "They can't just come here and kill people, just like we can't go there and kill people."

Hawk snorted. "I'm pretty sure they don't care."

"Because Faerie's Heart has awakened," Titus said, shifting. The movement inched him closer to Amiah and

I didn't know if he'd done that on purpose or not. "You have the Heart, you control Faerie."

"And by control Faerie, he means the very essence of the realm. You can remake it as you see fit, eliminate whole courts, kill thousands with a thought, and lock away the magic of the realm from others until they wither and die." It was a fucking nightmare and all the courts should have banded together to destroy it the first time it had manifested over two millennia ago.

But the court monarchs had been greedy. They still were. And only the dragons had had the wherewithal to lock it away.

Except that was all they'd been able to do. It would have taken the combined effort of half a dozen full sorcerers to destroy it, and even locking it away had backfired, linking all of dragonkind to the Heart, making them compasses to the keys that could release it.

"So how are you involved in this?" Cassius asked, turning his hard glare on Titus, who didn't notice because he was still staring at Amiah.

"Dragons have an innate connection to the Heart," I said. "They—"

Titus's gaze jumped to me and for a second he had the same look he'd had when he'd realized he was the last dragon.

God. I was the worst friend ever. I'd let him suffer in captivity and now I'd reminded him he was alone.

"Titus can find the keys to unlock the Heart. No one else can." The demonic magic inside me surged, making me gasp, and Amiah's hand slid from my waist up to my heart, her palm warm against my skin, as if even in sleep she was trying to heal me. Except all she'd done was remind me of how much I needed to fuck someone. "The courts won't stop coming after Titus until the Heart goes back to sleep."

"And when will that be?" Cassius asked.

"I don't know," Titus replied. "No one does."

"That's not the worst of it." I set Amiah's hands back in her lap and turned her slightly away from me. With luck, she'd keep her hands to herself until Hawk's magic had left my system — hopefully by finding someone to sleep with and not having to wait it out for the long fucking hours it would take to work its way out of my system. "The Shadow Court will only come after me and Titus. I'm not familiar with this team, but so far, they've behaved like the other Shadow Court teams I've seen. They stay in the shadows and strike quickly and efficiently."

"There was nothing about staying in the shadows in Lincoln," Hawk said.

"Because those other guys forced their hand," Cassius said, showing his combat experience by seeing through the chaos of that fight. "They couldn't afford for the spring fae's greater numbers to overwhelm Titus. In fact, it looked like they were willing to let Titus get away to ensure the spring fae didn't get him."

"The spring fae's team isn't as powerful as the Shadow Court's, but they have greater numbers and they don't care who sees them," I continued. "They'll also go after everyone involved with Titus even if Titus is no longer around."

Hawk rubbed his face, his expression growing more concerned. "Why the hell would they do that?"

"Information. Leverage," Cassius said, his voice low. "Possibly to cover Titus's tracks. If the others going after him don't know or can't find who he's been in contact with that could give the Spring Court an advantage."

"Two more points for the angel," I said.

"Jeez. Fuck this." Hawk sat forward. "I'm not just up and leaving my life. There has to be something we can do that's better than waiting for who-knows-how-long for this to blow over."

"I agree." Cassius glanced at Amiah and his angel glow flared.

I had no idea how she hadn't figured out he was in love with her. It was painfully obvious. Honest-to-goodness in love, not just wanting to sleep with her. Of course, there were times it seemed that she wasn't even aware of — or perhaps didn't want to acknowledge — her own sexuality, so the fact that she was oblivious to Cassius's desires shouldn't have surprised me. And while almost every angel I'd come across was uptight, Amiah took that to a whole other level... which was why it was so much fun to keep pushing that particular button.

"We can't take on all the courts," Cassius continued. "What are our other options?"

"You should kill me," Titus said. "That will solve everything. That will keep everyone safe."

"Really? Have you forgotten what Balwyrdan is like?" No one was sacrificing themselves to this ridiculous cause. "Even if you're dead, he'll come after us out of spite so your death would be a waste, and that doesn't account for the other monarchs and their seneschals or warlords. We hide until the Heart goes back to sleep."

"And what about in five hundred years or a thousand or whenever it reawakens and I go through this again?" Titus asked, his voice low, *still* not looking away from Amiah. Jeez.

Maybe I should have told him to be her pillow. And maybe he was just as horny as I was and was staring at her because she was the only woman in the room.

"The last time I lost my kin and then I lost my freedom," he said. "What will I lose this time or the next?"

"No one is killing you." The light in Cassius's eyes flared. "Amiah would kill herself trying to save you and I won't let that happen. If it's a race to get the Heart then we have to win."

"You want to go after it?" I couldn't have heard that correctly. That was crazy and everything I knew about Cassius said he didn't do crazy. "Going after the Heart would make us bigger targets. The minute the courts figure out what we're doing it won't just be the Spring Court coming after all of us, it'll be all of the courts, and Amiah will be in the middle of it."

"Amiah is in danger regardless," he said his voice hard and icy. "There's no guarantee that we'll be able to hide until the Heart goes back to sleep. It needs to be destroyed or lock away for good or we need it for leverage. Whatever we do, it means we have to get it. What other option do we have?"

"I vote for the option that doesn't get me killed," Hawk said.

Cassius's eyes narrowed. "And which one would that be?"

Hawk glared back at Cassius, his hands clenched as if he wanted to punch the angel. "Not the one where we join a treasure hunt where the competitors are trying to kill each other."

"You're welcome to sit around and hope someone doesn't come after you." Cassius turned his attention to me. "If we can get the Heart, we can redirect the courts' attentions away from Amiah and Titus. What are the possibilities that you can destroy or permanently locked away this thing? No one should ever have absolute control over anyone let alone a whole realm."

I had to agree with that... and fuck, I also had to agree with his assessment of the situation. "I don't have the power to destroy it or permanently lock it away." Even if I wasn't infected with demonic magic, I doubted I'd be able to channel enough raw magic to destroy it or lock it away without burning up. "But you're right. The only play we have is to get the Heart."

And then pray it would actually be enough to protect us.

AMIAH

I WOKE TO SOMEONE BRUSHING MY HAIR OUT OF MY FACE, the caress cool and gentle, and a hot throbbing ache in my hip from my mating brand. I knew I had to get up and heal the guys, but I didn't want to move. I didn't want to face the reality of my situation, leashed to Titus and with a worse fate coming my way. I wanted to just savor this touch, this closeness. I missed it so much, felt so unsteady without it, and I had no idea if I'd ever get anything like what I had with Marcus with someone else.

"Time to get up," Sebastian said, and I looked up into his pale, almost colorless gaze. There wasn't a hint of mischief or flirtation in his eyes. This was the man who'd tried to reassure me when I'd first been panicking about the leash spell and offered me something to sleep in. His complexion was still gray, but not nearly as bad as before which meant he must have recovered a little magic as well even though he was still powering the concealment glyph.

"If you stay there much longer," Hawk drawled, "he's going to expect you to do more than just lie there."

Sebastian's lips quirked.

"He's what—" My brain kicked in, clearing my sleepy thoughts. My head was in Sebastian's lap, right beside—

Heat rushed across my face — not just with embarrassment — and I quickly sat up. Hawk might have inside knowledge of my desires, but no one else needed to know them. I could only pray that once the spring fae could no longer track him, he'd go on his merry way.

It was bad enough Sebastian kept teasing me. I didn't want to have to deal with two of them. And I doubted propositioning Hawk and arranging for something later would get him to stop.

"How are you feeling?" Cassius asked, now sitting at the edge of the cave-in where we'd entered, his breath shallow, likely to ease the pain of his broken ribs and possibly the nasty burns on his torso.

I closed my eyes and focused on my magic. It welled in my palms, hot and warm and thick. Almost at three-quarters of what it should be, which was a little more than I anticipated I'd recover with six hours of sleep.

"I'm good. Unless any of you've lied to me, I should be able to heal everyone and have a little to spare." If, of course, I was smart about how I used it. And I was going to be smart because I had no idea when I'd need to heal them again.

I dropped my gaze to Sebastian's thigh. He was the closest. Might as well heal him first. He'd bled through the makeshift dressing and bandage, but the blood that had pooled on the floor beside him had dried, which meant he hadn't lost much more while I was asleep.

Blood oozed from the wound when I untied the bandage and I quickly pressed my hands against it. Even though I had enough magic to push my power through clothing, directly connecting with the injury was always the best.

My magic swelled into my palms, warm and strong, and, while concentrating on controlling its flow, I pushed it into the wound. It slid between his cells, thick and viscous, tugging them together and mending muscle and flesh before a thread split off toward the next most serious wound, a cut in the back of his shoulder. My magic split again and again and soon every injury was sealed shut and I pulled my power out of him.

"The wounds will still be pink and a little sore," I said, sitting back on my heels, "but I'd rather hold back as much magic as possible just in case."

"Just means you'll have to come back to finish the job." Sebastian flashed me his wicked smile, making my body heat, and I rolled my eyes at him, trying to hide the fact that his proposition excited me more than bothered me.

I really had reached my breaking point, and it was getting harder to care about the fact that I wanted to throw years of restraint out the window. I wanted more of the sensations I'd gotten from Hawk, but I also wanted to be touched and kissed and held more. So much more it was getting harder to remember that I needed to be careful and not get too close to anyone who could be a potential soul mate.

I got up and sat beside Cassius, who tensed when I placed my hands on his bare skin, probably anticipating the pain of a quick healing.

"I'll go slow. There's no need to do this quickly," I said. "We've already spent six hours here, what's a few more minutes?"

"Yeah," he said, his voice gruff, and he drew in a shallow, shuddering breath that did little to relax him.

Without waiting for another breath — I didn't need him to relax and I doubted he would — I pushed a gentle thread of magic into him. It flowed straight to his broken ribs, enveloping the bones and knitting them back together.

Again, I concentrated on slowing the flow of magic and withdrew it once all of his ribs were mended but before completely healing his burns. Now they looked like they'd been painful a month ago instead of only a few minutes, and if I didn't finish healing him, he'd have thick ugly scars marring his stunning body, but he wasn't going to be leaving a blood trail, which was the point of the exercise.

I moved to Titus next, who kept his gaze locked on the ground by his feet, refusing to look at me. He also tensed when I touched him to confirm he wasn't bleeding, but I didn't press either issue. As much as he'd held me after the pain of the failed attempt to break the leash spell, we didn't know each other. He didn't owe me or anyone eye contact let alone anything else. And while I didn't know exactly what he was feeling, I suspected he was still dealing with a mess of confusing emotions from his captivity and recent escape.

With everyone healed, we found concrete stairs at the back of the room that led up to what once was an opulent foyer of a fancy hotel, and walked out onto an abandoned street.

Less than half of the buildings still stood and there wasn't a soul in sight. And thank goodness for that because two of the guys were shirtless and everyone was covered in blood making us stand out.

The sun was well past noon, the day hot and humid, and it continued to sink as we made our way back through the ruined and deserted streets to Sebastian's car. No one wanted to call a taxi — if one would even drive into the neighborhood — and no one wanted to call a friend.

I was filled in about our situation, about how more fae were after us and would be after anyone we had contact with. Cassius had sent a text to Chris telling him not to dig too deeply into the mess at Left of Lincoln and that he and I had to go dark for an undetermined amount of time.

I couldn't imagine how hard that had to have been since that meant Cassius was abandoning his job again. We were clearly breaking the rules, and we'd surely get written up again or fired this time, especially since he hadn't given Chris an explanation.

The idea of disobeying protocol made my insides churn, but not nearly as much as endangering someone just because I talked with them.

Hawk and Sebastian had both cleared their schedules, and Sebastian had told Nova to leave town, which was why we were walking back to the sedan. They, like

Cassius, had destroyed their phones and scattered the pieces as we went, leaving us without a way to communicate but also safe from being tracked that way.

I tried not to think about how I was even more trapped than I was before or about the reckless plan to go after Faerie's Heart. Except that meant thinking about my aching need, which wasn't any better, or my throbbing brand, which was even worse.

It took us an hour to get back to the car, and we piled into the oven-on-wheels with me in the back with Hawk and Cassius — thankfully with Cassius in the middle and me cramped against the door so I wouldn't have to sit beside Hawk.

It didn't take us long to drive back to the Quarter. But instead of returning to Sebastian's underground garage, we parked at the end of an alley in the middle of Squatter's Row.

The Row was a neighborhood on the far side of the Quarter that, because the supers' population was still relatively small, had yet to be redeveloped. Most of the buildings were in good shape, having survived the war like the rest of the Quarter, but had no electricity, gas, or running water and weren't supposed to have tenants. However, those who didn't care about the lack of utilities, or had no other choice, had taken up residence in many of the buildings.

For the most part, the JP ignored the area, letting the individual species police their own and saving their resources for more powerful and dangerous criminals. But that meant most *businesses* in the Row offered less than legal services, and I was pretty sure we'd arrived at one such business since we needed illegal concealment charms.

Sebastian shut off the engine and turned to Cassius. "Don't be a dick and arrest Mavis once this mess has blown over."

"I managed to get in and out of the market without arresting anyone," Cassius huffed.

Sebastian quirked an eyebrow. "How much of that was because we ended up running for our lives?"

"I gave my word. I give it now." Cassius nudged me, and I opened the door and got out.

"And an angel's word is everything," Hawk said with mock innocence.

"It is." The light in Cassius's eyes flared. "So trust me when I say if you use your magic on Amiah again without her consent I will lock you up for assault."

Hawk snorted and slid out of the car with a grace that made me shiver with need. Only an incubus could make something so mundane look so sexy. "That would require you having access to a jail."

"Would you rather I just burn you?" Cassius got out and slammed the door, smoke curling around his hands.

Oh yeah, agreeing to all work together to get Faerie's Heart was a great plan.

"So now you're judge, jury, and executioner," Hawk said. "Didn't know *that* was the law."

"Extenuating circumstance," Cassius growled back.

"So we're all agreed," Sebastian said, heading down the alley. "You want to get it on with Amiah, you need Cassius's permission."

He did *not* just say that!

"There will be no *getting it on* with Amiah," Cassius insisted.

Oh, my God. And neither did he!

"There'll be whatever I want," I snapped. Jeez. Even with Hawk's seductive magic tempting me, I was perfectly capable of taking care of myself... or rather in my current situation asking someone to take care of me. "You don't get a say in who I do and do not have intercourse with. None of you do."

I jerked my head indicating they should follow Sebastian. Cassius stared at me, shocked, clearly thinking — and rightly so — that I was keeping open the possibility of having sex with Hawk, while Hawk's gaze turned hungry, clearly coming to the same conclusion. Titus still wouldn't look at me, and with a growl, he strode after Sebastian.

Heat seeped across my cheeks and I squared my shoulders. If I wanted to sleep with someone, I would. If I wanted to take a page out of Essie's book and take multiple lovers, I would... just as soon as I was free of my mating brand and the risk of being permanently bound to someone was gone. Oh, and we were no longer being hunted by all of Faerie.

AMIAH

I HURRIED TO CATCH UP WITH SEBASTIAN AND TITUS AS they reached a plain metal security door that opened into a long hall. A low light coming from everywhere and yet nowhere filled the hall along with a purple haze with a cloyingly sweet smell. Cool air that could only have been chilled by magic swept over my skin, drawing goose bumps, and a heavy sense of dread settled in my chest.

"Cut the theatrics, Mavis," Sebastian said. "You know it's me."

"And you're not welcome," a raspy alto replied as a woman with dark skin and wild dark hair barely contained by a gold multi-strand chain headpiece stepped into the hall.

She wore a billowy yellow blouse cinched at the waist by a black corset that drew the eye immediately to her ample cleavage, and a full gauzy skirt, also yellow, that, when she shifted, turned partially see-through, giving a teasing glimpse of her legs.

"No more referrals. No more angels and pretty boys

and whatever the hell you are." She jabbed her finger at Titus, making the numerous gold and silver chains around her neck and bracelets around her wrists tinkle and catch the dim light.

"I can pay," Sebastian said.

"You don't have enough money to pay me, after sending the JP here to make me cast illegal concealment charms."

The sense of dread grew, twisting in my chest, and I took an involuntary step back, bumping into Cassius.

Hawk shifted past me and a whisper of his seductive magic caressed my skin. "We'd be grateful on top of paying," he said, his tone clear that *grateful* meant he'd sleep with her. "We really need your services."

"Of course you do. You all look like you've lost a fight. Let me guess." She propped her hands on her hips. "You all need concealment charms."

"And a glamour for the big guy," Sebastian said.

Her gaze flickered back to Hawk as if she was seriously considering his offer. "No."

"It's a matter of life and death," Cassius said.

"With an angel it always is," she huffed.

"Mavis." Sebastian drew closer to her and her gaze slowly slid down his body as if she couldn't help herself from appreciating his fine physique and the tattoos swirling over it. "Do I need to remind you who holds the cards here? The wrong word to the wrong person..." He shrugged and the pale light emanating from his body rippled over him. "Take my money."

Her eyes narrowed. "I want the incubus, too."

"You've already turned him down," Sebastian replied

before Hawk could. "Take fair payment for the job and be done with it."

She glared at him and Sebastian cocked an eyebrow.

"Fine. Whatever." The sense of dread vanished, and she jerked around and stormed into a large room lit by dozens of thick candles.

Dark wood bookcases crammed with boxes and books and other magical paraphernalia lined the walls, and to the right sat a short length of stainless-steel counter, sink, and stove that looked like they belonged in a commercial kitchen. The counter was cluttered with jars, pots, and bowls, the sink full with dirty dishes, and a large pot sat on the stove. The element on the stove was off, but I had no doubt even though the building didn't have power, the element worked, powered by magic like her air conditioning.

In the middle of the room were an intricately carved wooden table and a matching high-backed chair. Mavis took a metal box with a complicated glyph carved on the lid from one of the shelves and sat. With a resigned sigh, she flipped open the box. Inside, on a bed of red silk, lay a thin knife, a small jar with dark ink, a thin paintbrush, and a handful of coins with another complicated glyph etched on them. Everything she needed to cast an illegal concealment spell.

"Who's first?" She pointed to a stool across the table from her.

"Titus, with a concealment and a glamour, then Amiah. Just concealment," Sebastian said. "They're leashed, so you're going to need extra juice."

Mavis's eyebrows shot up. "I'll need to use external

magic to set the spells." She flicked her finger and another metal box floated from the shelf behind her and landed on the table. "You're lucky I have a full orb. It's double for the two of them and I expect you to refill the orb."

"Agreed, but I can't refill it today."

"Of course you can't." She rolled her eyes at him and turned her attention to Titus. "You're up, big man."

"The glamour doesn't have to be significant," Sebastian said. "Just a shift in his facial structure, eye color, hair color, and a change of his essence. A wolf or bear would probably be easiest."

"Want to lean over my shoulder and watch me do it, too?" she asked as Titus settled on the stool across from her. "Give me your wrist."

Titus, his whole body so tense it broke my heart, set his hand on the table. Mavis flipped it over so the inside of his wrist faced up, dipped the paintbrush in the ink, and drew a simple glyph on his skin. Then she picked up the knife.

"Cassius should probably sterilize that," I said before she cut Titus. Given the pile of dirty dishes in the sink, I wasn't going to assume the blade was clean.

Mavis rolled her eyes. "Angels are a pain in the ass."

Yeah well, better a pain than have to deal with gangrene. I bit the inside of my cheek. She was going to cast a spell on me next. It was best not to upset her.

She handed the knife to Cassius who wrapped the blade with fire for a moment then handed it back to her. With another eye roll, Mavis made an incision through the glyph the diameter of the coin, hissed a sharp word, and set the coin in the blood oozing out of Titus's wrist.

"You might want to sit," Sebastian said, drawing up beside me and grabbing my elbow.

"Sit?" I didn't like the sound of that. I looked around for a chair or another stool but didn't see any.

Mavis opened the other box and pulled out a glowing marble filled with magical power. She clenched it in her fist, the light bleeding out between her fingers, hissed a long string of words, and the weight of the leash spell slammed into my chest.

Oh, my goodness!

My knees gave out and Sebastian caught me. He swept me into his arms, cradling me against his chest, and I fought against the spell's weight to regain my breath.

"You could have mentioned this earlier," I gasped. At least the air was still around me... although it felt thin. Or perhaps that was just because each shallow breath was a painful struggle.

"I should have," he said. He squeezed his eyes shut and the muscles in his jaw flexed. "Just concentrating on a lot of things right now."

"Are you all right?" Cassius asked, drawing close, the light in his eyes blazing.

I didn't know how to answer that. I was being crushed from the inside by a spell that every fiber of my being screamed I had to be free of.

Mavis hissed a few more words. The magic in her fist flared, blindingly bright making my eyes water, and the coin sunk into Titus's skin. The pressure increased, shooting agony through me, and I clenched my teeth against a groan.

Titus also tensed, and his breath grew ragged.

"Amiah?" Cassius asked.

"I'll be okay," I forced out. "It'll be over soon." *Please let it be over soon.*

Sweat beaded on the back of Titus's neck, his fingers extended into claws, and he dug the ones on his free hand into Mavis's table. The air around him wavered, like heat radiating off hot asphalt on a summer's day, and the pressure grew.

Dark specks crept at the edge of my vision, and my breath grew shallower.

Mavis hissed another word, and Titus's hair darkened to a warm brown and his essence shifted, now clearly saying he was a wolf.

Please be over. Please. I wasn't going to be able to take much more.

Another hissed word, and the pressure, along with most of the blazing glow from the marble, vanished. One minute I was being crushed to death, the next nothing. It made the world jerk, the sudden change jarring.

Mavis sat back with a gasp as I drew in desperate quick breaths, trying to clear my vision and steady myself.

"Next," she said, sweat glistening on her forehead despite the cool temperature. "And I don't want to hear any complaints about the glamour."

Titus stood and turned to face us. Except it wasn't Titus facing us, it was a still-big, but average looking guy. He now had brown hair and eyes and a slightly crooked nose. His once rugged appearance had softened and, if I really thought about it, he didn't seem quite as imposing as before.

"It's boring and perfect," Sebastian said, setting me on my feet by the stool.

I sat, my nerves thrumming and my chest still sore. I really didn't want to experience that pressure again, but I didn't have any other choice. Even if the plan was to hide until Faerie's Heart went back to sleep, I'd still need the charm.

Mavis cracked her neck and rolled her shoulders, and I placed my arm on the table while Cassius sterilized the knife again, my attention stalling on my bloody hands, the blood a mix of Cassius's and Sebastian's.

Mavis noticed the blood too and, with a hint of a smile, tsked.

"Let me take care of that for you." She closed her eyes, and the blood pebbled into droplets on my skin even though it was mostly dried. It rolled off my skin, onto the table, and gathered in the groove at the edge.

"Gee, Mavis," Sebastian said, "what do you take me for?"

"What do you mean?" she asked, batting her eyelashes at him.

Did that work with any man?

"Really?" Sebastian asked incredulously. With a sigh, he pressed a small glyph on his chest, lighting it up, and the blood evaporated. "You honestly think I'd let you get away with collecting my blood?"

"Oh, well, you know." Mavis shrugged. "I had to try."

"Sure you did, and I'll just accidentally say the wrong

thing to the wrong person." He cocked an eyebrow and her eyes narrowed all pretense of innocence gone. "Cast the spell, Mavis."

With a huff, she jerked her attention back to my wrist, painted on the simple glyph, and made her incision. She hissed the same sharp word from before, set a coin on the now-bloody glyph, and picked up the marble, which now glowed a third as brightly as before. Three more hissed words started her spell, and the crushing weight of the leash spell returned.

This time I did groan, unable to hold it back, and out of the corner of my eye I saw Cassius jerk forward and Sebastian put a hand on his chest to remind him to stay back.

Another hissed word and agony sliced through me with each panting breath. Specks of light and darkness flashed across my vision, and the room lurched.

I clenched my teeth and fought to hold on. It wouldn't take long. *Please, don't let it take long.* I'd never had a concealment spell on me before. I knew from talking with active agents that it was a pretty quick and simple spell. Surely my spell would be quicker than Titus's because he'd also needed a glamour.

The pressure swelled and I leaned onto the table, unable to keep myself upright. Then the coin sank under my skin, taking the blood and ink with it, along with the enormous weight from the leash spell and leaving no evidence that Mavis had cast the spell.

Gasping, I sagged against the table, tears I was *not* going to cry burning my eyes. At least I'd been right and it hadn't taken as long as Titus's spell.

Cassius tugged on my arm, urging me to stand, and helped me stagger to the stainless-steel counter, where I leaned against it, trying not to look like I was shaking. It was bad enough I'd looked weak since Hawk's tent. Much more and Cassius wouldn't want to let me out of his sight or go anywhere or do anything... which was just as bad as being trapped by a spell or a soul bond.

"You okay?" he asked, his angel glow bright with worry.

"Yeah. Sebastian will break the leash spell tomorrow and things will get—" Well, they wouldn't go back to normal, not with the Spring Court coming after us, but they would get better. I'd no longer be trapped. I could leave if I wanted to. It wouldn't be safe or wise, but I could. *Please, I had to.*

Except I wanted to leave *now*. My soul screamed. I had to be free. I'd sworn I'd never be someone's prisoner again, never be foolish or reckless enough for someone to take me and hurt me again. Never be so helpless.

I dropped my gaze, afraid he'd be able to see the fear squeezing my chest.

"Things will get... less restrictive," I said, awkwardly finishing what I was going to say.

He brushed a finger across my cheek, drawing my gaze back up to him, and tucked a strand of hair behind my ear.

The gentle action surprised me. He'd never touched me like that before. He barely ever touched me because touching wasn't appropriate for angelic friends, and the sudden soft contact ignited my desire... because everything right now seemed to make me yearn for sex, which then made me angry with myself. I had more control than this. I'd had over a hundred years of proof of my control.

"I'll make this right," he said.

"You're up, Cassius," Sebastian said as Hawk got up from the stool.

"I promise." A whisper of smoke curled around him and he took Hawk's place in front of Mavis.

Hawk sidled up to me, rubbing his wrist where Mavis had implanted the charm, his hellfire banked and his gaze appraising. "You are one complicated woman. When was the last time you got any?"

"Excuse me?" I don't know why it surprised me that he was so blunt.

"Sex," he said, lowering his voice. "You're awfully tense. When was the last time you had sex? And I don't mean the little treats I gave you today."

"You've already made your offer. Do you honestly think now is an appropriate time?"

"Baby, I'm an incubus," he said and a curl of his seductive magic caressed my cheek, mimicking Cassius's touch and making me throb with need. "There's nothing appropriate about me." He leaned in close, his demonic heat radiating from his body and his breath feathering across my neck making my pulse pick up. "And there's nothing appropriate about you, either."

"My situation is complicated." Why had I just said that? I should have just rejected him. Even if I wanted to take him up on his offer, now certainly wasn't the time.

"More complicated than being leashed to a man

wanted by all of Faerie?" he asked and his magic seeped across my chest and started to sink.

"Yes," I breathed. Oh, my goodness! I had to get ahold of myself.

"Which is why you need to do more to relieve your stress."

I squared my shoulders determined to resist his magic. "What I need is food and sleep." *And to get free.*

My panic surged, overwhelming my desire.

Hawk's hellfire snapped to tiny red pinpricks and he shifted away from me, his hands raised. "Hey, I'm not going to *make* you do anything," he said thankfully mistaking my fear for fear that he'd manipulate me into doing something I didn't want to do. "It's no fun if you don't really want it."

"So you think I wanted you to kiss me in the abandoned bathhouse?" I asked, realizing as I said the words how stupid they were. I hadn't expected his kiss, but I'd certainly wanted it, and Hawk with his ability to sense sexual desire knew it.

He cocked an eyebrow. "Pretty sure you wanted more than just a kiss. Pretty sure you still do."

Thankfully, Sebastian stepped close, rubbing his wrist like Hawk had, saving me from coming up with a response and drawing Hawk's intense gaze away from me.

"We're all done," Sebastian said. "Can you walk?"

"Yes," I replied, my voice still embarrassingly breathy.

I clamped down on my emotions and pushed past Hawk, hurrying down the hall, out the metal door, and into the stifling summer heat.

This was getting out of hand. I had to regain my control. Somehow. I just had no idea how.

Shadows filled the alley and dusk was starting to darken the sky. My stomach rumbled and exhaustion dragged at my senses. It had been a long day and I'd only eaten once and spent all of my magic twice. I was exhausted... which was probably why I had no self-control.

We returned to Sebastian's apartment in silence, the drive thankfully short, and the ride in the elevator grim and awkward. Everyone was worried. Yes, now we didn't have to worry about being magically tracked, but the spells, no matter how expertly they'd been cast, would only last for so long.

"Everyone should eat something before going to bed," I said as Sebastian unlocked his door and let us in.

"Speaking of bed..." Hawk purred with a sensual smile.

"You've got the couch in the living room, and you and I are using Titus's bathroom," Cassius said, striding past him toward the kitchen. "You're also going to be useful and help make dinner."

"Oh, I am, am I?" Hawk asked as he crossed his arms and narrowed his eyes. "I'm not even going to get anything out of it. Food isn't what I eat."

"It's okay," I said. I was too tired to deal with a fight between them and I was pretty sure Hawk, like Sebastian, would escalate the situation just to amuse himself. "I'll help you."

"No. You're going to sit and drink a glass of orange

juice." Cassius jabbed a finger at me. "You've expended your magic twice today and you look terrible."

Hawk snorted. "You should probably take that back."

"I'm perfectly capable of assessing my condition." Jeez, and now all I wanted was to prove him wrong even if the smartest move was to let him take care of dinner. But I wasn't helpless. I'd never be helpless again, and it made my insides squirm knowing he was doing something I was perfectly capable of doing myself.

"No, you're not," Cassius said. "You always push yourself too far."

"You did not just tell me I don't know my own body."

Hawk snickered and I glared at him which only made him flash me a heart-stopping smile.

"I'll help," Titus said. "Seirea— sorry, Sebastian, any suggestions?"

"Make whatever you want. I had Nova stock up the fridge and pick up more clothes for everyone before she left. It should all be in the kitchen." Sebastian rubbed his face and for a second his complexion was gray again... which it shouldn't have been because I'd healed everything that was wrong with him.

Or at least everything I could heal. There wasn't anything I could do for magic depletion.

He turned and headed to the hall leading to the bedrooms. "I'm going to get cleaned up."

"You should eat first," Cassius said. "We haven't eaten anything since breakfast. You can survive if you're filthy. You can't if you're starving."

"Whatever." He didn't turn around and gave Cassius the finger.

"Bane—" Cassius growled.

I set a hand on Cassius's arm. "Let him go. He used a lot of magic today, too."

No one, except for maybe Hawk who'd gotten more than enough sexual energy in the last little while, had much energy to cook anything, so we settled on sandwiches. All three guys — even Hawk — helped assemble sandwiches, and while Sebastian's kitchen was big, so were all three of the guys. So to stay out of the way, I ended up sitting at the kitchen table cutting vegetables for a salad.

Sebastian didn't come out to join us, and a worry that there was something wrong with him, something I'd missed started gnawing away at me. Maybe it was something deep, an infection that was slowly affecting him.

I'd been so concerned about the laceration in his leg and sealing shut all his other cuts that I might not have noticed it, and I'd pulled my magic out before I was finished fully healing him, trying to conserve it. If there had been the beginnings of an infection in any of his wounds, I could have withdrawn my magic before removing it and it could have been growing inside him since... well, since last night's fight.

Which was ridiculous. Surely my magic would have noticed it.

But the need to heal him twisted in my gut along with the selfish fear that if he was sick, I'd have to wait even longer to be free. And I had to be free.

I wasn't going to be able to get any rest until I eased the compulsion from my healing magic and the fear of being trapped, and I was too tired to fight either, so I grabbed a sandwich from the pile on the platter in the center of the table and stood. "I'm going to check on Sebastian."

"He's probably just fallen asleep," Cassius said.

I hoped so.

"Something you—"

I glared at him and he cleared his throat, making Hawk snort, not even trying to hide his amusement.

"Something *all of us* should do," Cassius finished.

"That's the plan," I said. "I'm taking him this sandwich then going to bed. Good night."

His expression softened, verging on that look I hated so much. Why did he always see me as the weak, pathetic angel he'd saved? Why could I never put that nightmare behind me?

Because it had been my own fault. I'd made a bad decision, first to go to the human realm by myself, then to keep healing those humans when I knew it would keep me weak. I never wanted to make a bad decision like that again, and yet I knew, if put in the same position, I would. I'd drain myself dry to save lives. I'd never been able to stop myself.

Which meant I couldn't allow myself to be put in that kind of position again. Ever.

I marched to the door at the end of the hall and firmly knocked. I doubted Sebastian was modest, but it was always polite to give fair warning. "I brought you something to eat."

No answer.

I strained to hear anything inside.

Nothing.

He probably *had* fallen asleep, and while it would be best if I returned the sandwich to the kitchen and went to bed as well, I couldn't ignore the compulsion to ensure he was okay.

I cracked open the door and peeked in. The lights were off and only a thin band of light from the barely open en suite door cutting into the room offered weak illumination. His bed was empty, the sheets still pulled up, and I could hear the soft rush of running water.

"Sebastian?" I called. "Are you okay?"

He still didn't answer and my need to heal twisted tighter. I had to confirm he was okay and that there wasn't anything else I could do to help him. He had, after all, saved my life. And I had no doubt we wouldn't be able to get out of this mess without him.

I certainly wouldn't be able to be free of the leash spell... or my mating brand.

The thought made my pulse race. It didn't matter if he was angry at me, so long as he wasn't hurt and could break the leash spell in the morning.

I stepped inside and closed the door behind me. His bedroom wasn't much bigger than his guestrooms and was done in the same white and blues as the rest of the apartment. Unlike the simple plain guestrooms, he had a large painting hanging on the far wall of a winter forest scape, a wide, masculine dresser with a stack of books and two small wooden boxes on top, and a large bookshelf also crammed with books. More books sat on a bedside table and in a pile on the floor in front of it.

I'd known he liked books — the man had a whole office with floor-to-ceiling bookshelves crammed with books — but it was always so easy to forget his scholarly nature with his brash flirtations.

"Sebastian," I called again, as I headed to his bathroom. "I brought you dinner."

Still no answer. Now I was really starting to worry.

"Are you okay in there?" I knocked on the door and it creaked open a little wider.

The air inside was humid. Mist had gathered on the large mirror above the sink and the glass wall of the large shower stall, but not enough to obscure my view of Sebastian's incredible body.

He stood with his back to me, his forehead pressed against the white tiles, the water rushing over his sleek muscles and the mesmerizing swirls of ink covering him. All of him. The ink encircled his neck, snaked down his spine, curled around one shoulder blade, and twisted on top of the other. A lattice of thin lines accentuated the firm muscle of one butt cheek and trailed down the back of his thigh, while a thick line cut along the curve of his other hip and wrapped around his other thigh.

My mouth went dry and my pulse picked up again for a completely different reason. He was breathtaking. I'd known he was. I hadn't seen him fully naked, but I'd seen enough to know he was in as good a shape or better than any JP agent I'd worked with, but this... This was so much more than I expected. I ached just looking at him.

AMIAH

My desire throbbed low within me, and I wanted to scream with the day's frustrations. I needed to regain control of my emotions, but I didn't know if I'd be able to do that, not while being trapped in this situation with Sebastian and now Hawk always around.

No. The best plan was to get it out of my system. Surely if I released this pressure, I'd be able to think straight again. Hawk would be my best choice. He'd already offered. Except there was no guarantee he'd be discreet, and I wasn't ready for everyone to know I'd invited him to my bed.

I bit back a groan. There was no good way to deal with this.

"Fucking hell," Sebastian gasped, and I yanked my attention back to him. I hadn't even realized my gaze had dropped to the floor. "What are you doing in my bathroom?"

Heat rushed across my cheeks and I turned my back to him. I'd seen many naked men before and I had no doubt many women had seen Sebastian naked, but given what I desired, looking at him was inappropriate. As much as I wanted to, I couldn't pretend I was just an impartial physician. "I came to check on you."

"So you just decided to walk into my bathroom?"

"You didn't answer when I called." I squared my shoulders, trying to draw on my cool professional persona and ignore my desires. "And you didn't get anything to eat."

"For fuck's sake," he hissed. "I'm fine. I'll get something to eat when I'm out."

"You're not fine. You're too pale."

"I'm supposed to be pale," he shot back. "I'm winter fae."

"You know what I mean," I said, shifting closer to the shower but managing to keep my back turned to him despite the urge to look... because I wanted to assess him, not ogle his gorgeous body. Really. "Just let me check you."

"I'm not a patient and we're not in your hospital. Go away."

"If you have an infection, it'll be easier to treat now than in the morning." I couldn't let it go. The compulsion to heal and my fears were too strong.

I set the plate with the sandwich beside the sink and walked backward until my back bumped against the shower wall.

"Let me check you." I reached my hand around the edge of the glass shower stall, even knowing I should comply with his wishes, that I shouldn't force my magic on him. But just thinking that made my compulsion twist tighter. "Please, Sebastian. A quick check, and I'll be gone."

"Amiah," he said, his voice low, filled with warning, and sounding like he stood right beside me.

Unable to help myself, I slid my gaze to the opening into the shower and my breath caught.

He did stand right behind me, his face inches from mine, and the desire burning in his eyes seared my insides. "You won't like my reaction if you touch me right now."

But I knew he didn't really mean it. He was just trying to get me to go away. He'd already made it clear that he could turn that look on and off with a thought, that he only pretended to want me because it shocked me.

This was just another tease and if I fell for it, he'd just make fun of me later. "We both know you're not going to do anything." I huffed trying to sound like the look in his eyes didn't affect me. "All you do is tease. At least Hawk has follow through."

I reached up to press my palm against his cheek and check him, but he seized my wrist and yanked me into the shower, pinning me against the tiles with his body.

Water soaked into my dress, plastering it to my body, and his erection pressed hard against my pelvis. My thoughts tripped. He did desire me... or at least he was sexually excited. I wasn't sure if it was because I was a woman or because I was me.

"You think I have no follow through?" He captured my head between my palms and smashed his lips against mine with a hungry, angry kiss. It stole all breath and thought. There was only my aching desperate need and my certainty that Sebastian couldn't possibly be my soul mate.

Somehow, I managed to regain enough conscious thought to slide a thread of magic into him. Absolutely no infection. He was tired and the lacerations weren't completely healed, but beyond that, there was nothing for my magic to fix.

He thrust his tongue into my mouth, and my thoughts scattered again. His fingers tangled in my hair and he ground his erection against me as if he needed to get closer. But the only way he could get closer would be to be inside me.

With a moan, I hooked my leg around his hip. The action tilted my hips and rubbed him against my clit, sending a shock of sensation zinging through me.

"Fuck," he groaned as he pulled his lips away and pressed his forehead against mine. His breath was ragged and his grip tightened in my hair. "Tell me to stop."

"No." I burned with a need that had only been growing since last night. I missed being touched and held, and I ached for more, so much more.

"You've been influenced by Hawk's magic." He shifted, the movement grinding him against me and making me gasp in pleasure. "*I've* been influenced by Hawk's magic. If we wait, it'll pass," he said, trailing his lips down my neck.

"Is that what you want?" I asked. Of course, that was what he wanted. He'd already made his feelings clear.

"Fuck no," he murmured against my throat. "But if *you* can't wait, you should go to Cassius. Not me."

"I've told you we've never slept together." I tipped my

head back and he reached behind my neck and unhooked the strap of my dress. "We're just friends and even if we weren't, he'd want a commitment I can't give him. I can't commit to anyone until my brand is gone. It'll make me love someone else."

"Maybe he's your soul mate." Sebastian slid his hands over my shoulders, slowly pushing the top of my dress down until just a fraction of material maintained my modesty.

"That would make it worse." My breath picked up with a mix of anticipation and fear. "I can't be trapped like that."

"Maybe I'm your soul mate. Having sex with me might seal the deal," he said with a ghost of his wicked smile.

"Do you honestly think we're soul mates?"

He raised his gaze to mine, his eyes filled with barely contained need, his body trembling. "Last chance to say no."

I captured his lips and gave him my answer with my body. He kissed me back with the same ferocity as before and pushed down the front of my dress. Sensation rushed through me, overwhelming everything else. There were just his lips on mine, his hand tangling in my hair, and his fingers tweaking my nipple. I was on fire everywhere our bodies touched and it was amazing, so much more than what I'd imagined.

My breath picked up and I dug my fingers into his scalp, not wanting to let his lips go. I couldn't get enough of the heat and hunger he inspired. I'd thought the kiss with Hawk had been incredible, and it had been, but it had only been a taste of what a kiss could be like.

"So wild it is," he gasped as he grabbed my rear and pulled me into his arms. "Let's get out of the cold."

"The what—?" I wrapped my other leg around his waist, realizing, through the heated haze rushing through me, that the water had grown cold.

He carried me to the bed, both of us still dripping wet, and laid me on the comforter. His lips found mine again, stealing my breath with a quick passionate kiss, before pulling away.

I reached to draw him back to me as he flicked his tongue over my nipple, sending a shock of sensation zinging through me, stopping my reach and drawing a surprised gasp. With a groan, he sucked my nipple into his mouth, building the throbbing need within me as he worked my other nipple with his hand, teasing it into a tight peak.

This was just as good as kissing. More so. God, I'd been such a fool. I could have been feeling like this for years. This was so much better than just pleasuring myself, and right in that moment, there was only him. No fear about being trapped by the leash spell or my brand, no thought about how I appeared or if he thought I was strong and in control. I wasn't in control. He was and it felt amazing.

He unzipped my dress and pulled it and my underwear off, tossing them to the floor, but didn't return to lie on top of me. Instead, he looked down at me with a heated hungry look that made my pulse stall. I'd never been naked in front of a man before, and I'd certainly never had one look at me the way Sebastian was looking at me now. I didn't care if he just wanted to have sex with me because I was a woman and not because of who I was. In that moment I felt beautiful and sexy and desired.

I slid my gaze down his body, drinking him in like he was drinking me in, and stopped at his impressive erection. I bit my lip. This was really going to happen. I was really going to have intercourse.

His lips quirked. "I have plenty of follow through."

"I can see that," I said, my voice breathy.

He tapped a finger against a glyph on his hip and activated it.

"I wouldn't have thought you'd need help," I said. It couldn't have been a birth control spell because angels could only be impregnated by other angels, so it had to be something else.

"This is for you." He pressed his palms against the insides of my knees and urged me to open for him. "A sound block." He leaned in, traced the vein on the inside of my thigh with his tongue, and settled his head between my legs.

Oh, my.

He flicked his tongue over my clit, making me gasp.

"The sounds you make tonight are mine, no one else's, and I have every intention of making you scream." His tongue swept over my clit again, and if I had a response, it vanished with the rush of sensation.

His mouth was even more amazing down there. He drove me crazy with his tongue, and with the spell blocking any sounds from leaving his room, I fully gave in, moaning and gasping my pleasure.

My breath grew ragged and my muscles began to tremble. "Oh, Sebastian."

He groaned and slid a finger inside me. Withdrew it and returned with two, pumping them into me, hitting a spot that made my trembling muscles start to tighten. With a hard suck on my clit, he made my muscles contract. Sensation crashed through me, radiating into every cell in my being and I cried out, not even bothering to try to hold it back.

But he didn't give me time to recover. My muscles were still clenching and my mind still spinning with my rushing breath and pulse as he moved up my body and pushed partway into my opening.

Oh, yes. I never imagined it could be like this.

"Shit, you're so tight." He squeezed his eyes shut and drew in long breaths to steady himself then slowly withdrew and pushed back in a little farther, his erection stretching me, urging my body to accommodate him.

The aching heat of need swelled within me again as if I hadn't just had an orgasm, and with another withdrawal and push, he fully sheathed himself inside me.

My breath hitched, my muscles already trembling again around him, and something in my essence clicked — not my mating brand, thank God. My skin grew luminescent similar to Sebastian's, making me moan, part in pleasure and part in embarrassment. It wasn't unheard of for an angel to glow his or her first time, but it didn't always happen, and I'd really hoped I wasn't one of the lucky few.

"Ah, fuck." Sebastian froze, his expression horrified. "You're a virgin?"

My pulse froze with him and my fears started to rush back in. *No. Please.* I didn't want this to end.

"It doesn't matter," I forced out. It shouldn't matter. *Please don't let it matter. Please don't stop.*

"Sweetheart, it always matters," he said. "An angel like you is a virgin for a reason, and I'm not that reason. You haven't been waiting for me. That's for sure."

"I'm not waiting for anyone." Not anymore. I rocked my hips, trying to urge him to continue. I didn't want to lose the trembling promise of another climax. *Make me forget I was a fool. Make me forget I'm going to be trapped forever. Please.* "Sebastian, make me scream."

I grabbed his head and urged him down to capture his lips in a desperate kiss. I needed my mind to stop whirling, to forget everything. I could taste myself on his lips and a shudder of pleasure whispered through me at the memory of his mouth on me.

He hesitated, just for a second, then groaned and kissed me back, plunging his tongue inside my mouth, ratcheting up my desire.

He kissed me until I was breathless and squirming and my mind blissfully empty. My core throbbed, my body teetering again on the edge of another release. With a groan, he sat back, still fully sheathed inside me. His hungry expression turned wicked, and he brushed his thumb over my clit, the sensation stealing my breath.

God, he was going to ruin me for other men. He knew just how to touch me, how to bring me close without letting me crash over, and he teased me again and again until I was gasping, the room spinning with my quick breaths, and my body was on fire, wound so tight I was sure I'd explode. Then he finally — thank God, finally! — seized my hips and started to move inside me.

"Oh, yes." This was what I wanted. This was amazing. The slide of his erection in and out of my body and the glorious friction. He fully possessed me, claiming me as only a man could claim a woman, just as I hungrily welcomed him in.

His pace grew faster and his thrusts harder. The promise of my climax spun tighter and tighter until every muscle in my body contracted and shattering bliss roared through me, tearing a scream from my throat.

Sebastian gave another few hard thrusts and tensed, his own release drawing a cry, sending another wave crashing through me.

"Fuck me," Sebastian groaned and he shuddered, which sent another, small wave rushing through me.

Yes, I had.

He gave me a fierce kiss and rolled off me, his chest heaving with his rapid breaths, and wrapped me in his arms, my back against his chest. I snuggled in, savoring the feel of his body pressed against me and the pulse of his life force thrumming against my senses.

This was the way it was supposed to be. This was right.

And oh my goodness, I'd just had sex.

With Sebastian Bane.

It had been amazing. So much more than I'd fantasized about. I was still spinning and glowing and floating, my body so lax I wasn't sure I'd be able to move. But oh my, goodness—

I'd had sex with Sebastian Bane!

How was I to know he'd actually cast a sound blocking spell? And even if he had, he was surely going to use this against me in the morning.

God, what had I been thinking?

I hadn't been, and for the first time in my life, I'd been free of my fear, my self-restraint, of everything. I hadn't thought of looking strong or of the nightmare branded in my skin. There'd only been his mouth and hands and body bringing me immense pleasure.

He pressed his lips against the back of my neck, his breath teasing my skin making my pulse pick up again and need throb between my thighs.

What was wrong with me? How could I crave more when I was still — literally — glowing from round one?

He hummed low in his throat, a sound of pure masculine satisfaction, and slid his hand down my belly and dipped his fingers into my curls.

I pulled away from him, need and panic a sudden whirling mix of hot and cold in my chest. "I should..."

I didn't know what to say. I wanted to let go again, stop thinking, and just feel, but my spinning thoughts were taking over and I couldn't push them aside.

I'd just made a horrible mistake.

No, I hadn't.

Sebastian had been everything I wanted for my first time and more, so much more. But at what cost?

"I should clean up." And take a moment to think. I had no idea how I felt about what had just happened. I just needed some time by myself to regain my mental equilibrium... as much as I— God! I loved being held in his arms like that.

He raised his gaze to me, his pupils dilated with desire, but his lips quirked in that wicked smile that said I amused him.

I scrambled off the bed and grabbed my dress. I didn't know where my underwear had gone but if I stayed to search for it, I'd have sex with Sebastian again.

And while a part of me was certain that wasn't a bad thing, the part that needed to be in control was having a meltdown. My pulse was already racing and my breath getting faster, and it had nothing to do with desire. I'd done something without considering the consequences. Again.

"You don't need to get dressed to clean up," he said. "I have an en suite."

"I know. I just— I need to think."

"That's a bad idea." His smile deepened, his eyes filled with mirth... and was that a hint of softness?

No. I was imagining it. I only *wanted* him to understand my fear, but logically I knew he didn't care. Which had been the whole point of sleeping with him.

I pulled on my dress. The zipper got caught in the wet fabric halfway up, and I didn't bother fighting with it, hoping I'd be able to slip into my room without anyone seeing me.

It shouldn't have mattered. I should be able to have sex with whoever I wanted whenever I wanted, and yet I was torn with so many conflicting emotions and thoughts.

I was supposed to be waiting... for someone I didn't want anymore.

I should never have given up control like that.

I should have picked someone more appropriate, someone who actually cared for me.

Except the fact that Sebastian and I didn't have an emotional attachment was the very reason I'd considered him. There were no strings attached with him. Now that he'd conquered me, this would likely be the one and only time we'd have sex.

And I had no idea how I felt about that, either.

I hurried out of his bedroom, pulled the door closed, and pressed my back against it, desperate to slow my racing heart.

That had been amazing.

And so foolish.

The lights in the hall and living room were off. Sebastian's apartment was dark and everyone had gone to bed. Which meant — thank goodness — no one would see me slinking back into my bedroom, and I had until morning to figure out how I was going to react to what I'd just done.

I squared my shoulders and headed to my room as Hawk stepped around the corner in the living room into the hall.

Oh, no.

My stomach bottomed out as realization hit me. I might have been able to hide what I'd done from Cassius, and if I showered I'd be able to hide it from Titus as well, but Hawk, with his incubus ability to sense sexual energy, knew exactly what I'd just done.

AMIAH

Hawk drew closer and the hellfire in his eyes flared, casting his beautiful face in flickering illumination and making him look dangerous.

"Why did you leave?" he asked, his voice low. "You weren't done."

"I was," I insisted, embarrassment heating my cheeks, even though I logically knew I had nothing to be embarrassed about.

"Oh, baby," he purred, leaning in. He brushed the back of his warm finger along my jaw and sent a shiver of aching need sweeping through me without even using his magic. "You weren't done."

"Yes. I was." I needed to get my thoughts under control, but I couldn't make myself push past him to go to my room. He was mesmerizing.

Like he was supposed to be. Because he was an incubus.

And as much as I'd said I was done, I wasn't. My body wanted to go back to Sebastian for round two and feel that all-consuming bliss again. But my mind wouldn't let me. I'd made a mistake. I'd lost control. I'd—

I shifted to put some space between us and my back hit the hall wall.

Hawk pressed close and, with a smirk, slid his hand under my skirt and up the inside of my thigh, stopping at the crux between my leg and pelvis.

My breath hitched, anticipation of what would happen if he just moved his fingers an inch reigniting my desire. I wanted him to touch me, wanted more, and that terrified me.

"Oh, no." He teased his fingers against my wet and swollen folds. Just a whisper of a touch, and my thoughts scattered. All the reasons I'd run from Sebastian's bed vanished, and, with just that touch, I was instantly trembling on the verge of an orgasm again. "You weren't done at all."

He slid two fingers inside me, and I moaned, my body melting into the sensation. *Oh, yes.*

"He wants you again." Hawk slowly slid his fingers out then pushed back in. "Even after you ran, he still wants you. But I think it's his turn to know someone else is fucking you. He can't sense it like I can, so let's give him something to listen to."

He brushed his thumb against my clit, sending another teasing tremor through me, and I fought to swallow a moan of pleasure.

It came out as a desperate mewl that deepened Hawk's smile. "Or would you rather he watched?"

The memory of Sebastian's hungry look when we'd been in Hawk's tent and the thought of him watching while Hawk pushed inside me rippled pleasure through me, torturously close to an orgasm but not quite.

"Fuck, yeah," Hawk murmured, increasing the pressure on my clit and sliding his fingers in and out at a torturously slow pace. "How about instead of watching, we invite him to join us."

Oh, God yes. I wanted that. I wanted all of it. Everything I'd learned about while I'd waited and prepared for my soul mate, and what better way to do that than with men as experienced as Sebastian and Hawk who were without a doubt *not* my soul mates.

My muscles clenched around Hawk's fingers and another orgasm swept through me. He captured my lips, swallowing my moan, and slipped a curl of his hot sensual magic into me that made the sensation swell. Stars flashed behind my eyelids, my release stealing all breath and thought.

"You're going to be so much fun," he murmured before sauntering away through the living room into the kitchen leaving me panting and trembling and clinging to the wall to stay standing.

Oh, God.

God.

That was—

And I was—

What was wrong with me? I wanted to call him back, wanted him and Sebastian so much it hurt, wanted the escape of not thinking and just feeling. No—

I sucked in a ragged breath. What I needed to do was think. My reasons for leaving Sebastian's bed hadn't changed, and I needed to figure out how to pull myself back together. Something, I wasn't going to be able to figure out in the guestroom any more. It was too small. I needed more space and sky to steady myself. I had to have sky.

I raced out the front door before common sense kicked in but managed to force myself to slow down so I could notice the moment the leash spell activated. It always started with a pressure before the air vanished. If I felt that, I'd turn around, but not before.

Please, don't activate. Please let the stairs to the roof be within the limits of the spell. I needed the sky too much. I needed to find my balance.

Thankfully, there was only a hint of weight in my chest, and I crashed out the metal security door onto the roof, the coarse surface rough against my bare feet and the summer's evening heat wrapping thick and humid around me. A mix of relief and desperation brought me to my knees.

There had to be something wrong with me. I wanted to go back to Hawk and Sebastian. I craved it. But the things I desired surprised me.

And yet just thinking about Hawk's proposition for a *ménage à trois* sent an aftershock rushing through me.

I wanted both of them. Together. But did I want *them* or just two men? I wasn't sure I'd feel comfortable agreeing to anything with men I didn't know. Except I barely knew Sebastian and I didn't know Hawk at all.

Which meant it wasn't them I craved, but sex... really? No, there was something about them that I trusted... or was that just because my control had finally shattered and my psyche needed to justify my desire for them by making me think I trusted them.

I swept my gaze over the Quarter's skyline. The lights across from me were tinged purple by the UV-blocking canopy which was attached to the side of the roof — marking this building as being at the edge of the vampire's section of the Quarter. The canopy rose up seven feet, stretched over to the roof across the street as well as the buildings up the street, protecting a whole, long block.

My insides squirmed, my worry and confusion growing. I'd thought seeing the sky would help, but with the glass canopy, I still felt trapped. Trapped by my fear and now trapped by my desires.

I couldn't take back what I'd done with Sebastian and I didn't want to. I'd hoped my aching need would go away if I satisfied it, but now I knew what I'd been missing, and I wanted more.

A part of me feared I wouldn't be able to get enough and another part feared if I propositioned Sebastian he'd refuse me.

As it was, Sebastian or Hawk would let it slip, and Cassius would know what had happened by the morning and would no doubt be concerned, since sleeping with Sebastian was out of character for me... because I wasn't a sexual woman.

Well, if I didn't want to go crazy and make even worse decisions, I was going to have to become one. I needed to own my desires. I was sure I could still practice some restraint, but I didn't want the celibacy of before. Surely I could convince the part of me that was still screaming at my lack of control that taking charge of what I wanted *was* an act of control.

The thought made my cheeks heat.

Taking charge meant being forthright and asking for what I wanted.

Funny how I could say what needed to be said in a medical situation no matter how blunt, but the idea of asking for what I desired embarrassed me.

I drew in a deep breath, trying to calm my fear. I was still in control. My destiny was still my own. Sebastian would break the leash spell and remove my mating brand and I'd be free. I had a lifetime to find my courage to ask for selfish things, sexual things, anything I wanted.

A footstep crunched on the roof behind me and I turned around, my heart pounding with the hope that Sebastian or Hawk had followed me.

But instead, it was the stern man from the market who'd been commanding the spring fae and their hired thugs. Behind him stood half a dozen shifters, their fingers extended into razor-sharp claws.

"Just the bait I was looking for," he said

Bait? My pulse leaped into a rapid tattoo. Bait meant he was going to capture me, use me. The thought shot icy fear through my limbs. I couldn't be someone's prisoner again. I swore. Never again.

My mind raced through my options. I didn't know how to fight and even if I did, there were too many of them. I had to flee. And flying was my best defense. I couldn't jump off the roof behind me — the way was blocked by the glass canopy — but I was still close to the side of the building. I hadn't gone too far from the staircase.

I bolted for the edge and release my wings. The leash spell wouldn't let me get far, but chances were none of these men could fly so hovering just out of reach would keep me safe until I could figure out how to get to Cassius.

The man laughed, the dark sound making the hair on the back of my neck stand up, and a sharp, sudden weight — too similar to the weight of the leash spell — slammed into my chest. I crashed to the rooftop before reaching the edge and the weight disappeared as quickly as it had appeared.

"How far do you think you'll be able to go?" he called.

I scrambled back to my feet. I just needed to get off the roof. It was only ten feet away.

The man's laughter grew and I put on a burst of speed as the weight slammed into me again. I hit the rooftop hard, spiking sharp pain up my right wrist in a failed attempt to protect my face. My cheek smashed against the ground and a fiery burn spiked through my knees.

The weight didn't go away and I heaved back to my feet, flapping my wings to help me rise. The edge was now only five feet away. If I could get there, I could fight the pressure in my chest and hold myself aloft.

But the weight swelled, stealing my breath, and yanked me around to face the man. He sneered at me, his eyes bright with pleasure, and he curled his finger at me in a come-hither gesture.

The weight jerked me forward a step. I heaved against it, flapping my wings, desperate to keep back. But it was as if a chain was embedded in my chest and fighting it felt like it was tearing out my soul with the same excruciating agony I'd felt when Sebastian had first tried to break the leash spell.

I stumbled forward another few steps, panting against the pain, fighting with everything I had. But I wasn't strong enough. I was weak. I was always weak. And this man was going to take me.

No, please. I couldn't go through that again. Even if it was just being trapped here on the roof while this man made his demands. My life for Titus's. And I had no idea what Cassius would choose. It wasn't right to give Titus over to this man, and the JP didn't negotiate with hostage takers, but Cassius's need to protect people was also strong. Would it be stronger than his need to follow the rules? He'd already turned a blind eye to the illegal activities in Lincoln and at Mavis's. Would he sacrifice Titus to protect me? And could I live with that?

I took another staggering step and another, my mind screaming — *fight. Resist. Be stronger. Stop. Please stop* — until I stood before him, straining to breathe.

I glared at him. It was the only act of defiance I could manage, and the man's sneer deepened.

"Grab her and let's go," he said.

"Go?" I gasped. I couldn't go. If he took me out of the radius of the leash spell, I'd suffocate. Titus would suffocate. "No, please. I'm caught in a leash spell—"

"I'm aware." The man flicked his finger and the air around me vanished.

I futilely gasped, instinct making me draw breath even though I knew there was nothing to breathe, and sagged to my knees. Dark specks crowded my vision and my lungs burned as the world began to spin.

The man grabbed my hair and yanked my head up to meet his gaze. Dark pleasure filled his eyes, making cold fear churn in my stomach.

"I've hijacked the leash spell." Then he flicked his finger again and the air returned — although the crushing weight of the spell remained. My fear grew, making me tremble no matter how hard I tried to hide it. This man wasn't just going to kidnap me. He was going to hurt me.

"I can't kill the beast, but I'll make him suffer through you until he comes to me and admits I'm his master." He jerked my head back, shooting agony through my neck and making me whimper. "We're going to have so much fun together."

CASSIUS

I LAY IN THE DARK ON THE COUCH IN BANE'S OFFICE surrounded by floor-to-ceiling bookshelves unable to get to sleep and my fire burning under my skin as I fought to contain it. With the exception of the window at the back — its UV-blocking glass tinting the Quarter's streetlights purple — and the fireplace across from me, there wasn't an inch of wall that didn't have a shelf filled with flammable material.

If I was smart, I'd go down to Bane's patio and relieve some of the pressure by releasing my flames on the concrete.

Except I didn't want to go that far from Amiah. It was already driving me crazy that she was out of sight.

Which was also driving me crazy.

I shouldn't have to literally watch her to watch out for her. She could be perfectly fine in another room.

But my need to protect her squeezed my chest and made my fire threaten to roar out of control.

She shouldn't be in this mess. She should be safe at

Operations, back to life as normal — or as back to normal as it was possible for her given she'd just had her heart broken.

But I'd failed her. Once again I'd been unable to protect the people I cared about. It didn't matter that it was Amiah's magic that had gotten her into this trouble by locking onto Titus. Somehow I should have been able to stop that, or gotten her out of the situation once I knew what a mess it was, or something.

I should have been able to do God damned something.

My fire flared, billowing smoke from my hands, and I clenched down on it, the heat searing my skin.

I couldn't believe I'd said we had to go after Faerie's Heart. Except no matter how I looked at the situation — and I'd spent all day trying to come up with any other solution that ensured Amiah's safety — there wasn't any option... if, of course, Bane was telling the truth.

I really wanted to doubt him, wanted him to be the lying bastard I'd thought he was before he'd helped my brother fight Lilith, but given how much he'd wanted us out of his apartment last night, he'd never come up with a story that forced us to stay together.

Which meant until we could get Faerie's Heart, Amiah was in danger, and even then, unless we could make an iron-clad arrangement with someone who I seriously doubted would keep their word, she was still in danger.

It also meant we were stuck with Bane. The man who made sexual advances on everyone.

God, he drove me crazy. He'd propositioned my

brother's mate and now he kept propositioning Amiah. Not that she'd ever say yes. He wasn't her type. He was a one-night stand guy. Have some fun and be done, and I doubted he even bothered to learn his lovers' names. He made no attempt to hide that, and if I knew one thing about Amiah, she was a full commitment kind of woman. She was careful with her heart, so damned careful, and she'd never say yes to his advances.

And really, he was the least of my worries. Now we were stuck with an incubus who didn't care who his magic affected.

I'd thought Essie's incubus mate had been a sexual harassment complaint waiting to happen, but he was restrained compared to Hawk. I couldn't feel the incubus's magic, but I had no doubt Hawk did little to hold it back. It was the only thing that explained why Amiah hadn't resisted his kiss in the abandoned bath-house, why it looked like she'd *wanted* him to touch and kiss her like that.

The thought made my heart clench and my fire flared again.

I jerked off the couch, strode to the fireplace, and shoved my hands inside.

I wanted to touch her and kiss her like that... well, not like *that*—

Actually. Yes. Exactly like that.

I wanted to kiss her, comfort her, and convince her that while I'd never be as passionate as a shifter, I could fulfill her desires and be a good mate.

Fire sparked from my hands, proving just how wrong I was. I couldn't be passionate. I'd burn her if I ever let go enough to show her how I felt. Hell, just thinking about her like that made it impossible to control my magic. How could I be a good mate if I couldn't even touch her?

I sagged to the floor, keeping my hands in the fireplace and letting my flames drip onto the cleaned concrete hearth and metal grate. I had to focus on my priorities: keeping her safe.

That was the only thing that mattered.

It had barely bothered me to see the stolen goods as well as the health and magic code violations at Left of Lincoln or at Mavis's. My need to protect overwhelmed everything else. I'd failed my youngest brother, Dominic, and I'd been useless protecting my other brother, Gideon. I couldn't fail Amiah.

Something banged against the floor out in the hall and I jerked up to my feet.

"Seireadan!" Titus roared. "Seireadan. She's gone."

My pulse skipped a beat. There was only one *she* Titus would be yelling about.

I threw open the office door. The bedroom door across from me — Titus's door — had been ripped off its hinges and lay half on the bed, while Titus, dressed in the sweatpants Bane's assistant had provided him, was already at the end of the hall. He shoved open Bane's bedroom door, revealing the naked fae scrambling out of bed. Of course the fae slept naked. Had Amiah walked in on *that* when she'd gone to check on him after dinner?

"She's gone," Titus said, his grip crushing the door-knob, his massive muscular chest heaving with rapid breaths. God, he was strong and dangerous. And another one I needed to protect Amiah from.

"She can't be gone," Hawk said rushing from the living room into the hall. "She knows the dangers of the leash spell."

Titus wrenched around to face Hawk and snarled. "She's gone. I can feel it."

I hurried into her bedroom and turned on the light. The bed was still made, and the scrubs Chris had brought over yesterday were still neatly folded at its foot. My stomach bottomed out and fire snapped from my hands.

"She's not in her room." I sucked my flames back before I burned anything and returned to the hall. "Would she be in the other room?" I asked, pointing to the only other door in the hall.

"That's my clean room for complicated spell casting. No furniture or windows," Bane said, pulling on a pair of slacks. "Would she be in there? Last I saw her, she said she needed to think." Bane's gaze flickered to Hawk before jumping to me.

"She'd want open sky," I said as Titus threw open the clean room door. "She'd go to the roof if she could."

"Would she risk the roof access being outside of the leash spell?" Bane asked.

"If she was upset enough." And God, she had so much to be upset about.

I shoved past Hawk and stormed out the door.

If I really thought about it, it should have surprised me that she hadn't gone to the roof sooner. Amiah's need for open sky was stronger than most angels'. I didn't know if it was the way she'd always been or if her captivity at the hands of that human had exacerbated the compulsion, but for as long as I'd known her, she'd sought out rooftops and large open spaces.

The others caught up to me and I fought to keep my pace even. There was no point in panicking. She was on the roof thinking. She probably just wanted some peace and time to think and was going to be upset we'd all come up to find her.

I pushed open the metal door and strode outside into humid evening air. Ahead stretched the wide, empty roof.

My pulse picked up.

Maybe she was on the other side of the stairwell.

"Amiah?" I called, heading around the other side.

She wasn't there, either.

I wrenched around, scanning the rooftop as if I'd somehow missed her. She had to be here. She couldn't be gone. Gone meant she was suffocating to death somewhere.

Titus groaned, clutched his chest, and sagged to his knees.

Panic seized my heart. If she was far enough away for Titus to feel the effects of the leash spell, she was in dire need. I had to save her. I couldn't fail her too.

I grabbed Bane's arm, not caring that fire raced over my hand and up my forearm. "Find her."

"Shit." He wrenched free of my grip, his fae glow undulating around him. "It'd be easier to concentrate if you weren't burning—" His attention locked on the rooftop a few feet away and his eyes widened. "Oh, fuck."

"What is that?" Hawk asked as he crouched in front of a shiny pebble. "It just lit up like the sun."

Titus's attention jumped to the pebble. All the blood

drained from his face and a wild fury filled his eyes. "He has her."

"Who has her?" I demanded.

"Balwyrdan," Titus snarled. "We have to find her."

"We have to be smart about this," Bane said, crouching in front of the pebble.

"If Titus is feeling the effects of the leash spell, she's suffocating," I snapped. Suffering. Dying. How long had she been gone? How long would she last without air?

We had to find her. Now.

Fire dripped from my hands, snapping and hissing around my feet. "There's no time to think this through."

"Balwyrdan is enough of a sorcerer to hijack the leash spell to force Titus to come to him. If she dies, he loses his connection to Titus." The muscles in Bane's jaw flexed. "No, he'll keep her alive until he gets what he wants."

"That's not better," Titus said, his tone dark.

I didn't like the sound of that. "He can compel Titus to come to him?"

"It's not like a compulsion spell," Bane said.

Titus groaned again, his expression tight with pain.

Bane jerked his chin at the pebble. "Touch the charm, Hawk."

Hawk tapped it with his finger. A burst of white light flared from the pebble and a life-sized flickering image of Amiah appeared on the roof.

She lay on her side, curled in a ball. Her hair veiled her face and she gasped deep ragged breaths. Dirt stained her dress, and from the angle of her arms, it looked like they were tied behind her back.

Relief whispered in my chest. She was alive. She had to be terrified — this was too similar to the nightmare I'd rescued her from all those years ago — but she was still alive. I could still save her.

I strained to see anything in the background that might tell me where she was, but everything except for her was out of focus and dark.

Someone chuckled, the sound dark and masculine, and a hand reached into the line of sight of the spell. He seized a fistful of her hair and yanked her head up and back, lifting her to her knees and straining her neck. She bit back a cry of pain and her hair fell away, revealing blood oozing from a broken nose and a right eye that was starting to swell shut.

My stomach bottomed out, and I jerked forward a step even though I knew I couldn't reach her through the spell. This was so much worse than before. That human had hit her, but that had been nothing compared to this, and whoever had kidnapped her now had only had her at most for a couple of hours.

The man from Left of Lincoln who looked to have been in charge of the spring fae stepped fully into sight.

"Balwyrdan," Titus snarled.

"Do you think the beast has found my little note?" Balwyrdan asked, his eyes bright with sadistic pleasure. "We should probably give him more incentive to find it, just in case he hasn't."

He flicked his finger and Amiah's body went rigid. Her mouth opened and closed like a fish out of water, gasping for air that no longer existed, her good eye widened with pain and fear, and her face turned red.

Titus collapsed forward onto his hands. His claws extended and dug into the roof, and his eyes squeezed tight with pain.

Balwyrdan flicked his finger again and Amiah gasped in a desperate breath, but he didn't give her time to recover and smashed her across the face with the back of his hand.

"Jesus," Hawk hissed, as she toppled over with a strangled cry.

"You can do better than that," the man said. He grabbed the front of her dress and wrenched her up, his other hand cocked back to strike her again, but the catch on her neck strap broke. She collapsed back to the floor, leaving the man holding the front of her dress and exposing her breasts. Her head hit the ground and lolled to the side, her face fully in the sight of the spell. Blood now oozed from a cut in her lip as well as from her nose and her eyes were unfocused.

With a huff, the man flicked his finger again and she went rigid.

Titus groaned, and I turned my back on the nightmare projected on the rooftop. My fire seared my insides and raced up my arms past my elbows, snapping and hissing and threatening to pull free of what little control I had and ignite my clothing. "Turn it off."

The sound of Amiah's gasps and sobs vanished, but continued to echo in my head, and I couldn't get the image of her beaten face or her ripped dress out of my mind's eye.

I *had* to go to her right now. Protect her. Except if I was going to save her, I needed to get my emotions and my fire under control. I knew next to nothing about this man or where he was or how many men he had. Rushing in without a plan would get her killed.

"Where is she?" Titus growled as he lunged forward to grab the pebble, but Bane snatched it up before he could get it.

"Don't tell him, Hawk." Bane jerked away from Titus, but the dragon seized his throat and yanked him forward.

"Give me the charm," he snarled. "I'm getting her away from that monster."

"Not until you've calmed down," Bane gasped, clutching Titus's wrist but not fighting back.

"He won't stop." Titus's pupils slitted and his body shook. "Seireadan, you know him. Suffocating her is for me, but the beating is for him. He's going to beat her to an inch of her life until he gets bored and then he's going to give her to his men."

Bane's expression turned icy. "But he won't kill her."

"Fuck man, that's cold," Hawk said.

"But right." I heaved my fire back under my skin, clenching it so tightly it felt like my blood was boiling. "What do we know about this guy?"

"He's a nasty piece of work," Titus snarled.

"No shit," Hawk replied. "We've already figured that one out."

"Bane?" I asked, giving Titus a hard look until he let the fae go. "Tell me everything you know." I was going to get Amiah back. Whatever it took. Even if that meant breaking every rule or burning down the world to do it. I would not fail her like I'd failed my brother.

TITUS

It took everything I had not to gut Seireadan with my claws and take the charm. Every instinct I had screamed at me to protect Amiah, comfort her, avenge her. I needed to hold her small fragile body and steady her soul, and once I had her, I wasn't ever letting go. She should never have had to experience the terror of captivity again let alone be beaten like that, and just knowing that even when Balwyrdan got bored with her, she was going to face the same torture and worse at the hands of his men, made me furious. I was going to tear that bastard to pieces and let her eat his heart—

Except she wasn't a dragon. She probably wouldn't want to eat his heart.

And she wasn't mine to hold on to.

She was Seireadan's. I don't know why he'd denied it this morning. Her scent was all over him along with the taunting smell of sex — recent sex — which made my beast furious and my cock hard. Of course, Hawk smelled of her arousal, too, although not nearly as much as

Seireadan, and that made my beast even more angry. She was Seireadan's and the incubus needed to keep his hands to himself.

I bit back a roar. They both needed to keep their hands to themselves. She was going to be mine and I would fight Seireadan and Hawk and Cassius and anyone else to keep and protect her.

Mine.

The roar escaped, a low, dangerous rumble in my chest that drew everyone's attention.

Fuck.

Not mine.

Not fucking mine. Why the hell couldn't I convince my beast of that? I didn't want *her*. I. Did. Not. Want. Her. I just wanted a female. Any female.

"Balwyrdan had at least two dozen men at Lincoln. He'll already have replaced the ones we injured or killed and added more," Seireadan said. "It looks like he still prefers hired thugs in an attempt to hide his court affiliation, so I suspect his new men are the same."

The weight of the leash spell slammed into my chest, stealing my breath and making the world tilt. I released a half groan half roar and dug my claws into the roof again to stay put. As much as I wanted to give in to my beast and stop Amiah's suffering, Seireadan was right. We had to be smart about this. I might not care if I died trying to save her, but rushing in could get her killed and that was unacceptable.

"Okay," Cassius said, smoke whirling around him, his eyes filled with the same burning rage I felt. "Tell me her location and a safe place to break the leash spell. Your apartment is compromised and we're not returning here once I get her back."

"Once *we* get her back," Seireadan corrected with an icy fury I'd never seen from him before, proving she really was his... and not mine.

"And *is* there a safe place to hole up?" Hawk asked, his expression grim. "We've all got concealment charms and there's another concealment spell on your apartment. The spells are good too. I can barely sense them or the glamour on Titus and only because I know to look for it. How did they find us?"

"Are any of us tagged?" Seireadan asked Hawk, who closed his eyes and drew in a slow breath.

"Not that I can tell," the incubus said after a moment.

"You're the most sensitive Sensitive I'd ever come across. Which means we aren't tagged. Someone has betrayed me, and that's a very short list." Seireadan ran a hand through his hair, the muscles in his arm bunching with the movement drawing my attention to the black glyphs swirling over his body. I wondered if they were a part of the glamour hiding his identity or real. Had he had all those spells inked onto his body? And why?

"If that's the case, then we find an abandoned building and regroup there." A flame flickered around Cassius's hands then vanished with a gust of smoke. "Hawk. I know you're still stuck in this mess, but I don't expect you to risk your life for Amiah. How about you meet us at the corner of Tyndal and Maingate. That whole neighborhood is abandoned but not completely rubble. Titus, you should go with him."

"Not happening," I growled, as the weight crushed my

chest again, stealing my breath and making me groan in pain.

"You're compromised. The moment Balwyrdan sees you, he'll suffocate Amiah and you'll go down. At best, you'll be useless in this fight. At worst a liability." Cassius turned to Seireadan. "Bane—"

"I'm going," I said cutting him off, "and I'm tearing that bastard to pieces."

I stood, fighting the pressure of the leash spell, and let my canines and claws extend in full to show Cassius how serious I was. I didn't want to, but I'd go through him to protect what was mine. And while a part of me knew he was right, that I endangered Amiah's rescue, my beast didn't care. Just like it didn't care that she was Seireadan's.

Cassius squared his shoulders and met my gaze without flinching. From the look in his eyes, he was well aware he was challenging me for dominance, and that only made my beast's fury stronger. "You'll get her killed."

"Seireadan already said Balwyrdan won't kill her until he has me," I said. "I'm glamoured. He can't recognize me."

"He'll know it's you the moment he activates the leash spell and you drop to your knees," Cassius shot back. "You're going with Hawk."

"Except Hawk is going with you, sparky," Hawk said. "You're going to need all the help you can get."

"I can manage just fine." Cassius's flames reignited around his hands. "Someone needs to show Titus where we're meeting since we can't come back here and he doesn't know the city."

"I'm going," I insisted, releasing just enough of my

beast to gain more height on him and widen my chest and shoulders. If I hadn't been glamoured, my red-gold scales would have covered my neck and hands as well.

Cassius stood his ground and molten flames dripped from his hands, setting the roof on fire around his feet. "You're not."

"I am." I grew another foot up and across, grateful for the elastic waistband on the jogging pants. A partial shift wouldn't disintegrate my clothes like a full shift would, but I could still rip them.

"For fuck's sake." Seireadan touched a tattoo on his chest. It flared to life and ice swept through the flames around Cassius extinguishing them. "I'll free Titus from his half of the spell so he's not a liability and I'll break Amiah's half when we get her back."

"It'll be harder to free them one at a time." Hawk frowned. "And won't Balwyrdan and the original spell-caster feel it and be able to find our location when you free Titus?"

"Not if I move the spell from Titus to the resonance charm instead of breaking it." Seireadan stood and headed to the stairs.

Hawk grabbed his arm, stopping him. "Except you're the foundation of the charm. That'll just move Titus's half of the spell to you."

"But at least it won't blow his glamour. We can't risk any survivors knowing what Titus looks like," Seireadan said. "The Spring Court isn't the only court after him."

"There won't be survivors," I growled.

"We still shouldn't risk your glamour being blown," Cassius replied, pulling the rest of his fire back under his skin, "and we'll give them a chance to run first. If they're just hired thugs they're not responsible for Balwyrdan's actions."

"Speak for yourself," I shot back. They were involved, they clearly hadn't done anything to stop Balwyrdan. They were just as guilty.

The muscles in Cassius's jaw flexed, but he turned to Hawk and didn't argue with me. "Hawk, you know where she is?"

Hawk gave a tight nod.

"Okay. Bane, move the spell, everyone finish getting dressed, and pack a small bag." Cassius headed to the stairs and the other guys followed as the leash spell slammed into my chest again. "We don't have time to waste and I want to scout the area first before we make our move."

Which was the smartest choice. But neither I nor my beast wanted to wait and it was getting difficult to rein him in. It wanted blood and I was going to let him have it.

AMIAH

THE DIMLY LIT ABANDONED RECEPTION HALL SPUN AROUND me, and tears I'd desperately tried to hold back rolled down my cheeks. Terror squeezed around my heart, and even when there was air to breathe, I still couldn't catch my breath.

I'd been taken.

Again.

And this man — his men had called him Balwyrdan — was a hundred times worse than the human who'd taken me all those years ago. He didn't care what I looked like. He wasn't trying to sell my services to an unsuspecting public.

Balwyrdan's fist smashed into my cheek with a sickening crunch, fracturing the bone. Agony exploded in my face and stars shot through my vision. My other cheek hit the dusty floor, and I prayed for unconsciousness. But I already knew Balwyrdan had experience beating someone like this. It had clear after his first few blows that he knew just how much force to use to take me to the edge of oblivion but never over.

I tried to shut my mind away from my body, curl my consciousness into a tiny trembling ball deep in the core of my soul and ride it out until Cassius came for me — *please, God, come for me.* But my concentration broke every time Balwyrdan activated the leash spell and my desperate need for air wrenched me back to the agony again and again.

Oh, God. Stop. Please stop.

I'd wanted to be strong and had glared at him defiantly at the beginning, but that had only excited him more.

Except I couldn't bring myself to be meek and obedient in the hopes it would stop the torture. Not again. Never again. That hadn't worked for the human, and even if it would work for Balwyrdan, I couldn't make myself do it. Not even to survive. I didn't want to be weak any more. I swore I never would be... except I was. I always would be—

No. I would survive this. I might not be able to fight, but I could still run... so long as he didn't break my legs. I wasn't going to sit around being helpless, waiting for Cassius to show up. One wrong hit and my broken ribs could puncture my heart or lungs. And given that I still had low reserves from healing the guys this afternoon, I didn't know if I had enough power to save myself from an injury like that because it took so much more to turn my power inward.

I couldn't wait. I needed to search for an opportunity,

any opportunity, to make my escape. I just needed to hold out until then.

He seized my hair and wrenched me up. The fear of another blow made my ragged breaths stall and all thoughts of biding my time, waiting for a chance to escape, evaporated.

"Sir," one of the shifters on the other side of the room called out.

"What!" Balwyrdan's attention jerked to the man who'd spoken.

The man nodded at the open doorway, and Balwyrdan tossed me to the floor, my head hitting the legs of the large stacked tables behind me.

With a snarl, he strode to the far side of the large room to the reception hall's wide main doors.

The pale glow from the half dozen magical fae orbs hovering at the ceiling flashed off of something metal, and Mavis with her gold and silver necklaces, bracelets, and chain headpiece sauntered through the entrance.

"You've been paid, witch," Balwyrdan said.

"But I didn't tell you everything, and now you know my information is good." Mavis flashed him a cocky smile and walked her fingers down the front of his chest. "For double, I can give you the dragon."

She could what—?

Realization cut through my whirling thoughts and the fear churning in my gut hardened and heated into anger. Mavis had betrayed us. She'd told Balwyrdan where we were— or rather from the sounds of it, where *I* would be. She was responsible for my fear and pain and now she was back to give Titus up and get more money.

Had she even bothered to ask what Balwyrdan wanted with Titus? Which was a stupid question. She clearly didn't care.

"For double, hunh?" Balwyrdan asked, his voice lowering and turning sensual.

Now I really had to escape. I had to warn Cassius. Without a doubt, Balwyrdan would take Mavis up on her offer, and she'd tell him what Titus now looked like.

I yanked my gaze away from them and glanced around the room. I wasn't sure how many men Balwyrdan had, but of the dozen in the room, the only one closest to me — fifteen feet away — was staring out the large bank of windows along the back wall that surprisingly still had glass in them. Beyond, lay a sloping field of grass and weeds with clusters of trees and bushes shrouded in darkness.

No one was watching me.

This was my chance.

I slowly rolled to my knees, trying to be as quiet as possible. My body screamed in pain and my pulse raced. *Please don't look my way. Oh God, please.*

"I should be charging you triple," Mavis purred. "But that faekin thinks he can keep sending angels and JP agents to my shop. I want you to teach him a lesson."

I shifted to bring one knee up but Mavis's gaze flickered to me, and I froze, my gaze locking with hers. There wasn't a hint of remorse in her eyes.

My heart thudded and each rapid breath sliced agony through my chest. Did she know I was trying to escape? Would she alert Balwyrdan?

Her smile deepened and she turned her attention

back to Balwyrdan. "I want you to make the faekin suffer. Something it seems you're quite good at."

I brought my knee up, ready to stand, and searched the room for my quickest escape route.

There. A door. A few feet past the guard at the windows. I didn't know if it was unlocked, but if I could get outside, I could release my wings and fly away.

No. Bad idea. Balwyrdan would see me and suffocate me—

My thoughts stuttered. He didn't even need to see me. The moment he realized I was gone, he'd use the leash spell to kill me or bring me back.

Why hadn't I thought of that?

Because I was in shock and pain and still reeling from the beating I'd taken.

All I wanted was to be strong and in control, but I wasn't.

For a second, I contemplated what my chances were that I'd be able to find Cassius and warn him before Balwyrdan suffocated me. He was still walking into a trap. Even if I died, perhaps I could save them.

Except would Balwyrdan be able to sense if I moved farther away from him, just like I knew when I'd moved too far away from Titus? How far would I be able to go?

"I usually don't hire my services out," Balwyrdan said, "but I may make an exception for you. How do you know the faekin will show up with the beast?"

Mavis gave a sensual shrug. "There's a chance he won't."

"Then you'd be losing out on one-third of your payment."

My throat tightened. There wasn't anything I could do to survive this or even help the guys except uselessly pray Balwyrdan didn't kill me before Cassius came for me.

"Oh, I can think of a few ways to get that one-third." She pushed her pelvis against Balwyrdan's and stroked her palms across his pecks.

More tears rolled down my cheeks.

It didn't matter what I wanted. I had no control. I never did.

"And what makes you think I'd take you up on your offer?" He slid his hand to her back. "What makes you think I'd even pay double for something I already have?"

"But you don't have the dragon." Mavis tried to pull away, but Balwyrdan tightened his grip, crushing her against him. "He still has my concealment charm and glamour on him."

"And when I first came to you, I asked you for the dragon," Balwyrdan hissed.

He grabbed the long knife from the hip sheath of the man beside him and plunged the blade into Mavis's heart.

Oh, my God!

Mavis screamed and tried to shove out of Balwyrdan's grip, but he held tight, capturing her against his body, and twisted the blade, driving it in all the way to the hilt.

My magic rushed into my hands and locked onto the woman responsible for my suffering, turning my fear and rage to frustration.

"You said you couldn't give me the dragon," Balwyrdan said.

Mavis gasped, her eyes wide.

I gritted my teeth and fought the building pressure to move my battered body across the room.

I was *not* going to save her. Saving her would take all my strength, and I wasn't going to make that mistake again. Just because I couldn't run, didn't mean I couldn't try to hold out until help arrived. It was the only thing I had left in my control.

God, I couldn't even control my own magic.

Balwyrdan yanked out the knife and slammed it back into her chest, drawing another scream. "And now you say you can give me the dragon."

A part of me hated how selfish I was. I had the power to save her and I'd picked me over her. But picking me also picked Cassius, Sebastian, Titus, and Hawk. Wasting my power on someone who'd betrayed us, whose greed was the reason she'd been mortally wounded meant not having the power to save one of the guys, and that was unacceptable.

My power burned up my forearms and heaved at my soul.

Save her.

No. Not at the expense of the guys.

Mavis weakly struggled to break free and clawed at Balwyrdan's hand, her mouth opening and closing on gasped words too quiet for me to hear on the other side of the room.

"You think I'll just accept your lie and pay you again?" he demanded, yanking out the blade and plunging it back in. "What made you think I was the kind of man who would play that game?"

Save her.

The pressure burned past my elbows and squeezed my chest. It heaved me up and I threw myself forward, curling into a ball and pressing my forehead to the floor to keep from moving.

She's dying. Try. I had to at least try.

No. I won't save her. Please. I can't.

My power surged and impossibly, a thin thread, just enough to assess injuries, connected with Mavis even though I wasn't touching her. I could feel her life force draining from her, pooling in her blood at Balwyrdan's feet. The pressure to go to her, heal her, screamed through me and my body struggled against my will to sit up.

Go. Save her.

Mavis screamed again, and the sharp burst of being stabbed shot through my connection to her. I wasn't touching her. I wasn't even looking at her. I shouldn't have been able to feel her pain or her life force. But it was there, inside me, overwhelming me, snapping, and writhing, desperate to stay alight, begging me to use the power I'd been born with to save her.

Another scream and slice of pain and Mavis's life force stuttered, flared, and went out.

The fiery pressure inside me vanished, replaced with the trembling ache of backlash. I tried to bite back a sob, but it escaped anyway. Frustrating useless tears leaked from my eyes. I was never going to be in control. If I wasn't someone's prisoner or trapped by my mating brand, I'd still be a slave to my power.

"I told you to run," a quiet, emotionless voice said.

My heart leaped into my throat and I jerked my head

up to face the demon-vampire, the sudden movement sending agony screaming through me.

He crouched beside me, his handsome sculpted features just as emotionless as his voice, but his fangs were fully extended and his hellfire angry red pinpricks in his black eyes, revealing a wild hunger — the kind a predator had for its prey. His attention dipped to a cut on my cheek and he swallowed, the muscles in his throat flexing with the movement.

My breath picked up, making my pulse pound faster, which I was sure only made me look like a more appealing meal. It was against the law for a vampire to feed on someone without his or her consent, and with the plethora of humans more than willing to experience the euphoria of a vampire's bite and legalized blood houses, very few broke that law. But I doubted this vampire, given how emotionless he'd been when he'd decapitated that man in Lincoln, cared about laws.

Balwyrdan kicked Mavis's lifeless body, now lying on the floor with the knife still in her chest, and glared at the man beside him. "Get rid of this."

The hellfire in the demon-vampire's eyes flared and he shifted closer to me.

I shivered, half in fear and half at his lifeless essence. I didn't mind vampires, they were who they were, but they always felt wrong to me. Empty and cold. I couldn't *feel* them like how I felt others, like they didn't have a proper life force even though they still had a soul.

"Where is that beast?" Balwyrdan flicked his finger without even looking at me and the air around me vanished.

My body seized, my lung screaming for air, and darkness swirled through my vision. I collapsed forward, tears rolling down my cheeks, and my fear swelled. After this, Balwyrdan would yank me up by the hair and hit me again and again. *No more. Please.*

"I want a report from the men outside," he said and my air returned.

I sucked in a ragged breath, shooting more agony through my chest, and squeezed my eyes shut. I had to shut myself away, had to endure this until help arrived.

But a cold hand grabbed my wrist and fear shattered my concentration.

"Please," I begged, ashamed that the word had slipped out.

Something yanked against the rope binding my hands and the pressure keeping them back vanished.

My eyes flew open and I met the demon-vampire's gaze. His hunger was gone, replaced with a hard, emotionless expression. He pressed something into my hand as someone outside the main door yelled, then he darted into the shadows behind me with his enhanced vampiric speed and disappeared.

My thoughts stuttered. He'd freed me... sort of.

But why even free my hands?

Orange-red light flashed somewhere beyond the bank of windows, and my heart skipped a beat. Had Cassius finally come? *Please, let this be Cassius.*

The men in the room all started running for the door.

"Hold your position," Balwyrdan snapped still standing at the doorway.

The orange-red light flashed outside again and someone screamed.

I glanced at what the demon-vampire had given me. It was a small switchblade, the blade only a few inches long. It didn't make any sense that he'd give me a weapon now when he'd tried to kill me in the ring park, and I wasn't sure I'd be able to use it. With my surgical knowledge, I might know the most effective places to cut, but I didn't know how to fight. And since resisting my magic and refusing to save Mavis hadn't resulted in a serious backlash, I still risked my magic locking onto whoever I cut.

"Let them walk into the traps."

My pulse stuttered. *Them? Traps?* It wasn't just Cassius who was coming to my rescue?

"Then I'll kill everyone except the beast," Balwyrdan said, striding toward me.

I shoved my hands behind my back, praying my skirt hid the knife. With my lack of experience, I'd only be able to get one strike. But if Balwyrdan was close enough that strike could kill him.

It would have to kill him. Fast.

It was the only way to prevent my power from wanting to save him.

And I was *not* going to save him. Taking his life would stain my soul — the act went against the very essence of my being — but if it meant saving Cassius and the other guys, I would pay the price, the consequences be damned.

AMIAH

B<small>ALWYRDAN</small> <small>STRODE</small> <small>BACK</small> <small>TO</small> <small>ME</small> <small>AND</small> <small>SEIZED</small> <small>ME</small> <small>BY</small> <small>MY</small> hair. With a snarl, he yanked me to my feet, wrapped his arm across my chest, his hand capturing my throat, and jerked me tight against his body. "Looks like Mavis was right. You are valuable."

My pulse pounded with fear and hope. Outside people yelled and screamed, but everyone was out of sight. All I could see were the bursts of orange-red light from Cassius's fire. It cast long flickering shadows across the lawn in front of the windows of human-like shapes jerking and running in the throes of battle.

Someone roared, the sound filled with fury and pain, and for a second, I thought it was Titus. But it didn't sound right. Not as deep as the roar I'd heard before. Which meant it had to have come from one of Balwyrdan's shifters.

Please let it be one of Balwyrdan's shifters and not Titus.

"Sounds like they even brought backup," Balwyrdan

chuckled. "Or was there always a bear or wolf in your little group?"

A ball of fire tossed a large gray wolf across the lawn into the thick trunk of a lone maple tree near the door where I'd originally hoped to escape. Flames caught in the dry grass and weeds and swept around the wolf, burning fur and flesh, before Cassius — still out of sight — sucked the fire back into his body, leaving a charred corpse without a hint of life force.

Bile burned my throat. It had happened so fast my magic hadn't even had time to lock onto the man. At least the shifter's death had been swift. But for Cassius to kill so quickly and violently...

Was this what it had been like for him during the war? No wonder he'd come back hard and icy.

Another scream tore me away from the horror of Cassius's power.

Was that one of the guys? Please don't let it be one of them. I couldn't let any of them die. Not to save me. *God, why had I wished for them to come for me?* Surely they'd already figured out they were walking into a trap. Cassius had experience with these kinds of things, and Sebastian, while full of himself, was smart. They had to know. *Please, let them know.* I had to find a way to tell them. I couldn't just stand there, helpless. There had to be something I could do.

Anything.

Please.

Blinding white light lit up the lawn outside and someone screamed in agony.

My heart leaped into my throat and Balwyrdan chuckled.

"I wonder which one of them walked into the trap." He wrenched my head back to look me in the eyes, his gaze filled with the same dark pleasure he'd had when he hit me. "The new shifter? The faekin Mavis wanted tortured?"

A blast of fire raced over the lawn in front of the windows, and a nauseating mix of relief, guilt, and dread churned in my gut.

Cassius was fine. Was Sebastian? Titus? Hawk?

"Well, the angel is still conscious."

The strange roar that could have been Titus sounded.

"And so is the new shifter."

Which left Sebastian and Hawk.

One of Balwyrdan's men ran into sight at the far edge of the windows. Cassius's fire whip snapped at him and he jerked out of reach, falling onto his butt. Two more men appeared, one wrenching out of the way as Hawk lunged at him, while the other swiped at Hawk. Hawk leaped to the side and the man's claws narrowly missed his shoulder.

More fire flared just out of sight and someone screamed, then Titus lurched into view and tossed a charred body, the clothes still on fire, through the window on the far side of the room.

The glass shattered, sending shards skittering across the floor, and the corpse tumbled all the way to the main door.

Titus's gaze locked on me and with a snarl, he

stormed through the opening. Hawk, Cassius, and —
thank God! — Sebastian rushed in behind him.

They were alive. *They're all alive.* And they were
terrifying.

Sebastian, the least terrifying of them, without any
blood on his clothes and a gray complexion, had a hard
and calculating expression. Without a doubt, he wouldn't
hesitate to kill any of Balwyrdan's men, and he probably
already had.

Beside him, stood Titus, his hands and arms covered
in blood up to his elbows and his T-shirt soaked with it.

Next was Hawk. Blood splattered his shirt as well,
although not as much as Titus's, and coated his hand
holding a wickedly curved blade. He, too, looked ready to
kill anyone who stood in his way.

But most terrifying of them all was Cassius. Molten
fire dripped from arms and hands fully engulfed in
flames, and the inferno raced along the top of his wings
all the way to the tips. His body shook, and from the
searing ferocious look in his eyes, he shook from a rage
that was on the verge of slipping his control.

I'd never seen him so angry before. I hadn't even
known he was possible of such rage. Rescuing me this
time wasn't compelled by justice but by vengeance, and
God help anyone who stood in his way.

Cassius took a step forward and blinding white light
flashed around them. Dark thick strands burst from the
ground, capturing them in a magical spider web. Hawk
and Titus slashed at the strands, but more strands swept
around their arms, immobilizing them.

Balwyrdan huffed. "That was too eas—"

Cassius yelled and his fire exploded into a massive fireball that ignited the web. Flames rushed through the strands sending ash to the floor and thick black smoke to the ceiling, freeing the guys without burning them, which was an extraordinary demonstration of Cassius's control.

"Let her go," Cassius said. He didn't even offer to let Balwyrdan live like I'd expected.

Balwyrdan's men who'd been told to hold their position tensed, shooting nervous glances at each other and waiting for Balwyrdan's command to attack.

"Hmm. Which one do you think is the beast?" Balwyrdan asked, his voice filled with dark mirth as if his spell hadn't just been burned to a crisp. "I know he isn't the angel or the faekin. It would be too obvious to make him a wolf, so my guess is the incubus."

Cassius's fire billowed from his wings. "Let. Her. Go."

"Give me the beast," Balwyrdan said in a mocking singsong, "and you can have her back."

"This isn't a negotiation," Cassius growled.

"You're right, it isn't." Balwyrdan released my throat and flicked his finger.

I gasped in a quick breath just before the leash spell slammed into my chest and the air around me vanished.

Sebastian groaned and pressed a hand to his chest.

"Come now. Which one of you is the beast?" Balwyrdan released the spell and slammed it back into place with so much force my knees gave out. His grip in my hair tore at my scalp, and I fought to regain my balance without grabbing his hand and giving away the fact my hands were no longer bound.

Sebastian screamed and dropped to his hands and knees, his chest heaving with desperate gasps.

"You took the leash spell?" Balwyrdan asked, his tone sharp with surprise, and air flooded back around me as if he needed to concentrate to keep the spell active. "You. You little faekin," he said incredulously. "*You* manage to take the spell and warp it enough so you wouldn't suffocate. You must have had help. That witch must have double-crossed me and helped you take on the spell."

"No help." Sebastian climbed back to his feet, his fae glow so weak it was barely visible, and shrugged. "The last dragon isn't coming, either. He's already left town and you'll never be able to find him."

"So I'm what?" Balwyrdan asked with a dark chuckle. "Just supposed to hand her over?"

"Yes," Cassius replied.

"You really didn't think this through." Balwyrdan jerked my head back, spiking agony through my neck and chest. "If I can't get the beast with the leash spell then I have no use for her."

I gasped in a quick breath, knowing what was coming, but the leash spell pounded into me, stealing what little breath I'd managed to get. Cassius bellowed and rushed toward me, but Balwyrdan's remaining men ran to meet him.

My body strained to breathe, gasping against nothing, and my lungs started to burn.

Titus and Hawk dove into the fray, Titus slashing the neck of a big, bulky man with his claws, sending blood spraying everywhere, while Hawk ducked under a similar swipe to his neck and sliced his blade through his assailant's gut.

My magic exploded under my skin, locking on Titus's man, then jerking to Hawk's for a second when Titus's man died.

Cassius seized the man closest to him with his fire whip and tossed him through another one of the large windows. He turned to head to me, but another man jumped in his way, slicing his right biceps before Cassius tossed him aside with his fire whip.

Flames danced along the floor on the verge of getting out of control, and Balwyrdan's men still blocked the way of all the guys. They were getting closer and there were only about six assailants left. But dark specks crowded my vision, and my body shook with the effort to stay standing. I was running out of time, and even if the guys could take out all the men right now, none of them were close enough to get to me before I passed out.

Titus roared and ripped out another man's throat. Hawk slashed at his assailant, but the man jerked out of the way and rammed his fist into Hawk's side. Cassius sucked in his fire before he burned the abandoned reception hall down around us as another man lunged at him, managing to slice through his fire whip with his claws. With a yell, Cassius sent a blast into the man's chest, tossing him into the stacked tables behind me.

Balwyrdan stiffened and Cassius's gaze locked with mine. His eyes were filled with rage and soul-crushing terror. He knew he wasn't going to be able to get to me in time, knew Balwyrdan was going to kill me.

He raised his hand, his whip hissing and crackling.

Balwyrdan would still be able to kill me before his whip connected, but it was the only option.

I knew it. He knew it. And Balwyrdan could see that too.

He jerked me closer, wrapping his arm across my chest and using my body as a shield. The room darkened and spun around me, and I had no idea if Cassius was going to use his whip or not. All I knew was that I had to get away from Balwyrdan or break his concentration or something. I *had* to do something. Now.

I yanked my hand out from between our bodies and without a deadly place to strike, sliced the blade through his arm.

He howled and seized my hand before I could cut him again. Air rushed back around me and I gasped in a ragged breath. But he wrenched my hand back and broke my wrist, exploding agony through my hand and arm.

"You need to do more than that to get free," he sneered, and the leash spell pounded into me again, just as his blood splattered on my bare foot and my power instinctually connected with him.

The wound was deep, but not deadly.

And that didn't matter. It was all I needed.

I shoved my magic into him with a forceful blast, making him scream. The leash spell sputtered out and his grip loosened. I wrenched free of his hold and tried to scramble out of the way but only managed a few staggering steps before my battered body lost its balance.

Sebastian caught me and yanked me back. We fell to the floor, me half in his arms, as sudden ferocious heat seared my back.

Someone screamed, and I turned to see Balwyrdan fully engulfed in a massive pillar of fire. The inferno burned so hot he barely had a chance to move before he dropped to the floor and burst into a pile of ash and glowing embers.

Cassius sagged to his knees and all of his fire, the fire that had consumed Balwyrdan and the flames dancing over his skin, went out. He'd used a lot of his magic and it was amazing he was still conscious. Hawk stared at him, wide-eyed and pale, as Titus killed the last of Balwyrdan's men.

I couldn't tell how badly everyone was hurt, but my magic hadn't locked on to any of them so none of them were in mortal danger.

Thank God. Oh, thank God.

With a groan, Cassius sucked the remaining fire in the building back into his body. He shuddered, heaved his wings back in as well, and pulled off his T-shirt. Somehow he'd managed to get through that fight with just that cut on his biceps, only the ugly red burn scars from his fight in Left of Lincoln marred his torso. Of course, he hadn't held back, hadn't cared if he ran out of magic or who or what he'd set on fire. I doubted anyone had managed to get close to him.

"Here," he said, tossing the shirt to Hawk who caught it in his free hand. "Give that to Amiah."

Hawk knelt beside me, his gaze filled with concern without a hint of sexual invitation even though I was half naked.

The look made my throat tighten with frustration. It

was the same look Cassius had given me all those years ago when he'd first rescued me.

"Can you sit up?" he asked.

"Yes," I insisted, even though I had no idea if I could. I didn't want to move. I wanted to pass out until my body stopped hurting. Except the only way I'd stop hurting was if I healed myself and that was going to take time. A lot of time… that I didn't want to spend topless.

I struggled to rise, shooting blazing agony through me that made the room darken and lurch, and left me panting.

"Jeez," Sebastian said. "You just had the shit beaten out of you. Stop trying to do everything yourself."

He helped me sit, and I held up my arms, my muscles trembling even with something as simple as that, and Hawk dressed me. Biting back a moan, I sagged against Sebastian, gasping shallow breaths and fighting my tears.

I wasn't strong. I'd never be strong.

I'd never be free.

Titus crouched beside Hawk with the same pitying expression. "Can you break the leash spell?"

"We should move someplace safer first," Cassius said, his head bowed, his body language saying he wasn't going to move anytime soon. "We don't know who betrayed us. We could still be in danger."

"It was Mavis," I gasped. "Balwyrdan killed her."

"Good," Titus growled.

"Does that mean your apartment is safe again?" Hawk asked. "Wait." Hope flashed in his eyes. "Does that mean I can go back to my life? Sparky barbecued that monster and we killed all his men. The bitch who betrayed us is dead and the spring fae don't know about us anymore."

Cassius groaned, pushed up to his feet, and staggered to the rest of us. "Are you willing to risk that?"

"Hell, yeah." Hawk's gaze jumped to mine for a heartbeat but he yanked it away and stood before I could figure out what the look meant. "This situation is fucked up, and you're all insane."

"There were more than just spring fae at Lincoln," Sebastian said, gingerly stroking a lock of my hair out of my face and drawing my attention to his pale eyes. His expression was still tight with pain and his complexion gray. "Let's break this leash spell."

"I can wait." As much as I wanted to be free — *now now now* — he was in no condition to cast anything... and if it was going to be as painful as the last attempt, I wouldn't be able to handle it. "You're too pale."

"Winter fae, remember?" His lips quirked. "And while I love the fact you can't go more than a hundred feet from me, I'm pretty sure Sparky here hates it."

Cassius bristled at his words. "Call me Sparky again. I dare you."

"So you don't care that Amiah is stuck with me?" A hint of Sebastian's usual wicked gleam lit his eyes. "Just the nickname."

"I didn't say that," Cassius shot back.

"Sure sounded like it to me," Hawk said.

"It's not an either or." Cassius crouched and held out his hands. "Give me Amiah and let's get out of here."

But before Sebastian could hand me over, the air a few feet away burst into a shimmering liquid mirror. A pale tiny woman in a dark flowing gown with gossamer wings and the same bluish-white and silver coloring as Sebastian stepped through. Two enormous identical men taller and broader than Titus who looked like they'd been carved from ice followed her and took up position behind her. They carried long spears and wore a strange shimmering breastplate that could have been made of ice, and loose white pants.

Cassius jerked to his feet and clenched his hands as if to summon his fire, but not even a hint of smoke curled from his skin. Titus extended his claws and snarled, and Hawk widened his stance, ready to fight.

"Fuck," Sebastian groaned.

"Faekin," the woman said. "You've been summoned to the Winter Queen's court to swear your allegiance."

Something shifted in the shadows on the far side of the room behind the woman, drawing my attention, and I met the demon-vampire's solemn gaze.

"I've already sworn my allegiance," Sebastian said.

The woman's eyes narrowed. "You have not."

"Yeah, well." Sebastian shrugged, the movement making me gasp in pain. "Tell her majesty, thanks but no thanks."

"This wasn't a request." The tiny woman clapped her hands and the air turned to liquid magic. It crashed around us before any of the guys could attack, sweeping us into a ferocious whirlpool and sucking us in.

We were going to Faerie whether we wanted to or not. Right into the realm where everyone wanted to capture or kill us, and the Shadow Court's assassin knew exactly where we were going.

Don't miss the next book in the series!

FATED WINTER
Angel's Fate: Book Two

Freedom is further from her reach than ever before...

I've been taken. Again. *God, not again!*

This time all of us — me, Sebastian, Cassius, Titus, and Hawk — have been abducted, dragged through a portal into the Winter Court where the Winter Queen wants *Prince* Sebastian to take his rightful place as heir, a title he abdicated the hell out of 300 years ago.

Now that the queen has her unwilling prodigal son back in her grasp, she won't let him go. Ever. And if she learns the truth of who we really are, she'll kill the rest of us.

The only thing blocking her end game: me and Sebastian's lie that we're married — bound together by powerful fae magic that can only be broken by death. And as an angel unable to give Sebastian children, I'm not exactly the queen's first choice for her son's bride.

I'm worse than back to square one. The guys will do

anything to protect me, and we've only got a small window of time to get out of the Winter Court before the assassination attempts begin.

OTHER BOOKS BY TESSA COLE

)